THE ENIGMA STRAIN

THE ENIGMA STRAIN

A HARVEY BENNETT THRILLER

NICK THACKER

The Enigma Strain: Harvey Bennett Mysteries, Book #1
Copyright © 2014 by Nick Thacker
Published by Turtleshell Press

PROLOGUE

Alexei Expedition

Northwest Territory, Canada

1704

The sound of another exploding tree caused Nikolai Alexei to jump.

He heard the men behind him snicker, but he did not care to address them. It was not worth his time, and besides, it was poor leadership to acknowledge such pettiness. His father had explained the odd occurrence to him on a wolf-hunting trip when he was a boy; the frozen tree sap inside the trunks of the pines would expand, causing the bark and wood to explode. He had often lain awake at night, counting the rippling explosions as they worked their way through the wooded area around their cabin. He knew the sound well, but it still took him by surprise when it happened, even now.

He grumbled to himself and marched onward through the knee-deep snow.

He enjoyed this land. It reminded him of home; of the countless miles of deep black forest, filled with the same animals he used to hunt, the same trees he used to climb, and the same bitter cold he used to long for with fresh blankets of snow thick enough to halt a horse. He remembered the smells, too—the ripe evergreens and the sheer emptiness of the air. He was more comfortable in the woods than any of his men, with the possible exception of Lev.

And yet their laughter frustrated him. It was not a sign of insubordination as much as it was a sign of their laziness. For three months they had made their trek over mountains and across valleys so high and so deep he had thought they would not make it to the other side with their entire crew intact. They had crossed tundra, plateaus, and wetlands, all without losing a man. Their hunting excursions were always successful, and most nights ended around a large bonfire with a deer roasting on a spit. Breakfast was hot soup, and they snacked on smoked meats throughout the day.

Nikolai had to admit that so far it was one of the more successful expeditions he had been on, and he knew God was smiling on them in this new land. But he knew also that it made them weak; it made them soft. They had grown fat and sluggish, covering less ground each day than the day before. Their energy and excitement had been replaced with a restlessness that had turned their stories and poems around the fire into passionless songs.

Without glancing back, Nikolai called out behind him. "Doctor?"

A short, thin man struggled through the snow but Nikolai did not slow his pace. "We will stop and make camp when we next find a clearing. The river is to the north, and we can fish there for as long as we like."

"Split the men into crews of two and three," Nikolai said, "and I will send them out in the morning to chart the area. These Cossacks will find pleasure in a change of scenery, and I myself will enjoy an excursion of a more solitary nature."

Nikolai was a man of his word; a man of integrity. He had promised the Tsar a map of the deep terrain of North America, and he intended to deliver it. His expedition had grown mundane, and it was time to bring it back to life.

"So you will wander alone through these parts?" the doctor asked.

Nikolai laughed. "I will take care to not lose myself in the fog, if that is what you are asking. Sometimes a man must wander, my friend," he said. "But rest assured, we will gather together after three days."

The doctor nodded and fell in line behind his leader. Nikolai was uncertain if this plan of his would do more good than endanger them all, but it was a risk he was willing to take. They had found nothing useful thus far; nothing the motherland would be inclined to return to claim. Cartography was their stated manifest, but he was under no false pretenses. By moving outward in smaller groups, the expedition could cover more territory and more ground than by moving in a single line.

So far, they had charted the great river to their north all the way from the sea, but they knew that every river began somewhere. Whether it was a lake amid the mountain peaks or from tributaries caused by glacial melt, he did not know.

And he did not care.

Nikolai Alexei was here for one reason, and one reason alone. His homeland sought riches, as did his men. All men sought more than what God had initially blessed them with. It was a man's duty to find what he was owed in this life, with all the more blessings to be bestowed upon him in the afterlife.

This new land was not known for its riches, but only a fool would think the Spanish had been capable of taming it when they came. This land was made for Russians. Only they understood it. This great unknown that had attracted Nikolai was an opportunity that he was not going to let pass.

PROLOGUE

Alexei Expedition

Northwest Territory, Canada

1704

When the first star appeared in the heavens above them, the men made camp, throwing oilskins over tent poles in a circle by the river bank.

They were slow, Nikolai noted. After the last few days' effort it did not surprise him, but it did not please him much either. It took over an hour to set up the ten tents and build a fire, but no more than ten minutes for the men to begin huddling around it.

Soon the moon rose, nearly full. A meal was prepared, a roasted deer and herb soup, and the men began singing.

But Nikolai had had enough. He broke away from the camp and lifted the moose skin hood up and over his head. This Siberian Yupik coat was one of the best trades he had made. The bitter cold tried to bite into his flesh, and the gentle wind threatened to chill his core, but he didn't notice. He made for a smaller clearing to the south that he had seen earlier, one with a rock outcropping against a higher mountain cliff. The river they were following had likely cut down into this valley they were currently in, and if he was lucky, it had left some interesting formations for him.

He reached the clearing and scared away a small beaver that would make a fine pelt when it reached adulthood, and stepped out into the open grassy area to get a good look at the outcropping. It appeared that the boulders were precariously situated around a hole near the ground, beckoning him closer. As he approached, he could see even in this failing light that what he had found was an opening to a small cave.

He had no light with him, but he ducked inside anyway. It was useless. He could explore little with just hands and arms.

Tomorrow, he would head here first thing, bring a torch and a few extra men. This was the type of cave that would have made a perfect shelter for one of the native tribes that might call this place home. So far, they had not encountered any such people, but he had no way of knowing if these indigenous tribes he had heard tell of lived along these rivers or not.

A light appeared behind him, flickering and orange. He could almost feel the heat of the torch as it grew brighter.

"Nikolai?" A voice said, softly. "Is that you?"

It was the doctor's voice, a little unsure.

"Yes, doctor," Nikolai said. He felt the excitement within him growing. "Bring the light! I would very much like to have a look at this place."

The doctor 'joined him and lifted the flaming torch up in front of them.

Scrawled upon the walls were dozens of paintings articulating dancing men and women around fires, hunting trips, and deaths.

So many deaths.

One particularly macabre image depicted a man and woman lying sideways next to each another, their arms crossed as in a representation of death. Six children were drawn below them haphazardly as if added at different times in the past.

Nikolai and the doctor gazed at the drawings, trying to decipher their meaning. Sections of paintings had been scratched out or painted over as if the original author had changed the story halfway through.

"I don't understand. Do you, sir?"

Nikolai didn't respond. He took the torch from the other man's hand and continued on deeper into the cave. A few feet past the first wall, the ceiling grew higher, and he drew himself up to his full height. More cave paintings decorated the walls to his left and right, and arrows were drawn near the floor. Farther on, and the small cavern twisted to the left and ended in a rounded chamber.

He swung the torch around this room, at first looking for a continuation of the path he was on. Finding none, he held the torch lower. Stacks of bones and skulls lay atop one another, of all shapes and sizes. Men, women, and children all lay close together, though arranged into what he assumed must have been families.

In front of these, he found baskets made from sinewy animal skins, with lids fashioned from skin and bones. The leatherwork was remarkable and he reached down to grab one. He examined it closely, handing the light to the doctor. Stamped into the sides and top of the basket were designs and symbols that he could not interpret. They swirled around the edges, leaving no section of leather untouched.

"Beautiful," he whispered. He twisted the top of the basket, finding the lid secured tightly, either by design or from years of rest. He gave the lid a harder twist and felt a pop.

The top of the basket came off, sending dust shooting through the air. He waved it away and dropped the lid to the ground.

He saw what was inside, and only then realized how heavy the basket was. He turned the basket upside down, emptying its contents out onto the cave floor. Hundreds of silver coins bounced on the dirt and rolled around.

"For the glory of..." the doctor said, his voice hoarse.

"I imagine this is the sort of thing we have come here for," Nikolai said. He scooped up a handful of the silver coins and held them up to the light. "Do you recognize these?"

"No. I have never seen such a design."

Upon the surface of each coin was a remarkably intricate design; either hand carved or stamped. It featured the bust of a native man, and Nikolai could even see the outline of a frown on his face. He was surrounded by what looked like fire, each wisp carefully measured and drawn.

"From the local population?" the doctor asked.

Nikolai shook his head. "No. The people here use the shells of clams as their currency, and most simply trade goods instead. This... must be from somewhere else entirely."

He flipped it over in his hand. The back was a reflection of the front, with the same native man frowning up at them. The fire, however, was markedly absent from this side. In its place were swirls and lines, which looked to be framing the man in the center.

"Fire on one side, wind on the other," Nikolai whispered. "A dichotomy. What could it represent?"

"What is in the other baskets?" the doctor asked. He reached for another, trying at first to lift it from the ground. The basket slid a few inches toward him but stayed on the floor. "This one is considerably heavier, sir," he said.

Nikolai reached down and twisted the lid free. He pushed the basket over with his right foot and watched as more silver coins tumbled out, identical to the one in his hand.

"Doctor," he said, "bring the men. And bring the satchels as well. I count at least twenty of these baskets. What about you?"

The doctor shook his head excitedly. "Perhaps more."

"If each contains even a portion of what is in these first two, it should be more than enough to justify a return home, do you think?"

The doctor smiled.

Nikolai wasn't greedy, but he felt the stirrings of excitement growing in his chest. He would share this treasure with his men without question, but he needed to be sure of what he had found. He moved to the back of the cavern, now standing directly in front of the pile of skeletons. Reaching down, he lifted the lid on one of the baskets that had been placed close to the back.

More dust spread outward from the freshly opened container, and he blinked and waved it away with his free hand. He moved the torch down closer to the top of the basket and peered inside.

It was empty.

Odd. He reached for the basket nearest it and lifted its lid too.

Empty, save for a few small tools.

He considered calling the doctor back, but stopped himself. *Why would they bury them here?* he wondered. *Why would they place a nearly empty basket next to a tribute to their deceased loved ones?*

Had someone come before him? Someone who had found the baskets and emptied what they could? It did not make sense. Anyone who had explored this cave before them would certainly have emptied it of its treasures. They would not have left anything of value behind, and they would not have put the lids back on each basket. Thieves were anything but tidy.

Yet these two baskets were empty? He looked again, this time lifting one of the baskets to eye level and turning it. He could see the fine sinewy lines of the bottom, woven together and sewn shut. A few tools shifted at the bottom; what looked like a few small pipes, a bowl made of clay, and some other small sticks and rocks.

He coughed and realized for the first time how thick the dust in the air had become. Waving his hands, he backed away from the burial site. He coughed again, and this time, felt his lungs strain with the effort.

He turned away from the room and walked back upward until the cave ceiling closed in on him. He stepped out into the small clearing. Night had fallen completely, and thousands of stars peered down at him. He fell to his knees, trying to catch his breath. He sucked in air, forcing his lungs back open again. He struggled forward then rolled onto his back in the snow.

Nikolai struggled to calm his thinking and shut his eyes.

Breathe. He willed himself to breathe, in and out, until he felt the dust clearing from his system. His breathing became normal and controlled.

Just then, he heard the footsteps of his men running toward the clearing. He stood and brushed the snow from his back. He lifted his head and walked towards the edge of the woods. "Have you retrieved the satchels?"

"We have, sir. Where is the cave?" The voice was Lev's, the huge bear of a man tumbling out of the woods first. His eyes were wide, and his breath was heavy, pouring out of his mouth and nose in great bursts. With scars on his face and body from a lifetime serving his homeland as a soldier and a woodsman, Nikolai enjoyed the man's company and trusted his skill as a dedicated naturalist who was as knowledgeable as himself.

Nikolai gestured to the entrance. The group, fifteen men in all, trotted past and soon emerged three at a time with their satchels heavy. The endeavor took only thirty minutes, and they joined Nikolai in the clearing when they were finished. Only four of the baskets had been empty, including the two Nikolai had found.

If the men were jovial before, they were near ecstatic now. They knew their leader was a fair and honest man, and they would each get a good portion of the discovery. The primary cartographer among them, Roruk, began scratching some notes into a small notebook he had produced from his pocket. He measured the edges of the clearing, counting each step as he went and drawing them into this book.

When he finished, he nodded to Nikolai and they returned to the main camp.

"We leave tomorrow," Nikolai said as the other men gathered around. "We have added too much weight to continue the expedition for now, and it will be a burden already with the water and food we must carry with us."

Cheers erupted around the fire and the men broke into song. Nikolai wondered how men could be so merry without the aid of spirits and drink, but he did not stifle the mood.

He silently stepped away from the doctor and Lev and entered his tent. As the leader of this expedition, he shared it with no other man, and he enjoyed the privilege. He slipped off his coat and nestled onto his cot.

The noise around the campfire grew, but Nikolai could hardly hear it. He felt as if his mind was on fire, as if his head was being held above a pot of boiling water. He started to sweat, and his hands and arms began to itch. Nikolai struggled to stifle the burning sensation, and considered calling out for the doctor's aid. Before he could, however, he drifted into a welcome and deep sleep.

PROLOGUE

Alexei Expedition

Northwest Territory, Canada

1704

Nikolai awoke the next morning to an odd sound.

Silence.

Pure, pristine winter silence. The quiet he had not heard since before they had left Russia. The quiet of his youth. Intense and intimidating. Nikolai would normally have welcomed it with a sharp sniff and a deep, satisfying breath, but this morning should not have been so quiet. An expedition with a group of almost thirty men guaranteed that every moment would be filled with some racket or another.

He threw the blankets off and stood. His head brushed the top pole of his tent as he opened the flaps. The fire had long since diminished, though wisps of cold ash rose with the gentle breeze, giving the appearance of smoke. The cluster of tents was situated in a circle around the fire, like spokes on a wagon wheel. His tent was the northernmost one, and separated from the others on each side by a few rows of trees. The tents were traditional, two vertical poles and a horizontal one resting atop them, with canvas stretched over it and staked into the ground at the corners. Each tent was immaculately placed, perfectly spaced, and set up to look exactly the same. His men were good men, Nikolai knew, and they cared deeply for these small details. But where were they? Why weren't they preparing for their long journey home?

"Doctor? Lev?" He called out. He entered the nearest to find the two men still asleep beneath mounds of blankets and furs. He kicked at the doctor's cot with an unlaced boot and asked again.

Hearing nothing in return, Nikolai pulled the blankets from the man's head. The outermost blanket, a thick woven fabric, caught on something and he struggled to pull it down. After a more forceful tug, the blanket fell away to reveal the flesh of the doctor's face eaten by a rash, red boils covering the surface of his skin .

Nikolai stumbled backward in disgust. A portion of the skin on the poor man's forehead had stuck to the blanket, glued there by dried tissue and blood. The doctor's eyes were open, but they were glazed over in death.

Instinctively, Nikolai clutched a hand to his mouth, struggling to hold back the vomit he felt rising in his throat. He pulled the blanket away completely, and found every inch of exposed skin on the doctor's body covered in similar boils. He turned to Lev's cot and made the same cursory examination.

More rash. More boils. More death.

Lev had also passed sometime during the night. Both men lay in their blankets, gazing up at the roof of the tent with blank eyes. Nikolai moved away. Closed the flap behind him. He looked down at his own hands and arms and noticed the same rash spread and thickened over most of his skin.

It was no longer itchy, but he felt the heat radiating from his skin on the places around his body that had been infected. Last night it was just his hands and arms. Now he felt it over his shoulders, neck, and upper back.

He checked two more tents, finding the same horrifying faces staring up at him in each. All of his men—all twenty-seven of them —were dead.

He was the sole survivor on an expedition that was now thousands of miles away from home, in one of the remotest places known to man.

Another tree cracked in the distance, and he knew that winter was about to set in for good.

1

Yellowstone National Park

Wyoming

Present Day

Harvey "Ben" Bennett eased the end of his rifle through the small space between the two bushes. He readjusted his left knee, moving a rock to the side of the bush he had crushed under his jeans. He held the rifle steady, using a stray branch as a platform. He watched the scene through the end of the scope.

The grizzly was busy rummaging through the food from an overturned cooler in the clearing. The female, small for her tage but no less dangerous, grunted in delight as she discovered bits of bacon and pancakes from that morning's breakfast.

The campers had long since fled, calling the main park line and complaining of a nuisance bear in the area. They were worried the bear would enter their camp and scare their kids, or worse.

Worried the bear would do what it was designed to do, Ben thought.

These types of campers were the worst kind. They left a mess, complained constantly, and ruined the sanctity of the ecosystem they'd stumbled into.

People from the cities treated camping like a luxury all-inclusive resort vacation. As if nature was designed specifically to please them. Ben hated them, almost as much as hated this part of his job.

Nuisance animals, everything from raccoons to grizzlies, were a major turnoff for visitors and tourists, and therefore a problem. People had no idea how to handle animals looking for an easy meal and tended to freak out and assume they were under attack rather than calmly leave the scene and find a ranger.

Ben slid a round into the chamber and took aim. He closed each eye in turn, checking the distance and trying to gauge where the bear would move next. His left eye provided him a view of the attached manometer as he peered through the scope, allowing him to adjust for pressure without losing sight of the target. The aluminum barrel and American Walnut stock felt warm in his hands; alive. It was a comfortable weapon, and Ben was satisfied with the department's purchase of these relocation tools.

He watched the bear's thick neck muscles throb as she tore off a chunk of cardboard from the pile of smelly trash she'd discovered.

That was the other thing Ben hated about these people. They had no intention of learning anything—how to cook, what to eat in the woods, how to find food—they just wanted the comforts of home in a temporary excursion from reality.

The bear straightened its neck slightly, and Ben suddenly caught a glimpse of her left eye.

It glistened with age, a sheen of gray sparkling in the corner.

Mo.

Ben recognized the grizzly from the other times he'd encountered her down here. He had helped a few crews move her only months ago last summer, and again two years prior to that.

Ben sighed, and focused on the air leaving his lungs. He sucked in a quick, small breath, and held it in. He counted to five and pulled the trigger.

The soft popping sound took him by surprise—it always did. The juxtaposition of the man-made machine he'd just fired was severely out of place in what was supposed to be a pristine environment. Yet here he was adding to the mess and he was immediately remorseful.

The bear bristled and sat straighter, her back still to Ben. She turned slowly, her head lolling around as the tranquilizer began to take effect. Mo wouldn't charge him. The projectile dart alone wouldn't have alarmed the bear any more than if a small branch had fallen on her, but Ben knew the two milligrams of etorphine and acepromazine maleate compound the dart had just injected into the side of the bear would be more than enough to drop it.

Ben waited, not wanting to alert the bear. Angering or exciting an animal just before they fell asleep would cause undue stress, and it may even put them in danger. After a few more seconds, the bear let out a low moan as she stood on her hind feet. She turned in an unsteady circle, then fell back to the ground. The grizzly lay down on the damp leaves, and her head fell to the forest floor.

Ben waited a full minute before stepping out of his hiding spot. He pushed through the bushes, not bothering to spread the brambles apart and crossed the clearing and stood over the animal.

"Sorry about that, Mo," he said softly. "Let's get you back up north again." He removed the small CO2 cartridge from under the barrel of the rifle and dropped it in his pocket. He crouched down and found the red feather-tipped dart protruding from the bear's left flank.

The dart was expensive and reusable, and the department prohibited rangers from leaving them in the parks, even if they were damaged or destroyed.

Ben unclipped the walkie-talkie from his belt and rotated the knob at the top.

"This is Bennett," he said into the device. "I've got Mo dropped up here; requesting assistance to get her cleared."

The radio crackled, then came to life.

"Okay, tag the location and stand by for location verification. We're sending out a crew—out."

Ben tucked his radio away and took out his phone. He tapped an app on the home screen and clicked around a few times, setting his current location into the device's memory, then turned on the GPS beacon.

Within minutes, a crew of four men and two women arrived at the campsite and began strapping the grizzly onto a board.

The rangers would move Mo to another area of the park with less human traffic. She would eventually wander down again, drawn to the enticing opportunity ignorant campers left her.

This was Mo's third repositioning, and Ben was worried it would be her last.

Don't come back down here, Mo, Ben willed the sleeping giant. *I won't be able to help you out again.*

2

The Chevy hiccupped over an invisible pothole in the road, and the aging suspension compensated with a clicking sound and a groan.

Ben pulled the truck to the left, easing it back to the center of the narrow dirt road before turning the radio up. The country song already blaring through the strained cabin speakers didn't need a boost, but it got one anyway.

"You really don't like to talk, do you?" Ben's passenger yelled. The young man sitting to Ben's right glanced over at him.

Ben kept his attention on the uneven road lying before them.

Out of the corner of his eye, Ben noticed Carlos Rivera turning back to looking out his side window. Over the past hour, Ben had said maybe ten words, and what he had said was mainly instructive, telling Rivera to "call in to base" or "check Mo" in the truck bed. To his credit, Rivera had dutifully done as he was told, but Bennett still hadn't warmed to him.

They drove on for another fifteen minutes, moving slowly over bumps and divots, until finally, Ben pulled off the road and began guiding the truck over a small plain toward the edge of the forest. Behind it, a small mountain lifted itself from the flat ground, shadowed by Antler Peak to the north. As they drove, Ben took in the surroundings—it was beautiful, pristine. He took a deep breath and turned the radio back down.

"No, I don't much care for talking," he said. Rivera glanced over. "You're a decent enough kid, I guess. Thanks for helping out today."

Rivera laughed. "Kid? What, aren't you like twenty-five yourself?"

Ben kept his eyes straight, looking out at the road. "Thirty-two."

Rivera nodded, a surprised look on his face, as they pulled up to the thick tree line. The section of woods in front of them stretched around the base of the mountain, ending about halfway up and turning into a scraggly patch of saplings and bushes. Ben maneuvered the truck backwards into a gap between two trees and jumped out. He unhitched the tie-downs on the side of his truck and waited for Rivera to do the same on his side.

Ben moved to the rear of the truck and started to pull the tailgate down.

"Did you feel that?"

Ben looked up at his partner. Out of nowhere, a heavy bass note rocked the ground at their feet, and Ben felt a pressure of sound vibrate through his head. The deep rumble grew to a deafening tremor, then quickly died, reverberating through the trees.

"What the—" Rivera backed away from the truck, looking to the east and squinting through a strand of trees. His eyes grew wide. "Ben. Look."

Ben followed the younger man's gaze. A smoking mass mushroomed from the horizon upward. The cloud billowed out, growing exponentially.

Neither man spoke. They just watched, glued to the spot.

Suddenly an earthquake tore through the trees, ripping roots and stumps from the ground and lifting the truck into the air and throwing both men thirty feet head over heels. Ben hit the ground so hard he felt his insides churn.

He forced himself to sit up, trying to get his bearings, but the tremblor would not stop. The truck lay on its side but he couldn't get to it even if it wasn't.

The ground had opened up. A widening gap in the earth drew a jagged line in the cracking dry soil and threathed to swallow the entire vehicle. Ben stumbled when he tried to stand.

We have to get out of here. Ben whipped around. *Where's Rivera?*

He wasn't at the truck. The bear's cage had toppled off the back and now lay upside down. Ben broke into a run and leapt over the widening crevasse.

Working frantically at the animal pen, he unlocked the padlock on the door and unlatched the two enclosures. He swung the door open and reached in.

Just as he did, he ripped his arm back.

Of all the things there was to worry about, and all he was concerned with was helping this bear survive.

Good way to lose a hand, he thought. He looked into the cage to find the grizzly unmoving, but breathing. The great beast was still unconscious.

The earth began to settle back to normal.

As fast as it had happened, it was over. In a mere thirty seconds the ground had lifted up, been pushed together with cataclysmic force, and fallen back down again. Trees had toppled over one another, trunks battered and smashed in half. Boulders that had rested in place for a millennia now sat disturbed, some cracked and broken.

And now, tranquility…

"Ben! Help!"

Rivera's voice came from somewhere on the other side of the truck. He ran toward it, skidding to a halt near the edge of the new fissure in the ground. Ben could see that the earth actually sloped downward for about twenty feet before it dropped straight down into an abyss.

Rivera was dangling over the edge, his white-knuckled fingers clawed around a tree root.

"I can't hold on," Rivera said.

Ben dropped to his stomach and reached down, grasping the other man's free hand. He gritted his teeth, summoning all his strength, and pulled.

The edge of the fissure wasn't solid rock, and as Ben pulled Rivera upward, the sides of the cliff eroded and fell away. Ben struggled with the angle for a half minute, then stopped.

"Switch hands. Give me your other arm," Ben shouted down to Rivera.

The young man's eyes burned with fear as he tried to do as instructed.

His arms shook as Ben willed himself to drag his colleague out of the hole.

And then, an aftershock, trembling through the woods.

The ground quaked again.

Ben lost his grip.

Rivera tumbled back down, swinging from the root with his other sweat-soaked hand.

Ben lunged over the edge to grab him, his finger glancing across Rivera's collar but missing him by mere inches. His hand slammed back into the wall of the cliff.

And then the tree root broke loose and snapped away from the dirt.

Rivera looked up at Ben as he realized in that instant what was happening.

The tree root fell away and Rivera with it.

Within seconds he was gone.

Ben called down to him.

There was no answer.

3

"What do you mean, *crack*?"

Ben looked up from the couch. "Crack. Fissure. Hole in the earth."

"Like a sinkhole?"

"Yes. Sort of."

"Then why didn't you just say sinkhole?"

"I didn't think of it," Ben said. "And it *wasn't* a sinkhole, technically. It was caused by some... explosion."

"And Carlos Rivera fell into it?"

Ben nodded, his expression blank. The officer sighed and turned to his partner. The second officer stepped forward, resuming the line of questioning. "And you said you two were moving—relocating—a nuisance bear?"

A man walked into the room. His large, round frame was unmistakable. Ben's boss, George Randolph, jumped in to the discussion. "A nuisance bear is a bear that's caused no harm or considerable damage and just needs to be relocated to a more remote area—"

The officer was not impressed. "This is Wyoming. We know what a nuisance bear is."

"Look, Mo, the grizzly, has three strikes against her now. We were trying to get her far enough away that she'll stay put."

The officers wrote everything down, the others muttering amongst themselves. Ben sat motionless on the lounge couch, the only remotely comfortable place in the entire room. The lights above the gathered local officers, park rangers, and staff burned down on him like the sterile lighting in a hospital wing. Ben felt trapped, out of place, and anxious.

The last time I was in a hospital...

Ben shook away the feeling. He knew it wasn't going to help his anxiety levels now to dwell on memories from the past.

All the staff on duty during the explosion had been summoned to this staff building to "debrief," as the local police called it. A fire and rescue team was on its way, due to arrive any moment. Ben also saw a few men and women milling about whom he didn't recognize, talking quietly to individual members of the Yellowstone team about the morning's events.

Government, he thought. One of the women walked toward him. Slim, fit, and wearing a tight suit that matched her demeanor—like the kind of person who took herself too seriously.

When the woman didn't deviate from her course, Ben almost said something he shouldn't have.

The words left her mouth before she'd even stopped moving. "May I ask you a few questions?"

Ben didn't respond. He glanced at her quickly, top to bottom, and aimed his eyes at the only window on this side of the building.

"Mr. Bennett, correct? Harvey Bennett?" she asked.

Again, he didn't answer.

"People usually call you Ben, though, right?"

Reluctantly, he nodded.

"Mr. Bennett, you're a ranger here at Yellowstone? You've worked here for thirteen years, correct? First as an intern of sorts, then moving into your current role."

These weren't questions. She was verifying information some subordinate had given her.

"Standard procedure would suggest you introduce yourself first," Ben said.

The woman wasn't sidetracked, and she continued. "You were nineteen, moved your life up here, and now live in a trailer just outside the park's perimeter. May I ask what you were running away from?"

Ben clenched his jaw and resumed staring out the window.

I wasn't running away, he thought. *I just needed space.*

"Later, then. What about Rivera? Mr. Carlos Rivera, twenty-five years old, from Albuquerque, New Mexico. How long had you worked with him?" The woman's emphasis on the word "had" was not lost on Ben.

"Are you going to ask any questions you don't already know the answer to?" he shot back.

The woman hesitated, before nodding. "Fair enough. Mr. Bennett, can you talk about what you saw up there this morning? The explosion?"

Ben thought for a moment. "Looked like a bomb. Mushroom cloud and everything."

"Right. And what reaction did you and Mr. Rivera have when you noticed it?"

"We didn't have time to react to it—there was an earthquake, and then..." He didn't finish the thought. She was wearing an ID tag he didn't recognize.. "Who are you with?" he asked.

"The Centers for Disease Control, BTR Division, local out of Billings, Montana."

Ben got off the couch and stood over her. "Listen, uh, CDC, BTR— whatever, lady," he said as he walked past her. "I've answered questions now for almost an hour. If you want more information, just read the reports." He walked through the gathering of people, heading for the door. He pushed it open and stepped down onto the patio, not looking back.

He heard the outer screen door slam closed behind him, then creak back open again. Footsteps quickly pounded down the steps. Within seconds, the woman was next to him. He didn't slow down.

"I'm sorry, Mr. Bennett, I know you've had a rough morning, but—"

"*Rough morning?*" Ben stopped and wheeled around to face her. "A rough morning is what Rivera's family is having. A rough morning is what the families of the—what, one hundred or so?—people who were killed in that explosion are having. I'm just trying to have *a* morning, but it's apparently not going to be possible."

"I—I know, Mr. Bennett, I just—"

29

"Stop calling me that."

"Okay, I just need to know exactly what happened."

"You *know* what happened. You and everyone else. A bomb went off and a lot of people died. There was an earthquake, the ground opened up and Rivera fell into it. What else do you need from me? I tried to save him, okay? I had his arm, and he fell. What? You think I'm a suspect in a murder investigation or something?"

She lowered her voice. "No, *I* don't, Ben. But my boss isn't the kind of man who will just let things be. He's going to ask some questions—some very specific questions—and I need to be able to answer them to his satisfaction. I just want to get back to Montana, back home."

Ben kicked at a stone at his feet, then met the woman's eyes again. "Where exactly is home?"

"Outside Billings, small town called Lockwood."

He thought for a moment. "Will you do me a favor, uh—what is your name again?"

"Julie. Juliette Richardson."

"Right. Just do me a favor, Julie?"

She waited.

"If you can make sure I don't have to talk to anyone else about this mess? I'll tell you what I know; that's all I can do. But I don't want to screw around with the other government types like you or anyone else. Fair?"

The corner of her mouth tugged upwards, almost into a smile. "I think I can work that out."

4

The club connected with the ball directly in the sweet spot. Josh Hohn watched it sail down the fairway, breaking left before landing and following the contour of the long par 5, as if the ball had been guided remotely. Josh smiled, knowing exactly what his boss, Francis Valère, would say.

He heard the older man standing behind him mutter a French curse word under his breath and then, in English, "must be that nice piece you are using."

Josh knew that his countless hours of practice and thousands of practive drives, as well as his commitment to fitness, were the real reasons he was able to send the ball just about wherever he wanted it. But the TaylorMade SLDR driver was a gift from Valère, and the man tried as hard as possible to make Josh feel bad about it.

"Well, you picked it, boss." Josh winked at him.

Francis Valère grabbed a driver from his golf bag strapped to the back of their cart and marched up to a bright pink tee. Placing his ball carefully, he took a few practice swings before launching the ball down the fairway. He watched it rise and get caught in a gust of wind that pushed it to the right. The ball landed close to a sand trap, bounced a few times, and came to a stop in the taller grass just before the tree line.

Josh laughed. Valère glared at him.

"Should have bought one for yourself, I guess." Josh shrugged.

"Said the man who is still trailing me by three." Valère returned to the cart and put his club away. He slid into the driver's seat. "Come on, that one is going to be hard to find."

Josh was already sitting in the cart and checking his cell phone. "You've got to be kidding me..." He glanced up. "You're not going to believe this. Looks like a bomb went off at Yellowstone. "

"Terrorists?"

Josh scrolled through an article on his smartphone, skimming the news article that he'd pulled from his feed reader. "I don't know. It says there was minimal damage, some casualties..." he paused. "Shit, I don't mean to be morbid, but if you're going to bomb a place, wouldn't you choose one a little more, uh, populated?"

"I suppose I would." Valère kept driving, keeping the cart on the path that stretched along the right side of Hole 13. "Unbelievable."

"I know, right?"

"I am talking about the ball. I cannot see it anywhere." He brought the golf cart to a halt and stepped out. "You want to help me find it?"

Josh returned the phone to his pocket and exited the vehicle. "What were they hoping to achieve?"

Valère poked around with his foot, trying to find where the white

Nike ball had landed. The grass was perfectly trimmed, left a little long to differentiate it from the short-cropped blades nearby. "What do you think they are working on?"

Josh thought for a moment, the question and change of subject taking him by surprise. "Who knows? Maybe they're actually taking a vacation, like you ordered them to." Josh knew his boss was talking about the two lab assistants who also worked for Frontier Pharmaceuticals Canada. Valère had founded Frontier Pharmaceuticals Canada only a few years ago with a massive personal investment and some venture funding from a couple of his friends. He'd hired Joshua Hohn as his right-hand man and partner, and Josh had, in turn, hired the two part-time university students to help with data and organization.

"You know them as well as I do, Hohn—they are probably hard at work curing cancer or creating the next *super*food." He stressed the word "super" with his thick French accent. Josh knew he meant it as a joke, as they'd often made fun of America's blind obsession with "super" fruits and vegetables. He loved creating hybrid plant fungi in their lab that included an extra dosage of a vitamin or two, then trying to get Valère to market it as the "next big thing." It was a fun game Josh played while working on the other project.

And their other project really *was* the next big thing.

For the past three years he had inched closer to the finalization of a very real "super" drug: an organic shell that could grow around the cell walls of microscopic organisms. The shell acted as a sort of flexible and semi-permeable "armor."

It was fascinating to Josh, to conceive of a lab-created chemical bonding molecule that actually fused to a cell's outer wall and added an extra layer of protection while still allowing the cell's internal functions to interface with the outside world. It would revolutionize the pharmaceutical world. The world of nanotechnology was almost upon them, and Josh knew his career would be solidified if they were successful.

So far, they had been. Their biggest breakthrough happened last week, at the end of a long stretch of over twenty hours in "The Dungeon," the nickname he had given their dark, cluttered workspace. Josh had called Valère frantically, almost tripping over his words as the test results poured in.

The nanocoating he'd applied had finally done what it was supposed to do—it stuck.

Valère finally found his ball near a tree stump that was lined up perfectly between himself and the hole. He cursed again, grabbing a pitching wedge from his bag.

"Going up and over?" Josh asked, clearly surprised.

"I do not have it in me to waste three shots and let you catch up." He took a few practice swings and set into his swing ritual.

The shot was beautiful—a perfect arc that carried the ball cleanly over the stump and straight to the middle of the fairway, mere inches from Josh's first shot.

"Well, I'm glad I didn't bet you that you couldn't do it," Josh said.

"I am not a betting man," Valère said.

"No, you're not, but you should be. With this product of yours, you could have been set."

Valère turned to Josh. "Rest assured, my friend, my exposure in this company is over and above anything I would wager out here with you. And do not forget, you have quite a stake in this as well."

Josh nodded. He had signed on for a half-million-dollar salary, in

Canadian dollars, and had taken an options contract as well in preparation for their inevitable IPO. Further, he had a small percentage share in the company's future profits.

Basically, both men were about to be rich beyond their wildest dreams.

"When I get back into the office next week, I have a call with our other two investors and patent lawyer, and from there I will make a decision about timing," Valère said.

"What do you need me to work on, then?" Josh asked. They'd arrived at the mid-point of the hole and walked to where their balls lay in the grass. "I'm guessing we'll need to set up some meetings with the bigger representatives and start on the marketing?"

"No, we will wait on the marketing. I need to get the sample to the investors, and they will start production."

"Production of what?" Josh asked.

"Do you remember my trip to the Northwest Territory that I took a year ago?" Valère asked.

Josh cocked his head. This was an interesting and sudden change of subject.

"I visited the site of a native tribe of people who have long since perished. There, we also found the remains of a camp, and what we assumed was a Russian expedition."

"We? I thought you went alone?"

"I met with my investors—as you know, we have been business partners for a long time."

"So this was a business trip?" Josh asked. He was growing more and more confused.

"Of sorts, yes. Anyway, we discovered the cause of death for these poor explorers. A plant that is capable of releasing a small amount of its natural defense mechanism into the surrounding air when disturbed. In its powdered form, I believe, it was used by this native tribe as some sort of hallucinogen. However, over time, that same defense mechanism turned into a quite lethal substance."

"You're talking about the sample you have in the freezer, right? Those boxes that were shipped back with you?"

Valère nodded. "We wished to *also* use this substance as a defense mechanism, just like the plant did. However, I needed to strengthen it; to improve its potency—"

"You created a virus?"

"I *discovered* one. In its natural state, its potency is barely enough to harm a small mammal unless it is ingested in large quantities. But with a few alterations and improvements—"

"What are you talking about?" Josh was horrified. "That's not a medical application, Francis—"

"It does not concern you what the application is," Francis said.

Josh stepped up to his ball and slammed his club down in a reckless swing. The ball flew off the ground, leaving a dirty streak of brown in the grass. He watched, his anger building, as the ball careened to the right and over the line of trees. Without turning back around, he began walking toward the trees to find it.

How could he do this? he wondered. Josh had been working with Valère for over three years, and he thought he knew the man. They both had been interested in *preserving* life through their work and science.

This sounded like the exact opposite.

He crashed through the thick bushes that marked the end of the golf course and the beginning of undeveloped land and kept walking toward a stand of pine trees he'd last seen his ball flying toward. As he neared the trees he could hear the sound of running water.

The trees stood like sentinels in front of a steep hill, standing guard over the cliff. The hill fell away at a steep angle down to a river, where he could see water tumbling over rocks and forming small rapids as it wound through the canyon.

What he didn't see, however, was his ball.

"I believe it landed farther up," his boss's voice called out from behind him. Valère had driven their cart to the edge of the course and walked to Josh.

"You can't do this, Valère. You can't sell us out like that. Who's buying, anyway?"

"It is not a matter of money—"

"Bullshit!" Josh barked. "Of *course* it is! Why else would you have kept this from me?"

"I told you, it is not something you should concern yourself with. This plan predates our arrangement, Josh."

Josh watched as his boss removed Josh's driver from his bag. He inspected it, examining the lightweight graphite build. "We have been working for a lifetime on this, and it is not something I will abandon before I am finished."

Josh took a step back up toward the hill, a pained expression on his face. "Seems like *you're* a terrorist. That's all this is. You smug, genocidal fool."

"You have your names for what I do, and I have mine. I am working on something *far* bigger than anything you can imagine," Valère said. "Something much more significant."

"You won't get away with it," Josh said. "You won't be able to run from it when you're done."

"I am not planning on running, Josh. I am here, and I will stay right here. And if I am removed, there will be another to take my place. And another."

Josh saw his friend and business partner watch him, as if he were examining a specimen. "It is truly a shame, Joshua."

"What?" Josh's eyes widened as he noticed Francis raising the golf club into the air.

Valère lashed out with the club and struck Josh in the head. There was a sickening smack, and Josh immediately fell to the ground.

Blood ran into and over his eyes. Coating his vision with a shade of red. Another second passed and he couldn't see at all. The pain was excruciating. His brain felt like mush. He couldn't think; he couldn't speak—

"It is a truly a shame to lose a mind such as yours, my friend. But you are wrong. I will get away with it. America is not united enough to save itself."

Josh tried to raise his arm, to do something to fend off the attack he knew was coming—

But he could not.

He could only stare with unseeing eyes as Valère bought the driver down and smashed it into his skull.

5

Ben and Julie sat tucked away in a back corner of the staff cafeteria where the peeling paint on the walls had gone unnoticed for years. The faint smell of fryers and old food mixed with cleaning supplies was off-putting and yet familiar at the same time. Unpleasant if you were a newcomer, oddly comforting if you weren't.

Ben sipped his coffee, black, almost too hot to drink, while he waited for Julie's next question.

"Did you know Rivera well?"

"No."

"That's it? That's all you've got for me?"

"If you hadn't noticed, I don't make friends too quickly."

"So what was the deal with this bear?"

"Mo."

"Excuse me?"

"The name of the grizzly," Ben said. "Her name is Mo."

"You named the bear?"

"Yeah, we give names to some of our frequent flyers. Mo's got three strikes now, but we got her moved up there pretty far. Hopefully she was okay after the, uh, incident."

Julie scrawled some notes in a miniature notepad she'd taken from her back pocket. Ben sipped his coffee, waiting for her to finish. He listened to the gentle commotion emanating from the front lounge, bits of conversation floating in from rangers and park staff.

"...Was probably nuclear, right?"

"No way, too small—I mean, could have been a test or something gone wrong..."

"...Government's probably gonna try to cover this one up and sweep it under..."

Julie looked up and caught Ben's eye. "This wasn't an accident, but it certainly wasn't a government test or anything. They're going to be all over this place within the hour. By tonight, Yellowstone will be crawling with FBI, CIA, DoD, every acronym you can think of."

Ben cringed. "What about BTR?"

Julie glanced down at her own nametag briefly as though seeing it for the first time. "Oh, BTR," she said, "Biological Threat Research division of the CDC. Not exactly top-secret, but it's a new program the CDC's trying to get funding for. We're keeping it quiet until we have some victories under our belt."

"Like trying to figure out who bombed Yellowstone?"

She snorted. "Well, more like trying to analyze the long-term negative environmental effects of possible radiation in the fallout zone."

"Hmm, not exactly tabloid-worthy."

"No, it's pretty unexciting stuff, and that's why it's just an idea at this point. But if I—*we*—can write up something worthwhile, they might just make it a formal department."

Ben nodded. "And your office is in Billings. Seems like a pretty small city for a CDC office."

"It is, and that was part of the attraction. It's a skeleton crew right now, just me and my team of five—"

A loud shout echoed through the corridor from the other room, followed by a growing commotion and more voices.

"Get him inside, on that couch!" one voice shouted.

"Who is it?" Ben heard.

The voices grew frantic, Ben heard the deep gravel of his boss, George Randolph, trying to make his orders heard over the din. "Get him down and get some water. Pull his shirt off and let's get a look at that rash—"

Julie was on her feet. Ben followed along on behind.

"How much is covered? Hands, arms?"

"And his head—look at his neck!"

Julie pushed on the swinging door to the hallway and barred Ben from going any further. "Wait. We don't know what that is, but it's not going to do anyone any good if we walk in there, and it's contagious. They've got enough people in there anyway."

"But—"

Her cellphone started ringing. "Richardson," she said as she brought the phone up to her ear.

After a minute, she banged the phone on the table.

"A bit one-sided for that to have been an argument," Ben remarked.

"My boss. Come on," she said. She didn't wait for Ben to follow as she slid out the cafeteria's rear exit, through the back of the commercial kitchen.

Outside, they were met by a bright noon sun and a red haze from the morning's blast.

6

Northwest Territory, Canada

University of Manitoba Archaeological Dig

One Year Ago

The rest of the afternoon faded quickly into evening, but thankfully, their excavation moved at a brisk pace as well. Before nightfall, the team of six—five students and the professor—had uncovered the remains of a camp.

Their excavations had revealed that the camp was arranged in a semi-circle around a central opening, in which one student found the remnants of a campfire. Another student found a nearly complete flap of canvas tent, with tie-downs and a large tent stake. Next to it, a small pouch containing five silver coins—a miraculous find, especially considering that the Native Americans who had lived in these parts had never printed any coins.

They shared the information about depth, soil density, and procedure as they went, and just as dusk approached, the team found three more tents, all collapsed in on themselves and preserved reasonably well beneath layers of the cold soil.

Together they marked, documented, and mapped the entire area, eventually creating a computer model of the landscape and coordinates.

But it wasn't the tents, or the artifacts, or even the coins that caused the most commotion.

It was what the team had found *beneath* those tents.

As two students carefully removed the canvas from the ground under the watchful eye of Dr. Fischer, what lay undisturbed beneath it for three centuries became visible.

The corpses of a lost expedition.

Some bodies were preserved better than others, but it was clear from the clothing, cranial structures, and some of the additional artifacts found nearby, that it was the fabled Alexei Russian expedition of the early 18th century.

Dr. Fischer was ecstatic; this was a discovery that, to him, surpassed anything he'd ever achieved in his professional career before now. He would write a book—maybe a volume of books—about this expedition, what it was attempting to accomplish, where it had been, and what had led to the eventual demise of these poor men.

Of course, there were questions to answer before these secrets would reveal themselves.

They had found pieces of maps, journals, and scraps of clothing, but they would need more to piece the story together. But now that Dr. Fischer had committed to exploring the nearby caves tomorrow, they had even less time to spend at this site.

He moved to another rectangular opening in the earth; a new hole they'd dug to continue their exploration. Another three tents were revealed, and another six skeletal remains were uncovered. In one, a student had removed a smoking pipe of carved bone and a small leather-bound journal. The student gave the pipe directly to another student, who was hard at work logging the items into the computer database and mapping the precise location they were found. The journal he handed to Dr. Fischer.

"Thought this might be interesting to you," the student said.

Dr. Fischer donned a pair of fresh latex gloves and held the journal delicately. He felt its worked leather surface, noticing the fine craftsmanship and attention to detail. After so many years, it really was remarkable.

Most remarkable, however, was the fact that some of the paper inside the journal was still intact. Dirty, smudged, and difficult to read, but intact nonetheless.

He held the journal open, barely enough to peer inside, as he did not want to damage the worn spine, but he moved the book around to let enough light in to see what was on the right-hand page.

"Anyone read Russian?" he called. "And good eyes? This is too small for me to see."

"Losing your vision already, old man?" one of the students yelled.

Dr. Fischer laughed.

Gareth, the student working the computer, stood and stretched. "I got it," he said. "I can use a break anyway. Anyone want to take over?"

Another graduate student fell in behind the computer screen and continued to document the dig site.

"You read Russian?" Dr. Fischer asked.

"Yeah, it was an undergraduate minor. Something I was interested in."

"Why?"

"Girl I met before that semester. I was hoping to impress her when I saw her again next year. Turned out she was German, but I kep taking the classes for fun."

Dr. Fischer shook his head. He handed the small book over to his student and waited.

"Okay, yeah, I got this. Pretty good handwriting, actually. Let's see... *'One more eventless day. Full moon last night and one of the men has caught a rabbit.'*" Gareth looked up. "Pretty exciting stuff, Doc." Some of the other students who had gathered around chuckled.

"Keep reading," Dr. Fischer said.

"*'One other place in my life I have found solace such as this...'* Can't read that word; I think it's a town or something. *'The wind whispers through our ranks; the snow crunches beneath our feet, and you would imagine it was the loudest noise in the forest.'*" He gently flipped through a few more pages. "A lot of this is more of the same," he said.

By now, the other four students were gathered around Gareth and Dr. Fischer, each leaning on a shovel or sitting on the ground.

"Skip to the end," Dr. Fischer said.

Gareth flipped to the back of the small leather journal. "Here we go. Last entry: *'It has made us sick. The baskets filled with that strange powder. No treasure is worth this. It has consumed us all. It is clear to me now that I am to die here alone..."* Gareth's voice trailed off just as the words of the journal entry had. His eyes were wide, surprise on his face. "Whoa. Pretty intense."

"Damn," another student whispered.

Dr. Fischer replayed the words in his mind, trying to commit them to memory. They'd found baskets somewhere. Somewhere close to where they now stood. Whatever was in them, besides these coins, was deadly. He looked up sharply, finding a young woman's face in the crowd. "Steph—did any of you find any of these baskets? Or more coins?"

She shook her head. "No, nothing like that yet..." her voice shook. "Should we be worried? You know we hear about live *Yersinia pestis* being found at sites once in a while."

"No, no, I don't think this is the plague," Dr. Fischer said. "Besides, the coins were out in the open, so they should be fine. But we need to change our plans a little. I'm not sure excavating any more of this area tomorrow is such a great idea."

The students nodded solemnly. Somehow, just knowing this information had changed their perceptions of this site. Knowing that it wasn't starvation or attack that had killed these men, but something sinister and hidden, had deeply unnerved them.

7

"David Livingston," Julie said to Ben as they walked across the parking lot, "is pretty much exactly what you think of when you think 'bureaucracy by the book.' He'd rather fail doing it the right way than succeed by not following the rules." Julie turned left and started down a row of parked cars, Ben in tow; sedans, small station wagons.

"He's not exactly the easiest person to work with, either," she continued. "Actually, you don't work *with* Livingston at all. You work *for* him. In his world, that means everyone's working against him, and it's up to him to right all our wrongs."

"Sounds like a bucket of fun," Ben said as they passed yet another Subaru Outback. "Which one's yours?"

Julie clicked the button on her key fob and a beep sounded from down the row. Ben stopped short. Ahead lay a monstrous Ford F-450, extended cab Lariat. Dark gray. It loomed over the minuscule Suburus around it.

Julie threw him the keys. "You drive," she said.

Ben wondered if it was Christmas. "Really?" He tried not to seem impressed.

She reached for the back door on the driver's side and opened it up, grabbing a laptop case and bag. "I've got some work to do. You, uh, think you can handle her?"

Ben got into the driver's seat and strapped in. He turned on the engine and listened to it purr while he waited for Julie to get in on her side. Once seated, he threw the truck into gear.

"Anyway, Livingston's making us do these reports." She opened the laptop. "He's got this idea that if we write everything down and email it to him, he'll be able to 'crack the case,' or figure out whatever it is we're supposed to figure out. It's pretty annoying, to say the least.

"So that call just now?" Julie continued. "He wants an *in-person* report every forty-eight hours. Can you believe that? He said if we can't make it face-to-face, we have to call in, but it 'won't look good.' I'm already up to here with processing, reports, and government forms, not to mention actually *doing* my job. And he thinks if I'm too busy to actually get to the office I have enough time to give him a play-by-play update over the phone?"

Ben listened as she vented, guiding the truck out of the parking lot and down the curved path leading from the staff facility. As he turned onto the main park road, he turned to Julie. "Where exactly are we going?"

She glanced back at him. "Oh, uh, I guess I should ask you first."

Ben waited.

"You have plans? I could use your help back at the office."

Ben couldn't hide his surprise. "Back in Billings? That's two hours away."

She shrugged. "Just over two-and-a-half, actually. I assumed you didn't have anything going on, what with the park needing to be closed for a while."

"I *do* have a life outside of the park."

"Really?"

Ben couldn't tell if she was being serious or not. "Theoretically," he said.

"I've got more questions to ask you," she said. "But I can't wait until after I get back. Livingston will want to know as soon as possible."

He drove in silence for a few minutes. "I'll need to swing by my place to pick up some clothes."

"Billings has a Target, buy some when we get there." Julie's head didn't even lift up from her computer screen.

"You buy 'em, if you want my help."

"Deal."

He hadn't expected that. "Look," he said. "I'll help you out for a couple days, tops. But just because I don't have anything else going on doesn't mean I want to play chauffeur for you forever."

"I promise. Just to the office, and then I'll buy you a plane ticket home—I can get my report prepared and sent on the way, and if anything comes up I can just ask."

"Okay then," he replied, uneasily. "But hold the plane ticket. I'll rent a car."

Julie didn't question him. They drove on in silence for another twenty minutes, finally coming to a gas station. "One other thing," Ben said.

"What's that?"

"This is your truck. You pay for gas."

8

David Livingston sat in his executive leather office chair and cracked his knuckles—an old habit. He ran his hands through his thick, oiled black hair and shifted in his seat. His computer dinged once with the sound of an incoming email, but he ignored it.

Clicking away from the news site, he read through the dossier on Juliette Alexandra Richardson, native of Montana. Other than a brief stint in California during and after college, she'd lived in Montana her entire life. He'd had his data lead, Randall Brown, send a copy to his office, where he scanned it and shredded the paper—a wasted tree and no doubt a waste of productive time. After five years at the CDC, he still had no idea why it was so damned difficult to just email everything. The data lead had tried explaining it to him several times—something about security and sensitive information, but it never took.

He reached the end of the dossier, not finding anything unusual or out of place. He shouldn't have been surprised—this was the third time he'd read it. It was similar to what his own looked like five years ago. Clean, simple, and without a black mark.

He had reached this point in his career through determination, hard work, and then bad luck. He'd first applied to the CDC as an investigator, hoping to land a job that allowed him to travel, study, and research the kinds of terrifying things the rest of world paid them to keep hidden. He'd started out following a team of scientists and biologists into the Andes but couldn't manage to get his name in the paper that was eventually written. After graduating and finishing his internship, he was passed over three times before landing a desk job at the Atlanta campus—CDC headquarters. He had toiled there for four years, e-signing his boss' expense reports and preparing meeting agendas.

Then his boss died. A man of sixty-one, a sudden heart attack left the department without a manager. Rather than replace him, Livingston found himself outsourced along with everyone else and the department all but shut down. Floating around, he landed a brief position as a "research specialist," effectively a news and media junkie who speculated on which outbreak or natural disaster would lead to the next Mad Cow Disease or Bird Flu.

During his tenure, there was none.

Finally, his luck turned—or so he thought. What appeared to be an opportunity to lead a brand new, recently brainstormed section of the CDC became the mind-numbing middle management job in which he currently served. They'd been relegated to the backwaters of the CDC—southern Montana—and asked to "provide guidance on environmental and biological threats to the nation."

In other words, he and his team were glorified storm chasers.

To Livingston, it was the worst place in the entire world.

Juliette, on the other hand, had come through his doors as a young CDC employee three years ago, still wet behind the ears with the usual "change the world" mentality. He wouldn't have picked her himself, but she had come highly recommended by people above his pay grade.

Plus, her looks certainly hadn't hurt her chances. Average height, thin, and cuved in all the right places, she was certainly what he would describe as "a looker."

Livingston pushed back from the desk and stood up, stretching his back and popping his neck. He pressed a button on the small intercom next to his computer and waited a moment.

"Please grab Stephens and tell him to come up here."

A woman's voice responded through his closed door. "Yes, Mr. Livingston."

Livingston knew his use of the intercom was an act of arrogance, but he didn't care. The intercom was a speaker that had been mounted on the wall outside his door, pointing down at the rest of the staff's desks. Their office space was so small that the only closed-door office rooms inside were his own and Julie Richardson's, which was currently unoccupied. The administrative secretary, technically charged to serve the entire staff of seven, had been given the nameplate "Executive Administrator" by Livingston, in order to help specify to everyone in the room who exactly she—and everyone else—*really* worked for.

When the knock on the door came, he waited a while, sat back down, then cleared his throat. "Come on in, Stephens."

Benjamin Stephens opened the door and stood on the threshold. He looked annoyed. "What can I do for you, Livingston?"

Livingston bristled—he wasn't a fan of people calling him just by his last name. He let it slide, but logged it into his mental file of personal grievances. "Thanks for coming so quickly."

"David, the secretary's desk is literally right next to mine, four feet from your door. If I didn't hear you over her intercom, I would've still heard you asking for me through the door."

Livingston ignored the response and motioned for Stephens to sit.

"I need you to do me a favor, Stephens," he said. "Richardson's out on assignment, and she was near Yellowstone Park." He paused. "You're aware of what happened at Yellowstone Park?"

Stephens nodded.

"Good. Well, anyway, she's out there traipsing around, trying to figure out how the regional environment will be affected by the radiation."

"I thought she was trying to study some fishing traps and the impact they're having on insects downriver?"

"She is—or she was. This is a little side project she came up with when she heard about the explosion. You know how she can be—overzealous and all that."

Stephens nodded again. "She's a hard worker."

"I want you to check in with her, like normal. You're her second-in-command on this team, and I need you to step up. She's not the kind of person to get excited about reporting back, but I know you understand why we do that."

"Yes, sir."

"Good. Get in touch with her and stay in touch with her. Stick to the traditional channels—send everything through SecuNet. Clear?"

Stephens hesitated.

"What is it?"

"Well, no, sir, I mean that's great, but I don't understand how this is different than how I usually run things."

"It's not, Stephens. I'm just *reminding* you, since your team lead seems to think she can invent the rules. I don't want you forgetting how we do things around here, okay? You get Julie on speed-dial, and you keep me updated on what she's doing."

"Right."

"Randy from Data is ready to go, and he'll get you set up on SecuNet if he already hasn't. All phone calls, emails, hell—even telegraphs, I don't care—go through Data."

Livingston watched his employee carefully, trying to read the younger man's expression. He knew that *Stephens* knew Randall Brown was on vacation, but he wanted to see how Stephens would react. Would he ask a follow-up question? Pretend that Brown wasn't away? Something else entirely?

It was one of many types of "power games" Livingston enjoyed playing with his underlings—watching them squirm as they tried to figure out how best to respond.

Stephens stood as Livingston was finishing. "Got it, sir."

In Stephens' case, Livingston was usually disappointed: Stephens had a fantastic poker face.

"Great." Livingston looked back down at his computer and pretended to be checking email. He waited until Stephens left the office, made his way over to a small cabinet on the wall at the back of the room.

He pulled out a decanter and poured himself a scotch. He'd made sure to specify in the employee manual that drinking was not allowed in the office, but he also believed that it was his executive right to be able to indulge in some of the finer things in life. He would have lit a cigar as well if it wouldn't smoke them all out of the small space.

9

Ben had been driving for the better part of two hours.

Julie was now fast asleep in the seat beside him. Her hair was tousled, poking up from the back where her tight brown ponytail had come into contact with the seat's headrest. She'd kicked her right knee up against the window, trying to curl into a position that was more conducive to sleep, her body pressed into a much smaller space than Ben would've imagined possible. She'd kicked her shoes off long ago. Thankfully her feet didn't stink.

Ben changed the channel to country music. An old George Strait song piped through the cabin.

Julie stirred and wiped her mouth.

"Didn't mean to wake you," he said.

She opened her eyes and blinked. "Oh, my God. I, uh, I guess I fell asleep," she said with surprise. She sat up straight, moving her leg back down and straightening her creased blouse. She reached up to her hair. "Oh, man, what a mess. I guess I was more tired than I thought. Sorry."

"Don't worry about it," Ben said. He was about to say something else but stopped himself.

"What?"

"Huh? Oh, nothing. Just, uh, don't worry about it. Go back to sleep, you obviously need it."

"No, I think I'm good." She noticed the music. "Country? Good choice for this road."

Ben thought for a moment. "Hey, back at the staff building. That guy they brought in? What do you think it was?"

Julie didn't answer at first. Ben wondered if she was collecting her thoughts, or still tired. "Yeah, I've been thinking about that too. The way they described it—at least what I could hear—it sounded like a rash. Maybe viral." She sighed. "I should have taken a look before we left."

"Viral? That's a leap. I was thinking poison ivy or something."

"Are you kidding? The way they were talking about it? Those guys were mostly all park rangers, right? You'd know a simple poison ivy rash, wouldn't you?"

Ben shrugged. "Sure."

"Besides, it was spreading. They said it was on his hands and arms, but then a few seconds later said they thought they saw it on his neck, too."

"What spreads like that?" Ben asked.

"Well I guess—if it's just a rash, it could be anything. Candidiasis, rheumatic fever, mononucleosis—chickenpox."

"Chickenpox? Really?" Ben looked skeptical.

"Sure—VZV, the varicella-zoster virus—if you don't get it as a child, can be super dangerous as an adult, especially if you're immune-deficient. But without getting a look at it, it's impossible to say. I'll be interested to see what the medical team has to say."

Ben waited a moment before asking his next question. "Except you don't think it's Chickenpox at all, do you?"

Julie didn't respond.

"This isn't some run-of-the-mill rash, is it?"

Julie didn't look him in the eye. Finally, she turned to him. "I think this is something else—something bigger. First the explosion, then this? What if both are related?"

Ben shrugged. "Depends on if anyone else has this rash thing, right? Might just be a one-off thing. A coincidence."

"Yeah, it just seems fishy."

They drove on in silence for a while longer. According to the news, ninety-three people had died from the explosion at Yellowstone, and countless others were now being evacuated from the park grounds. Early reports confirmed their suspicions: there was some sort of pathogen that appeared to be infecting some people.

"When will they get the results back on whether this is your fake Chickenpox?"

"We don't have a mobile lab in place yet, so they're airlifting the samples to Atlanta in the morning. We should get the results back in a couple of days. Why?"

"You think we can get our hands on a sample?" Ben asked.

Julie seemed circumspect. "Maybe. It won't be easy, but I think I could. Why?"

"If this *is* bigger than people realize, and we're talking about a fast-spreading disease, why are we evacuating the park and letting everyone go home when they could be infected?"

"Because we have no reason to hold them."

"Look," Ben said. "I might know someone close by who can help. If we can keep this boss of yours out of it…"

Ben watched her think it over.

"How fast would your friend get results back to us?"

"An hour. Two tops."

"I'll need to send Livingston *something*, so I'll see if I can get a sample from the park sent over, and I'll send part of it to the lab and the rest to your contact, if you trust him."

"Her. And I do," Ben said. "She's not working under any sort of traditional structure, so it should be pretty quick. Maybe it'll give you a head start."

"Of course. Who is this person?" she asked.

"Like I said," Ben responded, "just someone who might be able to help."

10

The computer in front of her chirped, signaling a new email. Amid stacks of books, unfiled papers, and other detritus from weeks of research, the desktop computer was almost hidden from view. Dr. Diana Torres found the mouse hidden under a sheaf of papers and shook the screen awake from its preinstalled screensaver—a never-ending ribbon of color.

She navigated across the desktop and clicked on the icon—the only app that was constantly running on this machine. Never much of a computer person, Dr. Torres often called in her research assistant to finalize and prepare her reports electronically. He chided her for the irony of it—a woman whose career was spent creating computer models of molecules and microscopic organisms was afraid of computers. She never let it bother her; it was all in good fun. But regardless of her methods, unorthodox or not, the research firm knew she was one of the best in the business at what she did.

Her position had only recently been finalized after months of contracting with the research firm. She enjoyed the work, mainly because she didn't have to put up with any bureaucracy or any of the usual corporate nonsense that had driven her from previous jobs. The firm had been established over forty years ago and had constantly been in a stage of growth. Still, Dr. Torres had been a "key hire," and was expected to take the firm to new levels in biological molecular research.

Dr. Torres double-clicked the email—no subject line—and began reading the body of the text. The email was short and to the point; just a request for help on a particular project. She brushed aside an old Wendy's burger wrapper and a half-empty Diet Coke that was lying in front of her keyboard. She rolled her chair closer to the desk and clicked on the "reply" button. As her fingers hit the keys to type a standardized answer to the request, she caught a glimpse of the sender's email address.

She did a double-take and read the email address again. She lifted her hands from the keyboard to think through her response. She reached over to the Diet Coke and brought it to her lips. She took a long, slow sip of the completely flat soda and read the email one more time.

> *I need your help on this one. Sending sample soon. Came from Yellowstone explosion. Please rush, will call soon.*

> *Ben*

Ben? She hadn't heard from Ben in over a decade. She knew he'd become a park ranger and had little to no access to the outside world most of the time. Still, she was stunned.

She took out her cell phone—a flip phone relic that she'd used for years—scrolled through the contacts. When she came to his name, she hesitated over the dial button. She'd never actually used this number. She stared down at the phone for another few seconds and then slammed it shut.

Not now, she thought. *Not yet.*

Thoughts raced through her mind. *Where was he? What was he doing? Why did he need her help, of all people?*

She sat in the chair for another few minutes, brooding. She didn't move until her assistant came in.

"Dr. Torres?" The young man's voice snapped her back to reality. She tried to wipe the surprised expression from her eyes but she failed.

"Dr. Torres—are you okay?"

"I—I'm all right," she said in return. "Just got another request. Something... I didn't expect, but we'll get going on it pretty soon."

"Sounds good. I can prepare equipment and send word down to Vanessa that some samples will be arriving. Do you have a date?"

At first, Dr. Torres didn't know how to respond. She eased out of her chair and walked toward the young man in the doorway. "Not sure, Charlie. Let's get everything set up now just to be ready. It's just going to be me and you on this one, understand?"

Charlie Furmann nodded without hesitation. The bulk of the company's projects were government funded, but the employed scientists were free—encouraged, even—to pursue personal interests and research projects when time permitted. Some of these projects, Charlie knew, weren't exactly public knowledge.

"I'll get everything set up this afternoon. I'll have Vanessa bring the package up personally when it arrives and leave it outside my office. The lab is open tomorrow night from about 8:30 until the next morning—shall I get it booked?"

"Yes, please. Thank you. I'm going to finish up here and head home. Don't worry about cleaning anything up; I'll be back in bright and early."

Charlie didn't say anything else. He left the room, closing the door behind him. Dr. Torres turned back to her computer and sat down in the chair. The screensaver had already resumed, and she wiggled the mouse to wake it up.

She stared at the screen for another minute, reading the email over and over again.

11

Northwest Territory, Canada

University of Manitoba Archaeological Dig

One Year Ago

It'll be any minute now, Gareth Winslow thought. He'd called in, just the way he'd been instructed, over three hours ago, just after he'd finished reading out loud the small journal they'd found. Dr. Fischer was ecstatic, mostly because their findings would verify and support his tenure.

He couldn't believe it himself, really. Some weird powdery substance that killed people? *That* was pretty exciting. But what was it? Spores, maybe? It was the ultimate question, but there was no way Dr. Fischer was letting any of them near the cave and the rest of the unopened baskets. It was way too risky, and besides, they didn't have the equipment to start a field analysis of whatever might be inside.

Still, Gareth knew everyone was curious. Beyond curious, actually.

Dinner was campfire-cooked foil packets filled with vegetables, and the conversation surrounding the bonfire in the middle of camp related to two topics: What was this substance and who put it there?

Theories ran from the dried remains of some mysterious plant the native tribes in the area held as sacred, or at least viewed as medicinal, to some extravagant assassination conspiracy by a Romanov-era traitor. Even Dr. Fischer, clearly playing along, threw in a far-fetched story of alien invaders using a cosmic element to start their takeover of the human race.

Gareth listened intently, as curious as everyone else, but he didn't contribute to the building exuberance of the conspiracy theorists. He wasn't sure what was in the baskets, but he knew it didn't matter.

Only a matter of time, he told himself again. *They should be here by now.*

As if on cue, his ears picked up the faint beating of helicopter rotors. It was low pitched and vibrated gently, seeming to emanate from within his body rather than from a machine flying in from miles away. As it grew in volume, a few other students picked up on it.

"Hey, shut up for a sec—you guys hear that?" one of the students asked. Everyone went silent, and only the crackling of the fire in front of them could be heard.

Another few seconds passed, and another student heard the noise. "Is that a helicopter? Out here?"

Gareth watched Dr. Fischer straining to listen— *he probably couldn't hear it yet,* Gareth thought—*but he will.*

Suddenly, Dr. Fischer's eyes opened wider and Gareth stood,

acting out his role. "It definitely is. Weird; I wonder where they're headed?"

Gareth excused himself from the group and walked over to one of the trucks in their three-car caravan. He opened the passenger-side door, reached below the seat, squeezing his arm into the gap between the truck's floor and the bottom of the chair, and felt around.

He found his prize. Slowly, he withdrew his hand, the dome lights inside the truck illuminating the small device.

It was black and silver, plastic with some metal components. A small rubber antenna extended from one side of the rectangular box, directly above a tiny button. He pushed the button, held it, and waited for a faint LED light to flash red once.

Done.

It was amazing what technology could do. The tiny GPS tracking device was now activated, and the inbound helicopter would stop tracking the archeology team's *expected* location within a grid of longitudinal coordinates and begin tracking their *actual* location. Their general coordinates had been posted on the university's internal boards months ago, but even Dr. Fischer was unsure where exactly their hunt for the Russian team would take them.

For that reason, the Company needed someone on the ground.

Gareth Winslow was brought onto the team to provide IT and administrative support—a part of archeology that hadn't existed a few years ago, when much of the data collected was shipped off and documented elsewhere. Using his interest in archeology and his undergraduate degrees in Computer Science and Technology Systems, he had assisted in building a suite of software tools that were helpful to archeologists, geologists, and geographers.

And since he was the one who had written the program, he was the perfect grad student to operate it. The recruitment interview with Dr. Fischer was short and sweet—they shook hands, Dr. Fischer asked if he was interested in helping out, and Gareth was in.

It was only after they'd started planning the trip that Gareth was approached by the Company. A shady guy in a black suit showed up at his apartment one day, knocked on his door, and gave him a check.

It was the largest paycheck that Gareth had ever seen his name on before, and he hadn't done anything to earn it.

"There's another one just like it after your trip," the man had said.

"For what?" Gareth knew that everyone had their price, but he wasn't about to kill someone.

"Don't worry," the man had said, sensing his unease. "Nothing illegal. The Company deals in information, and we've set up similar deals with plenty of other digs and research projects around the world."

"And what company is that?" Gareth had asked.

"*The* Company," the man had replied.

Gareth remembered nodding once, still consumed by the amount of money on the check.

"Okay, that's fine. I can live with a mysterious benefactor. But why not just go to the university? Or the expedition lead, Dr. Fischer?"

"We can't have a legal battle if there's anything of value found. You understand that. Plus, we need the expedition to run as smoothly as possible, without any hiccups along the way. Follow?"

"I do. You don't want anyone jealous that I'm making this kind of money on some low-profile dig."

The man had nodded in return. "Good. You understand. As I said, the Company is prepared to write another check in this amount if you successfully report any findings during your excursion." He made sure Gareth was looking at him as he finished. "You have a few days before you depart. I would suggest cashing the check first so you know we're not messing around, and then you'll be given instructions."

Gareth's hand had been shaking the entire conversation, but as the man finished speaking, he suddenly found a boost of confidence. "You got it. I'm in."

That was over a week ago, and Gareth was still riding the high of knowing what would be in his bank account one week from now. So much money it would wipe out his student loans and he'd still have enough left over to live life. He thought through the list of instructions he'd been given after he cashed the check, to make sure he wouldn't mess anything up.

It was a short list:

1. Participate in the expedition and do nothing to raise suspicion.

2. If any profitable or seemingly conspicuous items are found, email details to the address below.

The rest of the letter was a simple liability waiver, "*that by accepting and depositing the check the Company was hereby removed from any liability yada yada...*"

He'd sent the email after reading the journal for Dr. Fischer, using his laptop and satellite connection. Gareth mentioned briefly that they'd found "some sort of powdery substance that supposedly led to the demise of the entire Russian expedition..." and "we believe there to be more of the substance available in a nearby cave..." He sent it, and almost immediately there was a response. It was simple:

"We are converging on your general location. As the included battery will not hold much power, use the device only when you believe we are close to help us find your exact position."

Wow, Gareth thought. *These guys are on the ball.*

Now, as the helicopter's rotor wash grew, he knew they'd be on them in minutes. *Do I need to do anything to prepare?*

He placed the tracking device back under the seat of the truck and slammed the door. As he turned back to the campfire, he noticed the students and Dr. Fischer standing and looking around the sky, trying to figure out where the helicopter was coming from.

"There it is!" the Korean guy yelled out. Gareth hadn't bothered to learn any of their names—he knew they'd go home empty-handed, so there was no reason to become part of the team.

They all looked to where he was pointing. Southwest, hanging low over the tree line. If it weren't for the slowly receding hill they were on, they wouldn't have been able to see the bird at all.

Gareth examined the growing shape in the dusky sky. It looked dark, almost black, but that could be due to the lack of light at this time of day. It seemed to be sleek, too, not like the commercial helicopters he'd seen flying around cities. It was flatter, more military-looking.

Stealthier.

The copter finally drew near. It slid gently over the trees, slowing to their location, and began to descend. *Where the hell is it going to land?* Gareth thought. He looked around at their small clearing. The trucks, tents, and campfire were spread out almost evenly over the area, and he couldn't see where a helicopter that size would fit.

But the pilot had a different impression of the clearing. Gareth watched as the pilot masterfully guided the machine to a spot less than twenty yards from the campfire and then straight down to the grassy platform. He watched the skids land gracefully on the blades of grass, finally coming to a rest without the slightest bump or hop.

Before the copter had even hit the ground, though, three men jumped from its interior. Dressed in black and silver body armor and flight gear, they immediately began walking toward the group of students as the pilot finalized his landing.

It was hard to hear over the rotor noise, but the first man yelled over it anyway. "Gareth Winslow!" he paused and looked at each student and the professor, waiting for a response.

"R— right here," Gareth yelled.

The three men turned to him and met him halfway between the trucks and the campfire.

"Gareth Winslow?" the man said again. Gareth nodded. "Good. Take me to the location of the discovery."

"What is this?" Dr. Fischer yelled. "What's going on here?"

"It does not concern you," one of the men said. "Gareth, take us to the location."

Gareth snapped to attention, remembering his bargain. "Right.

Okay, come on. We're about a quarter mile away, through these trees."

He led the way, the three men and the rest of the group following behind. As they neared the cave, one of the men held up a hand and grabbed Gareth's shoulder. "Wait," he said.

Gareth watched him enter the small cave and return a minute later. He nodded to the two other men from the helicopter and began walking back toward them. He addressed the entire group of confused students and professor. "Who is leading this expedition?"

Dr. Fischer raised a hand. "I am. And do you mind telling me what's going on?"

The man eyed Dr. Fischer. "I see. And you have an idea of what might be inside that cave?"

"I—I guess. We found it earlier today, by accident. I believe whatever was in there killed the Russian expedition we came here to find."

"I understand that much, Dr. Fischer. But I'm asking if you have any idea what, *exactly*, killed them?"

Dr. Fischer thought a moment, then replied. "I have some ideas, but none that I'm entirely confident about just yet."

"I see." The man marched back through the group, the two other men following behind. He delivered orders without turning back. "Mark the location. Get me the coordinates saved and ready to go." The two men nodded and peeled off from the group, heading back toward the cave.

Gareth was now at the back of the line, watching as the lead man entered the helicopter once again. He heard him address the professor from the inside of the vehicle. "Dr. Fischer, would you care to join us? I would like to discuss your knowledge and experience with the items found within the cave."

"I'm not sure I feel comfortable—"

The man cut him off as he drew a pistol from a hip holster and aimed it squarely at Dr. Fischer's face. "Let me rephrase the question, professor, so that it doesn't seem so... *optional.*"

Dr. Fischer swallowed, then started climbing into the helicopter. "What about the others? The students?" he asked.

The two men reappeared, apparently having finished marking the coordinates, and jumped into the helicopter. Gareth looked around at the frightened students, and a growing wave of nausea filled him.

What have I done? he thought. The helicopter, filled with the pilot, the three men, and their professor, lifted a few feet off the ground. The students, wide-eyed and confused, began yelling.

"You can't do this!"

One of the men appeared in the open door of the helicopter and made eye contact with Gareth, just as he lifted something off the floor. It swiveled, held by some support mechanism, and swung out and stopped just outside the helicopter.

Gareth felt his blood run cold.

It was a gun. A *huge* gun. Gareth recognized the gigantic bullets, strapped together in a shiny gold chain of death. He took a staggering step back, trying to form words. *We need to leave,* he tried to say.

The words didn't escape his mouth. Instead, he felt himself being lifted off the ground and thrown backwards, hard, just as he heard a new noise. A *chug, chug, chug* sort of sound, but fast. He saw the gun's fiery tip burning as each round left the barrel and flew into one of the students. He wanted to close his eyes, but he didn't need to.

Everything went black.

12

As he walked past the newsstand just inside the door to the gas station, Ben noticed the tiny black and white television sitting on the shelf above it. It was set to a news channel he didn't recognize, most likely only syndicated throughout the small region of southern Montana they were in.

They'd stopped just past Red Lodge, on a stretch of highway that looked like it had been abandoned for a century. When they came to the service station, Julie had opted to stay in the truck while Ben ran in for some snacks and use the restroom.

He asked the attendant to turn up the volume. The old guy complied and Ben listened to the station's reporter on location outside the Yellowstone gates. The information wasn't anything new.

The explosion had, in fact, been a bomb, based on air sample analysis done on site and in a radius around the park. It was a type of thermobaric bomb, combining heat and pressure into a 5-kiloton explosion. Initial estimates postulated that the Yellowstone detonation was contained mostly underground, due to the vast amount of crust that had turned up around the site, as well as the relatively mild explosion. But it wasn't just the immediate effects of the bomb's blast that had the CDC and this news station worried about: the thin layer of crust beneath Yellowstone had been rattled, causing the cracks and earthquake-like effects Ben had experienced.

Ben set a candy bar and bag of chips down on the counter. He paid in cash and headed back out to the truck.

"Got you some chips," he said through Julie's open window. "Want to drive?"

"No," she said. "I'm enjoying being a passenger for a while." She smiled.

"I'm sure," Ben said. "Getting all that work done, catching up on your reading…"

"Just get in. We need to get to my office before tonight. Did you hear anything from your boss yet? What was his name?" she asked.

"Randolph. He just texted me. I'll call him back now." Ben swung into the lifted truck and started the engine. He slid his phone out of the cup holder in the center console.

The phone rang three times before Randolph picked up. The man sounded exhausted; breathing heavily, his voice raspy. *"Ben—that you?"*

"Everything okay?"

"No. No, it's not, Ben. There's—well, there's been…" Randolph took a labored breath. *"It's Fuller. He's—he's dead."*

Ben whispered the news to Julie. Her eyes widened. "I'm sorry," Ben said into the phone. "He was a good man."

"Whatever got to him, it's spreading."

"What do you mean?"

"I mean exactly what I said. It's spreading. Jumping, almost. We can't figure it out. It's fast. Much faster that we would have thought. Those of us who helped Fuller are covered in the rash, and our skin is starting to burn—me, Matheson, Frank, Clemens, everyone who was in that room. We've got it. We're quarantined inside the main building. Matheson passed out not too long ago, but—this is bad."

Ben didn't know what to say. "Listen, Randolph, you're going to be fine. You just—"

"Ben, listen. I didn't text just to keep you in the loop. We're in over our heads here. Two of my guys are already starting to hyperventilate, and there's a doctor in here that's checking everyone out. He pulled me aside an hour ago and told me it's some sort of viral infection, he thinks, and there's nothing he can do for us without quarantine facilities and better supplies.

"I wanted to see how you were doing. I don't know where you were when we brought Fuller in, but you might be safe from it. Did you get out of the park?"

"We did."

"We?"

"I'm with Julie. Juliette Richardson, from the CDC."

"Oh." Randolph paused, taking a deep, raspy breath. *"Okay, good. Well, stay away from the park, Ben. I'm not sure what's going to come of this, but if we can keep the contagion isolated long enough, we might be able to get a jump on it and figure out what it is before anyone else..."*

"Right. I'm headed to her office now. We're outside of Red Lodge,

Montana." Ben stopped for a second, catching himself. "Randolph —George. I—I'm sorry."

"Stop. Don't worry about it. Stay with that CDC gal and help her do what she can to stop it. Oh, and there's one more thing."

"What's that?"

"Fuller was at the lake when that bomb went off. He said he was close enough to feel the heat, and the pressure blast knocked him on his ass. But he wasn't hurt badly, and started walking back to his cabin when he felt the itching start.

"I'm starting to think it might have, uh, dispersed something into the air."

"How can a bomb do that?"

"I don't know. But he was the closest person to that explosion that we've talked to, and he's the first person who's died from this virus—whatever it is—that we know about. Understand?"

"I do, George," Ben said. He considered apologizing again, but thought better of it. *What was the point?* They were already dead.

He hung up the phone and hammered on the gas pedal, aiming the truck down the long highway.

13

Francis Valère poked at the food in front him. One of Quebec's finest restaurants and he couldn't get himself to eat.

Did killing Josh really affect him that much?

Of course it had, but it needed to be done.

He wondered if he needed to vomit again. The anxiety had risen immediately after their encounter on the golf course. Valère forcefully pushed the memory away and looked down at the plate in front of him.

Lobster, filet mignon, and the most decadent-looking chocolate mousse he'd ever seen stared back up at him. Not a bite had been taken from any of them. He used his fork to poke around the plate, pushing the meat to one side. He used another utensil to pile the lobster on the steak, forming a wall. It was a castle; a sanctuary now. If only he was small enough to fit inside...

"Are you alright, Valère?"

The voice snapped Valère back to the real world.

"Valère? Are you okay?" A second voice asked.

He was fine, but he needed them to assume he was struggling with his earlier decision. He had to hide the... *nervousness*. The anxiety that had plagued him since he was young.

Yes, I am okay, but I will play the role for as long as it is needed.

He looked up at his dinner guests sitting across from him. Roland and Emilio. He'd called the meeting on his drive back from the private golf course, suggesting this location for its world-renowned American cuisine, and for its semi-private rooms. One of his partners, Emilio Vasquez, the man now sitting across the table from him on his right, had called ahead and reserved the banquet room.

Even so, they'd chosen the table in the far back corner of the room. The waitress, a young blond woman in her thirties, had been instructed to enter the room only once every fifteen minutes. So far she'd performed well, never interrupting the men as they discussed the day's events.

The man to Valère's left didn't wait for him to respond. "Everything is taken care of?"

Valère nodded and finally spoke. "*Oui*, everything was accomplished. I do apologize, gentlemen, I seem to have lost my appetite."

Emilio smiled. "It is nothing, Francis. I remember the first time I, well, had to remove a *piece* from the chessboard. It is never an easy task."

Valère nodded once, accepting his friend's gesture. "Nevertheless, it is time to move to the next phase of our plan. We need to inform the media channels of our intention, and what is at stake."

The first man, Roland, swallowed loudly, trying to vie for their attention. While Valère hadn't touched his meal, Roland was on his second plate of dessert. Rotund, with rosy-red cheeks and jowls that hung nearly to his chest, the man was loud, invasive, rude, and liked by his peers for one thing, and one thing alone: his money.

They looked toward him. "We will wait."

Valère waited for him to explain. Never one to deny himself an opportunity to heighten the drama, Roland instead took a bite of a roll of bread that had somehow escaped earlier destruction. He chewed it no fewer than five times before speaking again. "We will wait to tell the media. We need to let the Yellowstone incident take center stage for a little longer. The news down there—hell, even here—is eating it up, and they're not letting go of it soon." His southern accent grew in strength, no doubt egged on by the three glasses of wine he'd already consumed, and he continued. "The more pressure that builds around this story in the States, the better off we'll be."

"We'll lose our opportunity," Emilio said. Valère nodded.

"No," Roland continued, crumbs falling from the corners of his mouth. "We'll benefit from this timeline. They have no idea what's gone on there, and they won't be able to get anything from the site without losing anyone they send in. We have the advantage of time, and we need to keep it."

Valère frowned. "That wasn't the plan. Why are we waiting? And what are we to do in the meantime?"

The fat man answered immediately, his mouth now full of vanilla pudding. "There are still loose ends to tie up. Something our contact at the CDC has informed me about. There's a woman there, digging around. Nothing major, but she's clever. More importantly, she's persistent. We need to get a jump on it, and make sure she doesn't talk."

The man to Valère's right looked upset. "No, we can't. It's too risky. Besides, the body count is rising, and for what? And what about the coins? I have heard that the students and that professor uncovered some of them."

Valère pitched in. "The coins are beside the point, and there is nothing left of the group that found them. There is no way to tie them back to us. As for the body count, I understand your concern. Believe me, I do. But think of the end result: it is the same."

"Then why the needless deaths? Won't there be enough of that?"

"Yes, my friend," Valère said. "But consider the alternative: we cannot let something leak before we're ready. Remember the rules: we control the means, we control the end. Nothing less, nothing more."

Valère and Roland nodded in unison. Emilio shook his head. "I am with you, but I do not agree. We risk more by trying to tie up these loose ends than we do in just letting them run their course. Can we not let this particular one go?"

"No. It's not a matter of risk, it's a matter of principle," Roland said. "I won't let anything like this slip. It's not in my nature to let things get out of my control."

They all knew that to be true, but the other man was still persistent. "If something happens, and this leaks before we're ready..."

"Let's vote on it." Roland spoke louder, obviously trying to control the conversation. "That was the agreement, was it not?"

"What is the proposition?" Valère asked.

"We take necessary action to prevent any of these *externalities* from becoming too knowledgeable. We postpone the media's involvement for another day and use that time to rehearse our strategy once again. The extra time will help settle us, and it will help our contingency do what it can to snuff out these little discrepancies."

"So," Valère said, "you suggest we use part of the allotment we've been given for containment and eradication?"

Roland smiled. "I do. What good is a dragon, then, without its fire?"

The two other men considered this. It would only take one more of them to agree with the man's decision before this plan would be enacted. Valère looked at the two men, measuring the addendum to their plan against the alternatives.

He pushed his steak around on the plate once more, toppling the castle and destroying his sanctuary.

"I agree. This is the best option for us at this moment." He looked up at Roland. "Alert your chosen men and deliver their objective."

It had been exactly fifteen minutes, and the waitress entered. All three men put on their most unassuming smiles as she hovered over them, refilling their water glasses.

1 4

The truck pulled up to the opening of an alley, and Julie told Ben to take a left down the narrow road. Run-down apartments and worn out buildings lined the route on each side as the truck bumped over potholes and through brown puddles.

"Seems like a pretty fancy place you've got here," Ben said.

The truck lurched over a deep pothole and bounced wildly as the suspension tried to compensate. Ben knew that any other vehicle would have suffered damage, but the massive lifted truck handled each bump and dip in stride. The alley curved to the left, and the truck and its two passengers found themselves facing a wide, squat warehouse. Made of metal siding and covered with a shallow steel roof, the warehouse fit in well with its dim surroundings. Ben slowed the vehicle and glided it toward the building, aiming for the small parking lot in front.

"No," Julie said. "Go around back. Park on the street." Ben didn't argue as he pressed the gas pedal and the truck lurched forward. "Most people assume this place is abandoned," Julie said. "We're okay with that, so we like to park on the street across from the health center."

They found a parallel parking spot on the street at the back of the warehouse, and Ben pulled the truck into the space smoothly.

"Wow," Julie said. "It took me about three weeks to be able to do that."

"Not bad," he said. "I'm surprised you can even see over the dash." He stepped onto the curb and waited for Julie.

She led him around the side of the warehouse and up a short flight of stairs. Her fingers brushed the keypad. She typed six numbers.

123456.

A small LED on the door blinked green, and the locking mechanism clicked.

"123456. Really?" Ben asked.

"Well, we're not the CIA," she said.

"Let's hope not."

She pushed the handle down, and the door slid open. Ben felt a wave of heat from the building's interior wash over them as they stepped in.

"Let me check in with Livingston first," she said. "If you don't mind waiting by the front door."

Ben shrugged. "Take your time."

She wasn't gone long. When she returned, she motioned for him to join her at the end of the hallway.

"He must be out golfing," she said. "Let's see if Stephens is in. He's my assistant, but we've got him working on another case right now. He'll at least appreciate that I'm checking in."

This time she headed to the right, and as Ben followed, he realized how small the office complex really was. The hallway intersected with another that ran perpendicular, but then opened into one large workspace. Half a dozen cubicles were sprawled in the middle, with two closed-door offices around the exterior. The fluorescent lighting was either on a dim setting or someone had neglected to replace many of the bulbs.

Julie led him to one of the cubicles and stopped in front of a thin man with his back to them.

"Hey, stranger," she said. The man spun around in his chair. "Hey, boss. Good to see you. How was the trip? Fishing traps and insects, if I recall correctly?"

"Something else came up, as I'm sure you've heard. This is Ben," she said. "Ben, meet Benjamin Stephens."

Stephens got up and extended his hand. "Nice name. Good to meet you."

Tall, wiry, and with black horn-rimmed glasses to match his disheveled hair, the kid looked as if he were maybe sixteen years old and on his way to a comic book convention.

"And what do you do, Mr. Bennett?"

Julie interjected. "He works at Yellowstone. Any news?"

"Not much," Stephens said. "It's all over the web now, though." He stepped to the side, revealing a triple-wide monitor setup full of open tabs and browser windows. Just about every one that Ben could see was filled with reports of the Yellowstone incident and explosion.

CNN, Fox news, Yahoo!, and the *Wall Street Journal.*

"I've been following it since it broke about four hours ago," he said. "You guys okay?"

"We're fine," Julie said. "We could use some coffee. Where's Livingston?"

Stephens walked over to the wall where an antique coffee pot sat empty. He placed a filter in it and added water as he spoke. "It's Thursday," he said, as if that explained everything. "He's golfing. Listen, there's more to it than just the Yellowstone incident."

Julie didn't understand "What you mean?"

"About an hour ago, a local news station way up in the northern part of Minnesota released a statement regarding some sort of debilitating virus that's already killed two people. Husband and wife, up near the border. He was out hunting, according to some neighbors, and she was waiting for him at home. Next thing they know, when the neighbors went to check on them, they were both dead."

Ben listened in silence.

"What makes you think it's related?" she asked. "Could be just some sort of seasonal fever. It is flu season."

"The bodies were found with a deep red rash covering their skin, and boils and welts over most of their body as well. The man was out in the snow, facedown. His wife was on the bathroom floor. Doesn't sound like any flu I ever heard of."

"That's awful." Julie glanced briefly at Ben. "Sounds like he was trying to combat the fever. With cold."

"Sounds a heck of a lot like what's going on at the park," Ben said.

"Rashes, boils, and a heat fever?" Stephen asked. The kid was obviously eager to confirm the details for his files, likely hoping the virus would turn into something significant that might lead to a promotion.

"Yeah."

"I'm sorry to hear that."

"Nothing we can do about it now except figure out what the hell this thing is." Ben said.

"Let's do it," Julie said. "Stephens, you know the drill. Anything you find goes through Randy's system, even though he's on vacation. Send me what you have curated and ready so far. Skip the duplicate content."

"Right," he said. "I've already started compiling it, and I'll send it through SecuNet later this afternoon. Hey—do you think this is going to get big?"

"It's already big." Julie said. "Let's just hope it doesn't get any bigger. An explosion that was obviously man-made, followed by *two* instances of whatever this virus thing is at the same time? Even if it's not an outbreak, it very well could lead to one."

"What do we do?"

"What we're trained to do," Julie said, as though she were a concerned parent, trying to console the hyperactive imagination of her child. "We find the source and stabilize the potent properties, then get it to the higher-ups for processing and propagation. Standard stuff. You know that."

The coffee machine behind Stephens began gurgling hot water down through the filter. Almost immediately, the smell of coffee filled the office air.

Ben licked his lips, just now realizing that he had driven the bulk of the journey from Yellowstone without so much as a sip of the stuff. "You going to pour that? I could use a cup."

"Oh, right," said Stephens, obliging. "Where are you two headed now?"

"Back to my place first," Julie said, "then we'll find this guy a hotel," gesturing to Ben. "Livingston won't cut his golf game short for anything short of a nuclear attack, but he'll be expecting all of us to work an all-nighter tonight if this thing blows up." She winced at her poor choice of words but continued. "Like I said, give me what you have whenever you can and keep it coming. As long as he's got information coming in, he'll stay quiet."

Stephens sank down into his chair. "Sure would be easier around here if you ran this place," he said almost under his breath.

"I would keep it down if I were you," Julie said. "Knowing Livingston, I wouldn't be surprised if he has this place bugged."

"Right" Stephens said, smiling. "But I've seen the budget for this operation—I think we'll be okay."

Julie turned and raised her eyebrows, silently asking Ben if there was more to cover. He shrugged. They took their coffees with them on the way out.

15

The evening sky turned to a bluish haze thanks to a gentle showering of rain and a near-full moon. Livingston clicked the key fob on his keychain.

The Mercedes-Benz was his pride and joy. He'd taken out a second mortgage on his condominium to ride in this kind of style, and he hadn't regretted a moment of it. As a government employee, he understood the irony and the juxtaposition of seeing a man of his status rolling around in a vehicle like this, but that was all the more reason to love it.

He'd always been fond of money. His first word, in fact, was "money," a story he loved sharing at parties and around the office.

Livingston headed over to the squat warehouse building that served as his temporary office. He liked to think of it that way: *temporary*. Everything in this life was temporary, he knew, but especially dead-end jobs like this one. He'd get to ten years, cash in his tenure play, and move on to a middle management job in a huge corporate bank or investment firm. Companies like that were always looking for management who weren't pushing for more and driving everyone around them to insanity. He'd fit in well at a company that needed an axe-man or a standard-issue pencil-pusher.

He'd also fit in well at a place that enjoyed the same type of indulgences.

Julie, Benjamin, Charles, his executive assistant, Laura—these people didn't understand him. He couldn't care less if they did or not, but he at least expected more respect than he got.

Wasn't a $400,000 luxury car enough to make an impression?

He tapped his six-digit entry code into the keypad, opened the door and breathed in the musty air. *God, I hate this place.* At the T-intersection in the hallway, he stopped to check his appearance in the long window of the lab room.

Tall, dark, and slightly heavyset, he wasn't a bad-looking man. Years of sedentary work had taken his college swagger and turned it into a waddling gait, but he still had a full head of brownish-blond hair and a proud jaw. He'd played hockey in college, but he'd lost his youthful spryness long ago, as well as a couple of teeth.

He hooked right into his office at the end of the hall.

He dropped his briefcase onto the chair next to the door and hung up his overcoat. He poured himself a double shot of scotch and opened the miniature freezer to find a cube of ice, and—

Perfect. Laura couldn't even remember to do that right.

He slammed the door shut and sat down at his desk. Like his car, the desk was an indulgence even the United States government wouldn't waste money on. He'd spent all $2,000 of his office decoration budget line item as well as another $1,500 of his own money to get this antique mahogany desk, complete with a hidden door beneath the top drawer.

He opened up the laptop in front of him and clicked around for the folder he needed. A prompt nudged him for the password. He entered the string of characters, the folder opened, and Livingston browsed through the list of pictures, sipping on the warm scotch.

Double-clicking on one particular image, Livingston sat up straight in his chair. It was a picture of Julie Richardson, smiling in a two-piece bathing suit at the local branch's company picnic. She was holding a volleyball under one arm and talking to someone off-camera.

He clicked on another. This time Julie was mid-serve, the volleyball inches above her right hand, and her body stretched out to its maximum length.

Livingston didn't know who had taken the pictures, but when Laura had given everyone in the office Dropbox access to them, he'd made sure to save them locally to his hard drive.

Another picture opened—Julie and Benjamin Stephens sitting at a picnic table across from one another. Julie's back was to the camera, and Livingston clicked the magnifying glass to zoom in slightly...

The phone rang.

He checked the caller ID. It was his daughter. He let it ring a second and third time, and waited for it to go to voicemail. He hadn't talked to Rebecca in almost a year, and he knew he'd regret not answering it later.

The answering machine picked up. He groaned as the sound of his own voice interrupted his thoughts. *"This is the voicemail box of David Livingston, Director..."*

At the beep, his daughter's voice punched through the low-quality phone speaker and into his office. *"Daddy? Hey, it's me... Just wanted to say hi. I figured you'd be working late again, but I wasn't sure."* The voice paused for a moment. *"Listen, call me back sometime. It's been awhile."*

Another pause, then the sound of a phone hanging up. Livingston swirled a sip of scotch in his mouth and stared at the conference phone on his desk. He swirled again, swallowed, then took another deep sip.

He squeezed his eyes shut tightly, holding them for a moment as the burn of the low-quality scotch ran down his esophagus. "I miss you too, honey," he said to no one.

He took another drink. Nine years since her mother had walked out. Nine years since she'd slept with that rat-bastard from the softball team...

He snapped his eyes open. Was he still alone in here? *Yes. Good.*

He sniffed, trying to shake off the feeling of delirium caused by the whiskey. *Get it together, Livingston. You're better than this.* He slammed the rest of the whiskey and set the glass on the far corner of his desk.

He needed a way to keep tabs on Julie without raising a flag in the data center. He thought for a moment, then sat back up and clicked away from the picture.

The image of Julie at the park bench disappeared, replaced by a browser window displaying the SecuNet homepage, an intranet server with a user interface for the company's secure communications and file storage.

He almost laughed out loud. Though SecuNet was secure enough for the CDC's standards, he knew all too well how *unsecure* the shitty browser was. A perfect example of "good enough for government work," the browser had been thoroughly proven unsafe by just about every web development and tech blog on the net, but it was the mandatory browser installed on every government computer, and it was a serious pain in the ass to circumvent it.

The page had a few options available, and he clicked on one toward the bottom in the first column. The site redirected him to a secure page, and he typed his username and password in the respective boxes and was soon faced with a new dialog box:

"Email Redirect: Choose Originator"

Being considered "executive" at a government organization did have its perks, even if it didn't pay well. Livingston entered Julie's email address, then added a second Originator email address entry for Benjamin Stephens. In the "Enter Forwarding Address" box, he entered his own email account and hit "submit."

The dialog box disappeared, and Livingston closed the browser window. The redirect would be "silent," meaning it would run invisibly in the background—neither of his employees would know they were being tracked via email—and it would be relatively untraceable. Only a seasoned IT veteran specifically looking for the redirect would be able to find it.

He stood, refilled his scotch, and sat back down at the computer. He smiled at his own ingenuity and went back to the folder with the pictures from the company picnic.

16

Dr. Diana Torres peered through the compound microscope, certain that whatever it was, she hadn't seen it before. The structure was different. This was not a normal virus. First, it appeared to have an integumentary system that protected the rest of the microscopic body from external elements and diseases. What she assumed was the capsid was studded with odd bumps and scrapes, as if the virus *itself* was infected. Secondly, while she recognized the lipid and protein structures that made up the bulk of the body, she couldn't quite place their configuration.

Finally, the entire inner cavity of each individual viral body was made up of the traditional nucleocapsid and capsomeres, but also other bodies she didn't recognize that seemed to be crammed in as well. While the overall structure was standard for a type of herpesvirus, it didn't fit any of the eight strains modern science was aware of.

She took another measurement and checked her notes.

"Varicella Zoster strain; assumption smaller form. Standard nucleocapsid and lipid envelopes; odd protein buildup differs from traditional strains."

"Most spherical virions 80 to 90 nm in diameter; largest observed 93 nm, smallest observed 73 nm."

The results were accurate; her measurements weren't off. Her assistant, Charlie Furmann, had reserved the lab space at 5:30 that evening and she'd been inside until now. She checked her watch.

7:30 PM.

The act of checking her watch suddenly triggered her body to announce that it was exhausted. She yawned and stretched her arms. Standing, she shut the light from the microscope on the long lab table in order to prevent any unwanted reactions in the sample. She slipped on her lab coat once again—essentially her entry key to the myriad of rooms, labs, and closets spread around the building. She rarely wore it inside her office, but it was considered bad form to walk around the campus without it.

It would also get her into the cafeteria on the main level; her chosen destination. The nature of the work at the research facility, as well as the personality types of those doing it, meant that the facility had 24/7 cafeteria access. The scientists and research assistants that populated these offices weren't governed by traditional 9-to-5 jobs, nor did they care for culturally accepted norms about when to sleep and when to work.

Torres stepped off the elevator on the main level. The halls were dimly lit, but the open doors to the cafeteria spilled light out into the corridor, beckoning. Another involuntary response in her brain reacted to the smell of food, hunger pangs running up and down her insides.

Surprised to find the cafeteria empty, she pulled out a small plastic bin of hummus and crackers and a 20-ounce bottle of Pepsi from the open-faced refrigerator and tapped her identification card on the credit card terminal. After the terminal beeped, she clipped the badge back to her lab coat pocket and walked back out into the hallway when she felt her cell phone buzz in her jeans pocket. She juggled the Pepsi around and reached for the phone. It was a text from Charlie.

"Where are you? Wanted to check in with this model."

She frowned, wondering why he had taken the time to send her a text message when he could have just waited for her to return. She sent a quick reply.

"Went to cafeteria. On my way back. What's up?"

She didn't wait for a response; instead, she stepped into the elevator and pressed the number for her floor. She found Charlie, his back to her, hunched over the microscope.

"What's going on?" she asked.

Charlie jumped and turned. "What is this, Diana? Is this the same sample that was sent over from earlier?"

"Yes..." Dr. Torres replied.

"Did they say what it was?"

"What do you mean? They sent over a standard laboratory-required specimen size for examination and classification. If they knew what it was already, they wouldn't have sent it."

Charlie nodded. "I guess I'm just confused..."

"About what?"

"Well, I don't understand why you would have mounted both samples at once."

Now it was Dr. Torres' turn to be confused. "Both? What do you mean?"

Charlie plugged in the external monitor display into the microscope's output line, displaying the image from the microscope on a 60-inch display hanging on the wall behind them. "Look," he said, using a wireless computer mouse to draw a circle around one of the spherical objects on the screen. "This is your virus, right? The 'Varicella Zoster' strain, or whatever?"

She nodded.

"Well, when you continue to zoom in, you'll see the standard components—nucleocapsid, lipids, different protein amalgamations, etcetera."

Dr. Torres nodded again, trying to hurry him along.

"But then if you *keep* increasing the magnification…" he paused to reset the microscope's magnification wheels, "you'll notice that the interior structure of the virion is completely crammed with foreign bodies."

"Foreign? How can they be? They're part of the virus."

"Right—but that doesn't mean they always were. The virus certainly doesn't *look* like it wants them in there, does it? They're all bulging at the seams, thanks to the spirillum pushing everything around."

Dr. Torres looked up sharply. "Spirillum? What are you talking about?"

He zoomed in further. As the microscopic components of the viral organism came into focus, she saw the unmistakable spiraling of one of the common bacterial shapes. The twisted object grew as Charlie pushed the microscope to its limits; the screen suddenly appearing grainy and slightly out of focus.

"Oh, my God," she whispered.

"You didn't see this before?" Charlie asked.

She shook her head.

"So, then, I'm guessing there weren't two different samples?"

Both scientists were speechless as they stared at the TV monitor. The fuzzy black and white image was unmistakable.

"No. No, Charlie. There weren't," she said. "We're looking at some sort of herpesvirus that contains a *living, breathing,* bacterial infection around it as well."

"So it's a virally infected bacteria?"

"No… it seems that they have some sort of symbiotic relationship with one another. I can't really explain it, but they *both* seem to need the other to exist."

"But that's impossible," Charlie said. "There's no way for the virions to provide livable conditions for the bacteria, and the capsid would need to have access to the world around it. And a bacterial cell is so much larger than —"

"I know," Dr. Torres said. "But we're dealing with something completely different here; something outside the realm of what either of us has studied before." As she spoke and stared at the screen in front of her, Dr. Torres grew increasingly confident that what she was looking at was in fact, exactly what she had said it was.

Impossible or not, what they were looking at was a *virus*, fully functioning and living *inside of* and supporting a bacterial cell.

"How is that possible? It's against the laws of nature."

Diana Torres looked up at Charlie. "It's possible because I don't think *nature* had anything to do with it."

17

Six Months Ago

Dr. Malcolm Fischer gasped. Sucking in a huge breath of air, he tried to swallow. It was painful; somehow, something wasn't right. He tried to look down, but had a hard time moving his head.

Weird.

He tried moving his hands instead. Nothing.

His fingers, maybe?

Nope.

Malcolm felt glued down, lying on his back. At least it was comfortable.

What do *I have control over, then?* he wondered.

He opened his eyes, blinking once, twice. He moved his eyeballs around; at least he could see.

He tried to make sense of his surroundings. Bright lights,

fluorescent. The kind used in offices and commercial buildings. Whitish walls, some sort of sterile color.

That was it.

Okay, what does that mean? Malcolm tried moving his body, his limbs—anything. Nothing would give. It was as if he were—

Am I paralyzed?

He considered it a moment. He didn't remember taking a fall, or any type of accident. Actually, now that he thought harder, he couldn't remember anything. There was...

A helicopter.

Oh, God.

The memory roared back into Malcolm's mind in a flash. *The students...*

He remembered being forced into the chopper at gunpoint, being pushed down into a seat and strapped in, then the gentle upward motion of the pilot's expert takeoff. They ascended only a few feet off the ground.

The gun.

The horrid sound of hundreds of miniature explosions rocking the gunman back and forth on the side-mounted machine gun.

The one he'd fired into the students. *His* students.

Intense pain seized him, but he couldn't tell if it was merely psychological. He closed his eyes again, breathing. Still, his hands and legs and arms wouldn't move; *everything*, was frozen in place.

Where am I?

Just then, he heard a beeping sound. It had grown louder—or had he just now noticed it?

He pushed his eyelids apart and tried to look for the source of the sound. As his eyes opened, the beeping grew more intense; quicker.

He heard footsteps. Running.

"...Patient experiencing some sort of shock. Possible reaction..."

Voices drifted in and out. They were in the room.

Who were 'they?'

Malcolm was growing agitated. He wanted answers, and he wanted to be able to *move.*

"He's awake!"

More footsteps.

Now he could hear multiple people—three?—moving around his bed.

I'm in a hospital. It must be. I'm paralyzed.

"He's no longer comatose?" one voice asked.

"No, he's got his eyes open. The new cocktail they sent down must have done more than just keep his muscles from atrophying."

The voices were hurried; frantic.

"Okay, let's get some Codeine into him; he's probably going to be a little rough around the edges."

"Got it. We're keeping him up?"

"No, no. That's just to hold him over until he goes under again and his musculature calms down. It shouldn't be long."

Malcolm heard a popping sound, followed by the smell of something bitter. Some sort of chemical. A bag of liquid suddenly passed directly in front of his face. He saw a strange assortment of letters and numbers, then a few letters that his brain computed as words.

Global. D-something Global.

"Ok, right. Medesinsk is going to be here tomorrow morning, and we need to get him back down." Another pop, followed by a sloshing sound, reached Malcolm's ears.

He tried to speak, but he wasn't sure he had control of his vocal cords. It didn't matter anyway, as he realized he couldn't even open his mouth.

A small hand pulled his chin down then placed a hand over his throat gently, another hand reaching for his shoulder. He felt two — three — hands on him, and then saw someone placing a needle into his IV line.

"It won't matter —I've already reported that we've achieved success."

"Yes, I know, I read the report," the first voice said. "Still, they won't want to see him awake. They'll need him under for the final round of testing, so there's no reason to let him become too aware."

Malcolm tried to piece things together. He *was* paralyzed. Waking from a coma, anyway. His body felt... good. Weakened, but usable.

"How'd he wake up?" the second voice asked. It was a woman.

"It's a standard reaction to the chemical; almost like developing an immunity. Most subjects awaken after four to six months. He made it to five and a half."

"Can we up the dosage?"

"No, a higher dosage will likely kill him. Keep the mg count steady; just track it closer. Any increase in heart rate or changes in sleep cycles, have someone come in and check it out."

"Got it."

Malcolm heard them finish up, then leave the room. He was left to his own thoughts and the slow, methodical beeping noise.

He suddenly felt the pricking of thousands of nerve endings flaring up in his neck and head, as if needles just below the surface of his skin were trying to poke their way out. It was painful, but it meant something else.

He could move his head.

It was the same feeling he'd had when a body part fell asleep. He could feel the line of nerves crawling up and around his face. Slowly, painfully, he tried to move the outer muscles in his face—cheeks, lips, ears. He thought he could feel the slightest of motions.

His face continued to "wake up." He'd have preferred the traditional feeling of being awake, rather than the feeling of millions of ants crawling over his skin, but he didn't argue. He moved his mouth.

Using an unbelievable amount of energy, he tried lifting his head. *Yes!* It was moving. His head was lifting up from the bed, slowly, surely...

It fell. He could hold it no longer. His head fell back into the pillow.

With a deep exhalation, he recovered and tried again. A little farther this time.

Now he could see his body covered in a sheet, his feet poking out from the bottom. Beyond that, there was the door to the room he was stuck inside. It too was that skeletal white color.

Again, his head fell back into the pillow.

This is good, he told himself. *I'm getting stronger each time.*

As Malcolm tried for the third time, however, he realized they'd injected him with something. No doubt *multiple* things.

He was probably only minutes away from passing out again.

I need to get out of here.

He lay back for a few extra seconds, summoning energy, then tried once more to lift his head.

He wanted to scream. Pain seared through his skull, worse than any migraine he'd ever experienced. *Don't. Stop.* He chanted to himself over and over again. *Don't. Stop.*

Through sheer will, he forced his neck to articulate, and glanced down at the maze of tubes that were inserted into different parts of his body. He had no idea what they did or what human bodily function they were intended to perform. Some appeared empty— maybe those were waste tubes?

Others had clear liquids running through them, and a few had deep crimson liquid coursing through them.

He didn't have much choice. He could still only move his head, and he didn't have the luxury to wait around for more of his body to wake up. He looked down and to his right, noticing a small clear tube that had been inserted into the soft skin underneath his upper arm, just below his shoulder.

If I can reach that...

He struggled again, forcing his head forward and down. *A little more...*

His lips were on the tube now, but there was no way his teeth were going to reach that far. He needed a little more. *Millimeters* more.

Come on, Malcolm. He willed himself to push forward again. The pain was unbearable, his face flushed.

Just a few millimeters more. It had to be.

Don't. Stop.

He exhaled the last of the air that was in his lungs, and his face inched forward just enough. He felt the cold steel of the IV line's end hit his mouth, and he clamped down. He didn't care what he yanked out, as long as he disconnected *something.*

Yes!

He bit down as hard as he could, tugging on the tube with his with his teeth. His shoulder throbbed, but he didn't stop. Until—his head fell back. He waited a moment, letting his body regroup. Finally, he lifted his tongue up and felt for his prize.

It was there, cold steel and clear plastic tubing. It bumped up against his mouth as it fell, and he was ecstatic.

He'd done it.

He could see the plastic tube out of the corner of his eye, disappearing off the side of the bed and around the room somewhere, its contents no longer able to enter Malcolm's body.

He smiled—or what he thought was a smile—and closed his eyes again.

Only a matter of time...

He waited for the drug's effects to wear off; waited for the prickling line of needles to expand their reach, overtaking his body with the beautiful gift of motion. Any moment now, and he'd be able to move again.

What was that?

He felt something, or rather, understood something. It wasn't a feeling as much as a sort of *knowing*. His body was crashing, falling again. He felt the line of needles receding, going back down into the surface of his body.

No!

Just a little more time.

But it was not to be. Malcolm's body was going to sleep again. He could do nothing but lay, helpless, as his eyes closed out the world around him. He could hear his breathing, feel the rising and falling of his chest, but it was odd, as if it were not his own body that was controlling it.

To be sure, he tried lifting his head again. *Nothing.*

He couldn't cry out, couldn't make a sound. His mind was shutting down, sending him to sleep once again, and he couldn't think…

18

"Anything yet?" Dr. Torres said, her frustration really starting to fizz as she waited on Charlie to return with the results of their latest test on the sample.

"Not yet," Charlie muttered under his breath. They'd put the sample through a battering ram of tests—the standard lab-required composition, attributes, and plausible generation tests, as well as a few others Dr. Torres ordered hours ago. Charlie was still finishing up the last of these—a test to determine any possible effects external forces might have on the sample.

Charlie returned to the table carrying a Petri dish with a swab of the sample inside. Transferring the sample from an observation plate to the dish had made prescribing tests so much easier.

"I don't understand why you won't just send an email to Levels 4 and 8," Charlie said as he set the dish down on the table in front of her. "What can possibly go wrong by getting more people involved?"

Dr. Torres grabbed the dish. "Come on, Charlie, you know the rules. This one isn't company sanctioned, so there's no way we're doing that."

"Yeah, but don't they encourage us to take on private jobs?"

"They do, but only if they can maintain the standpoint of plausible deniability for any of their scientists' clients' work," she answered.

"Seems like a backwards way of doing business, in my opinion."

Dr. Torres sighed. "Well, in *my* opinion, it seems like a good way for them to stay out of trouble. You and I both know that there's enough non-sanctioned work going on here that's ended in all but disaster. One of those leaks, and we've got incriminating evidence on our hands. For all of us." Dr. Torres gave Charlie a look that was supposed to mean the conversation was over, but Charlie continued.

"I get it. The company won't take credit for anything unless it ends in dollar signs for them."

"Welcome to America, Charlie."

Charlie let the insult slide. He'd been raised in Idaho and had lived in just about every small town there was. Hope, Irwin, Twin Falls, and his parents now lived in Mud Lake. Now that he worked in Twin Falls, it seemed like Charlie was going to spend the rest of his life inside the borders of his home state.

He'd grown up like most normal American boys. Street hockey in the summer, pond hockey in the winter, with other random sports thrown in during the off-season. He was of average build, not tall but not short either, making him an ideal candidate to fill out a team roster for just about any sport he tried out for.

Much to his father's dismay, however, sports were not Charlie's strong suit. Before football practice and after school during the fall semesters, Charlie spent his time in the science club at his local high school. What his parents thought —and hoped— would be a just a phase, turned out to be a career choice for the young man. He enrolled in night classes at the local university while only a junior in high school, convincing his parents that it would be good for his future. While it was certainly useful later in life, the truth of the matter was that Charlie was actually just interested in studying robotics, something his local high school did not have a program for.

He ditched the robotics studies after his first semester in college, opting instead to study microbiology. After graduating summa cum laude, he was quickly tapped for an internship at a local clinical research firm, then a pharmaceutical company, and finally as an assistant to Dr. Torres.

Charlie enjoyed the job; Dr. Torres was a good boss, and she treated him appropriately—hard enough that he was challenged to continue learning, but friendly enough that he knew she still cared about his education. It was because of this relationship, and Dr. Torres' leadership, that he was able to succeed in the role while gaining worldly experience at the firm. As even-keeled and mild-tempered as he was, however, it was on nights like these that Charlie wished he were working somewhere else.

Dr. Torres just wouldn't stop. They'd been at it for over six hours straight now, with no end in sight. He enjoyed discovering and learning just like any other scientist, but he also enjoyed sleep. Furthermore, he could already feel himself growing hungry again.

"Hey, chief, it's getting late," Charlie said. He hated to play that card, but he was long past his ability to be effective.

"Huh?" Dr. Torres said softly as she stared down at the sample and the associated report. "Oh, right, I guess it is getting a little late."

She looked at her watch.

10:57 PM.

She pushed her glasses back onto her nose and straightened the pile of papers in front of her as she stood up from the table. "Are you heading out?"

Charlie had worked with Dr. Torres long enough to know what the question really meant. *Had enough? Can't handle the grind of* real *science?*

He had also worked with her long enough to know how to handle the situation. "Yeah, exactly." He laughed. "We've done every test in the book and all the reports are there in front of you. I'm happy to stay and read them to you, but I'm pretty sure you've got it covered on your own." He half-smiled from the left side of his mouth. It was enough to tell Dr. Torres that he was seriously tired, but not serious enough to tell her that he didn't care. "Plus, you know that I'm only an email away."

She nodded. "Let me finish up here, and I'll be on my way out, too."

When Charlie left, Dr. Torres found herself alone in the sprawling state-of-the-art laboratory. Just another specimen amid the gadgets, tools, and instruments that she could only guess were used by others in the building.

The laboratory she worked for had been around for over forty years, and from stories she'd heard, it had been successful from day one. Operating in the black each and every fiscal year. They could afford sparing no expense for their top-notch scientists. Dr. Torres was no exception and she knew it.

There were scientists working here she had never met, who had been published in every month of every trade journal she subscribed to. There were also scientists who had spoken at every conference she had ever heard of. These were her peers, and nothing less was expected of her too.

Dr. Torres enjoyed her position at the company. While she was certainly not the most tenured, nor the most esteemed scientist in the building, she knew that the only way she could improve was by challenging herself. World-renowned or not, working somewhere where you were only a number among many other numbers caused you to strive for more than you thought you were capable of. Most days, Dr. Torres felt this way. It was the reason she had come this far in her career, and it was the reason she was not slowing down yet.

She grabbed a stack of papers and the small Petri dish from the table and carried them down the hall to her office. Charlie had affixed a lid on the Petri dish and taped it shut, complete with a label signifying what the sample contained.

Unknown s.248—sample 248.

The viral/bacterial infection that she'd been sent to study.

Back in her office, she placed the sample on the far wall next to her personal microscope kit and took the report to her desk. She placed it on the stack of papers that she had scattered all over her desk, careful not to cause any to fall to the floor. She moved a few Styrofoam cups and plastic takeout trays to the trash next to her chair and sat down in front of her computer.

Her email was still front and center on the screen. She clicked on the last message she'd received and replied.

>To: Harvey 'Ben' Bennett <hbennett1419@yahoo.com>

>From: Diana Torres <diana.torres@focalresearch.org>

>Subject: Re:

>Body: I think we've figured part of this out. Report attached; p-protected. Use my bdate with his first name.

Miss you. Are you ok?

She read through the email to make sure it included the attachment and the information he would need. She was still surprised by the recipient, though not as overwhelmed as she had been when she'd first heard from him.

It must be more than ten years, she thought. She couldn't actually remember the last time they'd spoken on the phone. Still, it was amazing to hear from him. These weren't exactly the best of circumstances, but she knew that if he was contacting her, it must be something important.

Just then, she heard footsteps coming down the hallway. Was Charlie coming back?

No, she thought, *Charlie was wearing sneakers all day.* These footsteps were clearly made by either a heeled woman's shoe or a man's dress shoe. Her ears perked up as she listened to the sound, now growing louder.

It lacked the purposeful quickness of a woman in high heels, and it seemed heavier. *Who was visiting her?*

She knew for a fact that no one else on her floor was currently in. After three or four trips to and from the lab on the fourth level, she could tell in a quick glance up and down the hallway that there were no other lights on besides her own.

The footsteps continued toward her open door. She stood up from the computer, forgetting about the email for a moment and turning toward the door.

Just as she turned, a man entered the space inside the doorframe.

"Dr. Torres?" The man asked. His voice raspy; not quite that of a lifelong smoker, but one that seemed tired or weary with age.

She nodded.

The man stepped in and took a long, slow glance around.

"Can I help you?" Dr. Torres asked.

The man's eyebrows abruptly lifted, as if he had forgotten that he shared the room with another occupant. "Ah, yes. Dr. Torres, it's great to meet you." He extended his right hand forward. She reluctantly reached for it and allowed him to grasp it. His hand completely enveloped her own, though he did not squeeze tightly. "I'm here from the CDC, which, as you know, is currently operating in a crisis mode."

"Well, I—I didn't exactly know that," Dr. Torres said, still caught off guard. "Do you mean the explosion at Yellowstone?" Charlie had filled her in about the day's events when he came in this morning, though she still hadn't checked for an update.

The man smiled. He retracted his hand and placed it in his pants pocket.

"Yes, in fact, that is exactly why I'm here."

19

"What's your name?" she asked.

Rather than answer her question, the man simply put both hands in his pockets. "We're following this thing as well; trying to stay ahead of it."

"Do you know what this *thing* even is?" Dr. Torres asked. She sat back down in her leather desk chair and steepled her fingers thoughtfully..

"We're guessing it's some sort of bacteriophage; T4, Coliphage, something like that." He motioned to a chair. She nodded once, and the man pulled it out and sat across from her. "But the lab results haven't come in yet. That's why I'm here. I wanted to know if you'd figured anything out yet."

Dr. Torres couldn't even begin to fathom how he knew she'd been working on it.

The man smiled. "The package that was delivered. A colleague of yours received it and sent it to you, but was prudent enough to document your research and testing phases as well."

Charlie, she thought. She swallowed her anger, remembering that her assistant had only been doing his job. All of the lab techs and assistants at the company had been instructed to keep a record of any and all testing done on-site on any materials that could be considered "potential threats." While she'd wanted to keep their work quiet until she could prepare a final report, she hadn't considered asking Charlie to bypass this security step.

"It's okay, Dr. Torres. This type of thing happens all the time. You don't want to make any mistakes in the research phases and potentially damage your career. Even if you *had* kept this one hidden from us, I'm not here to reprimand you."

Dr. Torres nodded. "May I ask why you *are* here?"

"Information," the man said without hesitation. "Like I said, we need to keep ahead of this one, especially if it's some sort of bacter—"

"It's not."

"I beg your pardon?"

"It's not a bacteriophage," Dr. Torres said. "Actually, it's exactly the opposite."

"What do you mean? The symptoms we're seeing in patients suggests that it is some sort of bacterial-viral combination."

"Well, you're right about that," Dr. Torres said, turning around in her chair and opening a file on her computer. "It's bacterial *and* viral, but not in the sense of a bacteriophage. Rather than a virus attacking and piercing a bacteria, we've recognized the exact opposite. A bacterial infection within a larger virus."

The man stood up and began pacing the office. Dr. Torres chose to continue.

"It's a standard form of a spirillum bacteria, only crammed inside the shell of another body. I've never seen anything like it before, really. It's quite ama—"

The man spun on his heel. "And who else has been working on this project with you?" he asked.

"J—just my assistant, Charlie Furmann."

"I see. And do you have the sample here with you?"

Dr. Torres fidgeted in her chair, suddenly feeling uncomfortable. Her eyes flicked to the test tube on the table, then quickly back to the man. "I'm sorry—can I ask again why you're here?"

The man had already begun moving to the table. He reached down and grabbed the small glass vial just as Dr. Torres stood up from the chair.

"Hey! Excus—" The man held the tube away from Dr. Torres with his right hand and lifted his left arm. He swatted the back of his hand at Dr. Torres' face, catching her just below her left eye.

Dr. Torres stumbled backwards, stunned. Tears welled in her eyes. She gasped. The man continued moving, retrieving a pair of latex gloves from his pocket. In one fluid motion, he stretched them on over his thick fingers and walked to the small lab sink.

"What are you doing?" Dr. Torres asked as she regained her balance. "Wait!"

The man threw the vial containing the sample down into the sink. It shattered with a loud crash, launching glass into the air. The man was already moving toward the open door. He reached for the handle and stepped out into the hallway.

Dr. Torres watched him reach into his coat pocket and remove another vial, this one containing a clear liquid. He held the tube up in front of her.

"Dr. Torres. I am sorry it came to this. However, rest assured your research and time will not go to waste." He threw the sample down. The hard floor obliterated the glass vial, and the clear liquid bounced upward and onto Dr. Torres' feet. Before she could react, the man slammed the door shut, and Dr. Torres heard the clicking sound of his shoes retreating down the empty hall.

She ran to the door and tried to open it, fumbling and slipping over the now-wet floor. Finally, the handle gave, and she nearly fell into the hallway. Her breathing labored heavily, but she pushed on down the hallway regardless, following the sound of the man's shoes. Just as she reached the elevator, it dinged.

The doors slid open. A shocked Charlie Furmann stared back at her. "Dr. Torres—are you okay?"

Her eyes were wide and wild. She backed away from the elevator, putting space between herself and Charlie.

"I—I..." she stammered. "Yes, I'm... I'm fine. Go home, and I'll call you tomorrow," she said. She turned away from Charlie and the open doors of the elevator, and stumbled to the stairs at the end of the hallway.

20

Juliette Richardson and Harvey Bennett drove to the other side of town leaving Julie's office behind. Julie behind the wheel. Ben cooped up in the passenger seat. Just as they passed the city limits and left the metropolitan area, the high-rise apartments and multi-floor office buildings slowly changed into larger, flatter buildings and individual houses on suburban streets.

"I moved out here after living in the big city for ten years," Julie said.

"Big city?"

"San Francisco. I was right in the middle of everything," she said. "It was great at first, but it wears on you after a while."

"Yeah, I bet," Ben said.

Julie laughed. "Well, sure, I guess *any* city's big to someone like you."

Ben thought about that for a moment before responding. "I didn't always live out in the middle of nowhere," he said. Before Julie could interject, he added, "But I guess I always wanted to."

They drove on, passing yet another neighborhood filled with one- and two-story houses painted either brown, tan, or beige. White picket fences separated them from one another, and perfectly manicured lawns signaled a strict HOA governed the neighborhood.

"So the park is a great job for you," Julie said.

Ben nodded, looking out the window. For the first time during their trip, he was only a passenger in the vehicle. Julie had offered to drive from the office to her apartment.

"It is," Ben said. "I guess, I mean it was."

"It's going to be fine," Julie said, trying to convince herself more than anyone else. "We'll figure this out."

After passing the neighborhood stretching over the road on their right and left, Julie turned onto a smaller country road, and Ben could see the houses and white fences receding in the distance. Fields and farms now replaced the neighborhoods on each side of the road.

"I thought you lived in an apartment," Ben said, noticing the herd of cows.

"I do," she answered, "but it's just the upstairs room of a converted barn. I rent from the family that owns it."

While she spoke, she took the next turn down a gravel road. Up ahead, a crop of tall pines surrounded a house and a few out buildings, among them a large barn which didn't look like it had been kept up for many years.

"It looks worse on the outside," Julie explained apologetically.

"They stopped using it as a barn in the '70s, but converted it back in 2003. It's completely renovated inside, and has everything I need."

Ben shrugged. "You don't owe me an explanantion."

Julie pulled into the long driveway that led to the farmhouse and barn, and the truck lurched over potholes strewn over the single lane. "It's quiet and it helps me relax."

Ben's phone buzzed in his pocket. When he reached for it, he stared down at the number for a moment before answering. "Hey. H—How's it going?"

A few moments later, "What? Are you okay—how long ago?" He listened again. "Where are you now?"

Julie looked over at her passenger as the truck slid onto a gravel driveway in front of the barn. She shut off the engine and waited for Ben to finish his conversation.

"Don't be ridiculous. I'm coming—I'll leave now." He hung up and stuffed the phone back in his pocket.

"Where are we going now?" Julie asked.

"*We're* not. You've got work to do here."

"Like hell I'm not."

"I have to get to Twin Falls."

"We're in this together, remember?"

He didn't actually remember when they'd decided they were in this together, but he let it go. "Listen, that was Diana Torres, the person I sent that sample to. Something's gone wrong."

Julie remained quiet.

"She's infected, and I need to get to her…" his voice trailed off.

To her credit, Julie didn't intrude by asking more questions. "Ben, I'm sorry. I'm going with you. Let me get some stuff from the house, and then we'll get to the airport."

"No, I don't fly."

"Your friend's in trouble, and you won't fly?"

"I—I can't."

"Don't be a baby."

"I don't need this right now, okay? Besides, it's less than a day's drive from here. Plus, it doesn't sound like there's much I can do about it."

Julie looked like she wanted to ask, in that case, why it mattered that they go visit her. Again, she was quiet.

"That's fine, you can come. Hurry up in there—we need to get on the road."

21

Six Months Ago

Dr. Malcolm Fischer gasped again.

I'm alive.

His eyes were open, blinking, as if trying to clear a veil from in front of them. The room was the same, but it was darker now. The ceiling lights were off, but some light source from outside was trickling in under the door.

He lifted his head to see. *Yes, that's where it's coming from.*

And then: *I just lifted my head.*

Malcolm wondered if he was dreaming. *How do we check that?* Then he remembered. He lifted his right hand and pinched his left.

He could feel it.

There were no pins and needles this time, no probing behind his skin. He was awake, and fully conscious. He blinked a few more times and tried to sit up.

He let out a groan as his right arm pushed off the bed. He looked down at the location of the pain—his shoulder. There was a large purplish welt where he'd ripped out the needle with his teeth, and he could see that he hadn't done a great job: the small metal needle was still resting on his skin, the end slightly poking into his arm.

He reached with his left hand and gently slid it back. It came out easily, leaving a spot of blood behind.

He swung his legs off the table, waiting for the slightest noise.

No beeping. No instruments in the hospital room seemed to be trying to alert their masters that their subject had awoken.

He put his feet on the ground and tried to stand up. Malcolm's body collapsed immediately. He laid prone on the floor for a moment before trying to stand up again.

How long have I been here? He tried to remember. The last time he'd woken up, he'd been asleep for six months. *Not enough time to have completely atrophied. Plus, didn't they say they injected something that would help my musculature?*

He forced himself to stand again. Shaky, but he was balanced. He focused on the tubes that were mainlining into his body. He noticed a reader on his finger—wasn't this the one that tracked his heart rate?

If he removed everything, he knew the machine would start beeping again, sending the alarm that his heart had stopped.

What to do?

He couldn't start switching off the machines, either. They were obviously going to be tracking the data, if the machines suddenly went offline one after another, they'd be in here in seconds.

He looked around. Nothing to use as a weapon, really, unless he was James Bond.

And he wasn't James Bond.

Besides, what could he do? There were at least three doctors around, and possibly the beasts who'd brought him in. Three- or more-on-one didn't sound like good odds.

He did have the element of surprise, though. Unless there was a silent alarm emanating from one of the machines, they—whoever they were—had no idea he was awake.

What had they said? "The chemical usually renders the patient comatose for around four to six months" or something like that?

He thought about it for a moment. They had also said Medesinsk was coming tomorrow morning. If they *had* come, they surely would have noticed the giant welt on his arm, and the misplaced needle that should have been sticking properly out of it.

That meant he had only been asleep for a few hours.

He'd done it.

Malcolm did a small fist pump, more to test the motion of his right arm than anything. He was awake, but he still needed to get out of there, and fast.

At least before tomorrow morning. Hopefully *long gone* by tomorrow morning.

Again, though: what could he do?

He took another look around the room. The many computers and instruments hooked up to him wouldn't *all* alert anyone if he started fiddling with them. The ones that would, he could only guess at. Then he noticed the computer connected to one of his fingers. It was on a rolling cart, and he couldn't see it plugged into anything.

He hobbled over to it, using the bedrail as a support. Sure enough, it was a standalone machine. Battery powered.

He looked at the screen. It *looked* like a heart rate monitor, from what he could tell. There were numbers flashing on every inch of the screen, but the majority of it was a continuous graph, with peak appearing every second on the right side.

Well, what do I have to lose?

He started taking the rest of the trackers and monitor tubes off his body. *Disgusting.*

Next were the needles poking through his chest, arms, and legs. Finally, the clip-like things that were connected to his fingers.

All except the heart-rate monitor.

He hoped that was the only one that would alert his captors. Why wouldn't it be? They expected him to be completely comatose, after all, not an alert, mobile prisoner.

He checked the wheels on the cart and began pushing it toward the door. Malcolm checked the handle, found it unlocked, and pushed the door open. He hobbled behind the cart, careful to not let the tube fall to the floor for him to trip on.

It *looked* like a hospital wing, except one with no one else in it. It was a little creepy, actually, he realized. Not a soul was anywhere to be seen, and the only lights that were on were the emergency lights that ran up and down the hall between the brighter fluorescents.

He wheeled the cart to the end of the hallway. Unlike what he'd expected of a "real" hospital, there was no T-intersection here. The hallway ended in what seemed like a janitor's closet in front of him. He checked the door. Locked.

He needed a plan, and fast. He couldn't exactly wheel the heart monitor computer out and down the front steps, but he had no idea how to disable it without sounding an alarm somewhere. If he shut it off, he was almost positive an alarm somewhere in the building—no doubt where the nightshift was still working—would sound, and his jig would be up.

Unless...

He thought for a moment. *It might work...*

But where?

He hobbled along, faster now, turning the cart around and pointing it back the way he came. He pushed past his old room, noticed the door open, and pulled it closed. *Can't be too careful.*

He continued to the center of the hallway and found his T-intersection. He was in the top of the "T," and this stretch of hallway in front of him was short—likely just a bridge or covered walkway to another section of the hospital. He entered it, noticing the floor curve up in a gentle arc.

He walked slightly uphill until he reached the center of the bridge, then stopped in front of a door. *Electrical 2-A.*

He was on the second floor, and this was the electrical closet for building A, which was either the one he'd just come from or the one he was about to enter. He hoped he'd chosen correctly as he tried the door. This one was unlocked, and he pushed the cart inside.

A light switch on the wall next to the door flicked on a single overhead bulb, enough to light the space in a dim yellow bath of light. Finding nothing at first besides a few mop buckets, some brooms and dust pans, and a shelf of cleaning supplies, he was about to leave When on the right-hand wall he found an electrical panel, the kind that housed the fuses and breakers, The whole unit was easily as tall as he was.

Okay, he thought. *Let's get to work.* Whatever he tried, he couldn't disable the monitor from signaling that he'd been tampering with it. But he could, however, try to disable the system on the *other* end, so that it wouldn't receive the signal.

He opened the panel and looked inside. Standard stuff—each of the breakers was labeled with cryptic text that would only make sense to the electrician who'd installed them.

67A.

46-49B + J34.

It was a good thing he didn't need to understand any of it. Was there a master anywhere?

There. At the very top of the panel, right at eye level, was a large breaker that reached almost across the entire width of the panel. He pulled it as hard as he could and felt the pop as the breaker handle hit the other side of the panel. He thought he could hear a deeper *pop* from somewhere outside the room.

The light in the closet stayed on.

He looked around nervously. What if it hadn't worked?

He made up his mind. He reached up and started flipping off each of the individual breakers, one at a time, as fast as he could. If the master hadn't actually turned anything off, this certainly would.

He reached the bottom of the left side and started in on the right, this time working bottom to top. He got faster as he went, now using the palm of his right hand to flick sections off all at once. Somewhere in the middle, he hit the power breaker for the closet he was in, and darkness fell around him. He waited for his eyes to adjust, but they didn't. It was *dark*. Even the greenish glow of the heart rate monitor was useless.

Malcolm reached out again and felt for the rest of the breakers, using his left hand as a guide until he'd turned off the remainder of the switches. Satisfied, he looked down at the monitor waiting patiently next to him, like a pet. He ripped the clip from his finger, and a beeping sound immediately echoed from the machine. He spun the cart around, looking for a power switch.

There, on the top of the back panel, he found it. A standard I/O computer button. He pressed it, letting out a deep breath as the machine died. For good measure, he tried to hide it behind the mops and buckets that stood in a corner. It wasn't spy-worthy, but it at least wouldn't be immediately noticeable.

Now, he had to get out of the building. He assumed doctors and other night staff would be around soon, checking in on him until the backup generators turned on. He guessed he had less than a minute to get out.

Voices called out in the hallway.

"Yeah, I'll check it out. Probably a brownout or something."

"Okay, holler if you need anything."

Malcolm waited until footsteps raced past the closed closet door. Just as they receded up and over the bridge-like walkway, he opened the door and looked out. A balding man jogged down the other side, into the hallway to the room where Malcolm had sleept for the past six months. The man was only seconds away from realizing that his patient was no longer there.

Malcolm grabbed a mop, stepped out into the hallway and ran, trying to disconnect the mop head from its handle as he went. As he reached the entrance to the other building, the mop head fell off.

He burst through the open doors, only pausing to get his bearings. The electricity was out here, too—a good sign, at least until the generators kicked on.

"Anything?" he heard another man ask. The sound came from just ahead, around the corner.

Malcolm heard the clicking sound of a walkie-talkie, then the notoriously poor sound quality of another voice from the other end.

"Nothing. Lights off down here, too." A pause, then heavy breathing. "Checking in on 0-10-7... what the..." The voice continued breathing, then it shouted. "He's not here! 0-10-7-5-4 is gone! I repeat—"

Malcolm had heard enough. He had no idea if there was one man around the corner or twenty, but he took his chances. He flung himself around the end of the hallway, relieved to not have the burden of the heart rate monitor cart.

A lone young man in his thirties had his back to Malcolm behind a circular desk situated in the middle of an open atrium. This man was not a doctor, Malcolm realized. He was wearing a navy blue suit and black belt.

Rent-a-cop.

Malcolm kept running. Through the darkend atrium, shafts ofmoonlight piering the darkness through skylight leaving a odd silvery tint on the plants, and marble-art workwith its sharp light, like a modernist's interpretation of film noir.—Shadows cut through everything crosscrossing the pristine lobby.

Malcolm ran past a glass elevator and caught a glimpse of a sign glued to the side of the elevator shaft.

Floor 2.

And below it: *Drache Global.*

Drache Global—something clicked in Malcolm's mind. *That had been the label on the bag.*

By now, Malcolm was sure the man could hear him coming, but he didn't turn around. Instead, the rent-a-cop flicked the button on the walkie-talkie and asked again, "Hey, you hear me? What's up?"

The doctor tried to respond, but the connection either cut in and out or the doctor was inept at the use of walkie-talkies. The voice flickered. "—Patient... need assistance..." The cop tried to respond again, finally realizing that there were loud footsteps behind him.

It didn't matter. Malcolm was now within range of the cop, and he brought the mop handle up and over his head. He felt the burn in his right shoulder as his muscles voiced their discomfort, but he ignored it.

Malcolm felt a rage building inside him. *Six months. My team; my students.* Their faces flashed through his mind as the mop handle crashed down on the cop's head just as he spun around.

The handle connected with the man's temple, and a look of shock appeared on both the men's faces. The act of violence was unlike Malcolm, but he followed through. The mop handle broke in half, but the damage had been done.

The cop's head crunched sideways, and he fell from the stool he was on. He managed a quick gurgle of pain, but was silent as he fell to the marble floor. Malcolm dropped his half of the mop handle.

Without checking to see if the man was alive, Malcolm turned to the elevator. *There has to be...*

There. Stairs. Off to the left of the elevator shaft, he saw a small open entrance.

He went down the stairs two at a time, his body at once excited for the movement it was now allowed as well as struggling to provide it. He reached the bottom and found himself in a similar lobby.

Floor 1.

Drache Global.

No one was at the desk, but he didn't take any chances. He found a door to the left of the stairs that was labeled *L1–Garage,* and pushed it open.

A sharp snap of air hit him in the face. *Six months since I've felt fresh air,* he realized. He'd been asleep for just about all of that time, but his body knew. He drew in a deep breath and ran outside.

The parking garage sloped upward, and he now felt the strain on his muscles as he reached freedom. Ahead, he saw cars zipping by. The building must be on a busy road.

He ran, daring not look back. Closer.

The edge of the street was tantalizingly close.

Closer.

"Hey!"

He heard the doctor's voice yelling from behind. "Stop!"

Closer.

He reached the exit of the parking garage, thankful that the gate was an unmanned, automated machine. He dodged around it and continued running, forcing his legs to move faster.

Closer.

He'd made it. He reached the street, not pausing for traffic. Cars honked and swerved as they sizzled by, but Malcolm didn't notice.

He reached the other side, then kept running. Up another busy street.

On his left, cars raced past him. He held up a hand, waving —pleading.

Finally a car stopped. Malcolm slowed to a walk as the car's window rolled down.

"Need a lift?"

The voice from inside was that of a middle-aged woman, raspy from a lifetime of smoking. Her hair was tousled, but she wore a huge grin and unlocked the passenger door.

"P—please." He didn't know what else to say. "I... I don't know where to go."

The woman smiled larger. "I'd guess that. I'd say we get you some clothes, first."

Humiliation surged through Malcolm as he looked down at his body.

He was utterly naked.

2 2

For what seemed like the hundredth time in two days, Ben drove the truck while Julie snoozed in the passenger seat. As he pulled into the driveway that he'd known so well for so many years, he realized his hands were shaking. He raised one of them to his face, resting it near his eye, as if he were expecting to wipe away a tear. He parked the truck just in front of the closed garage door and stepped out.

Julie rose, yawning, as she opened the passenger door and stretched on the front lawn, she and the truck casting long late-afternoon shadows on the house.

"Is this her place?" she asked.

Ben was already moving toward the front door.

"So how do you know her, anyway?"

It was the second time she'd asked the question during their time together, and the second time he'd dodged it. "She moved here from St. Louis," He said, as though that answered anything.

He knocked but didn't wait for a response. The door was unlocked. He stepped inside, Julie following on behind. The house was dim, with low ceilings that sported 1970's style texture.

"Hello?" he called out.

A woman's muffled voice came from somewhere at the back of the house, so the pair walked down the narrow hallway until they came to a closed bedroom. Ben took a deep breath before knocking again.

"Stay away from the bed," the woman said when he opened the door. "The contagion is extremely potent."

Ben rushed forward, coming to his knees at the edge of the bed. He reached for the woman's hand and held it in his own.

"You never were a good listener, Harvey Bennet." She nodded her head but smiled at the same time. "How are you?"

Ben swallowed, trying to find his voice. "I—I'm good, Mom. What's going on?"

"Some sort of viral-bacterial combination, not unlike a bacteriophage," she said, glancing over at the doorway. "Who's your friend?"

—"This is Julie. She's with the CDC."

Julie's eyes widened as realization swept over her. She, too, approached the bed.

"Stay close to the door," Ben warned. "We can't have you getting infected with this stuff."

"It's okay," Dr. Torres said. "I can't explain it yet, but I believe it's safe… under some circumstances. Something about the dosaging, though I haven't yet cracked it."

"Still," Ben said. "Not worth the risk."

"Dr. Torres? It's... nice to meet you." Julie waved awkwardly from the corner of the bedroom. She stared at the large man beside the bed, doing all he could to not burst into tears.

"Mom, what happened? Was it the sample?" And then, just now realizing that there was bruise across her face, "Why aren't you in a hospital?"

"Slow down, Harvey. No, nothing like that. And you two both know a hospital can't do anything about this. It wasn't your sample." She took two breaths, each sharp and staggered. "I mean, it was the same strain, I believe, though not the sample you sent." Again, a breath. "There was a man. Said he was with the CDC too." She looked through pained eyes toward Julie. "Which, I now know, was a lie."

Ben stood and dropped his mother's hand. "Did he do this to you?"

Tears squeezed from his eyes, and Ben felt his face flush with anger. His eyes narrowed. "Mom. Who was it?" The words were clipped, on edge.

She shook her head again. "I don't know. I didn't recognize him. But that's why I think you're safe. It's... it was meant for me, and me only. He walked into my office and emptied your sample in the lab sink, then... then..." Her eyelids fluttered. She took another sharp breath and tried to continue. Ben suddenly noticed how red her skin appeared. He examined her neck and arms and found. They were covered in the same shiny, bubbling rash he'd seen back at Yellowstone.

"He threw it at me. A test tube full of something much more lethal." She took a breath again. "Listen, Harvey, I don't have much time."

"Stop it."

"No, listen. You know this by now but listen anyway. There's more to this than just a freak virus. The explosion, men pretending to be from the CDC—"

"Mom, we're going to—"

"Harvey, knock it off." The words were more intense than they had been, and Ben fell silent. "I don't care about any of that. I can't. I've got hours to live. You listen to me, okay?"

He nodded.

"Harvey, I love you. It's been over ten years since I've even heard from you, and you need to know that I love you."

A single tear fell down his right cheek. He couldn't bear to let Julie see him cry, so he kept his eyes glued to the bed and didn't wipe the tear away.

"I love you, and I never stopped loving you. After your—your father…"

"I love you too, okay?" He felt his voice shaking. *Was it noticeable?* He whispered. "I do. I'm sorry."

His mother's eyes were closed now, and she was trying to breathe peacefully.

"I'm sorry for everything."

He stood up from the bed and left the room.

Julie caught up to him in the hallway and followed him into the dining room, where he collapsed on an old leather sofa.

"—I don't know what to say…" she stammered.

Ben stared blankly at the flat-screen television that sat on a stand in the corner of the room.

"Ben," Julie said. She waited for him to look at her. "Ben, I know how this sounds, okay? But if we stay here, we might die."

"I'm staying here," he insisted. "You heard what she said. She thinks it's safe, that the stuff she was —"

"Ben! There's no way she could know that for sure. Listen to me. You *know* what's about to happen. If you're not infected yet, you soon will be. And then I will be. It's only a matter of time."

Ben knew she was right, but he didn't move from the sofa.

Julie finally came around the couch and sat next to him. "Can we at least go somewhere we can talk, okay? Somewhere we can figure this out together?"

She reached over and placed her hand on his.

This time, he nodded.

23

"Anything else?" The frazzled server gazed down at the couple in the booth with distain.

Juliette Richardson shook her head. "We're good, thanks." The server was gone before she could finish.

"I thought diners were supposed to have great service," Julie said to Ben over two plates of waffles and cups of coffee.

He shrugged, taking a huge bite of syrup-covered waffle. "They're known for their cheap food, I guess. Maybe good service is extra."

The diner sat just outside of town on the state highway they'd taken into Twin Falls. It was called The Family Diner, and Ben and Julie—the only two guests—weren't sure yet whether the play on words was meant to be taken seriously or not. So far, they assumed it was meant as satire. There wasn't a "family"—or even another person, besides their waitress—in sight.

"At least the food's good," Julie said, cramming almost half a waffle into her mouth. She guzzled coffee to wash it down, and only then noticed Ben staring at her. "What?"

He grinned. "As hard as this is…" he stopped.

"Yeah?"

"No, just… as hard as this is… I'm glad you're here."

Julie swallowed. "Me too. I mean, I can't imagine… I'm sorry, Ben." She took another bite of waffle, and this time added a forkful of sausage to it. "By the way, what's up with 'Harvey?'"

"That's my name," Ben said.

"Well, yeah, I picked up on that," she said. "But you don't go by that anymore. Why?"

He shrugged again. "I don't know. Dropped it after high school. Seemed like sort of a nerdy name, I guess. Ben's easier."

Julie considered this. "I like Harvey."

Ben stared blankly at her.

"I like Ben too," she added.

He looked down again at his plate, comparing his plate to Julie's. *She can really put it away,* he thought. He was almost embarrassed by how little he'd eaten.

"Hey, I have another question. Did Diana—I mean, your mom— did she have any assistants or anything? Anyone we could contact?"

"Always working, huh?" Ben's response was blunt.

"Oh my God, no, Ben… I'm sorry —"

He shook his head. "It's fine. Really. I'm shaken up, but this is good.

Let's keep moving; figure out what's next." He thought for a moment, using the lull in the conversation to take a deep sip of jet-black coffee. He winced.

"Too hot?" she asked.

"Too crappy." He swallowed, feigning choking. "Where'd you find this place, anyway?"

"Google Maps. Never steered me wrong so far."

"'Bout time to start using something else. Anyway, uh, I have no idea about her work. I've been in the park for over a decade. Man, it's been a long time."

A solemn look came over his eyes.

"Ben, it's okay. If you need —"

"No, I'm fine. Yeah, I can't think of anything. Hell, I don't even really know what she does. I remember she worked for a chemical company when I was a kid, but she took this job not too long ago."

"You spoke with her?"

"No, she'd email me quite a bit. I never responded more than once or twice, I think. I kept the email account open, though. Is there any way to figure out who she was working with?"

"I tried looking it up in the company directory, but they're pretty good about keeping their work and employees protected. I might be able to get some help from my tech guy, though." She took a sip of coffee, this time not using it to wash down her meal. From the expression on her face, she could clearly taste it better this time around. "Wow, you weren't kidding. This is rough."

Ben smiled, and he caught her gaze. He could almost feel her examining him, exploring the leathery-brown contours of a face that had rarely gone a day without being exposed to the sun and elements.

"Hey," she said quickly. "I have a question."

"Shoot."

"Why'd you leave?"

She didn't need to explain it; he knew what she meant. It was a fair question, but also the forbidden one, and she didn't dance around it or build it up.

He took a deep breath. *No one asks me that,* he thought. It had been years since he could even remember talking about it.

A light flashed in front of the diner. Another visitor had parked and was getting out of their vehicle.

Without realizing it, Ben was suddenly engrossed in the newcomer. He watched as the rectangular, boxy headlights flicked off—it was an older sedan—and the driver stepped out. *Tall, thin, can't see what they're wearing. No passenger.*

The visitor walked quickly, heading directly to the entrance. The man—Ben could now see him clearly—pulled the door open and walked inside.

"Good evening, go ahead and sit anywhere," the monotone voice of their waitress called from somewhere in the back of the restaurant.

Julie realized Ben wasn't paying attention to their conversation and turned to see what he was looking at. The man continued walking toward them. Ben locked eyes with him and began to stand up.

As he did, the man sped up. Ben's heart raced. The man was now only fifteen feet from their table and closing the distance fast. *Who is this guy?*

He watched the man reach into the pocket of his coat. Ben saw out of the corner of his eye another flash of lights, then another. *Two more cars.* He reached down and grabbed the closest thing he could find.

A salt shaker.

From the man's pocket, a gun. Small, compact. *.380. Enough to do some serious damage from this range.*

Ben didn't wait. He jumped to the side, throwing the salt shaker. It struck the gunman in the forehead, knocking him backwards a few steps. He dropped the gun, instinctively raising his hands to protect his head from further attack.

"Julie! Run!" Ben called out. He'd landed beneath some bar stools set alongside the counter of the diner. He struggled to his feet, feeling the painful throbbing in his hip.

Julie was on her feet, running toward the door, but the man was chasing after her. He overtook her at the diner's second exit, grabbing her waist with one arm. His other hand weaved up and around her left underarm. Julie was helpless, her arm completely pinned away from her body. She tried madly to swing it at him, but the man dodged the blows with ease.

Ben rushed forward, aiming for the attacker's lower back. Just before Ben collided with him, the man turned, exposing Julie's belly to Ben's tackle.

Ben was moving too fast to stop, and the three of them fell backwards out the diner's doors. They collapsed in a heap on the concrete sidewalk, but their attacker was on his feet almost immediately. He pulled Ben up and shoved him up against the tall glass window. Ben held onto the man's wrist, trying to wiggle free, but the man landed a solid punch to his gut.

He felt the wind get knocked out of him, and he caught a glimpse of Julie running toward the man before he was released and fell to the sidewalk. The man anticipated the attack, grabbing Julie's hands just as they fell toward his head. He twisted them sharply, and Ben heard her abrupt cry of pain. The man twisted harder, hugging her body close to his and moving his hands to her neck.

She was turned around, her back to his, so her punches had little effect. She danced around, trying to shove her heel onto the top of his foot, but the man was prepared for this line of defense as well.

The man's grip on Julie's neck grew tighter.

Ben blinked a few times, sitting up against the wall.

Get up. Come on, move.

He willed his body to work. His hip wasn't broken, but it was obviously badly bruised.

He heard Julie gasping for breath, her arms and legs flailing wildly.

Get. Up.

He forced his lungs to accept a deep breath of air. It was painful, as if someone was stabbing him in the chest.

Not as painful as getting choked to death, he thought.

He stood up. Julie's raspy voice broke through the gasps. "H—Help," she said.

He ran forward. His footsteps were heavy.

The man could tell he was coming. He was expecting it.

As Ben got within a foot of the man's back, an elbow caught him directly in the nose. Searing pain shot up his face, tears coming to his eyes. Ben stumbled backwards, nearly losing his balance again.

Just then he heard a shout. The lights from the other two vehicles became clearer.

Truckers.

Two men ran toward the trio, one of them shouting. "Hey! What the hell's going on over here?" One of the truckers saw the man choking Julie. He ran toward them, and the attacker released her neck. She sucked in cold air, falling to her knees on the rocky parking lot ground. Tears fell from her eyes.

The attacker was too late to protect himself. The first trucker had reached him and landed a blow across his face. He followed the attacker backwards as he struggled to keep his balance, but before he righted himself the larger truck driver punched him in the side. He doubled over, and the man kneed him as hard as he could.

The second truck driver had reached Julie, and he bent down to help her. Ben crawled forward, trying to regain his balance.

He watched as their attacker jumped to his feet and began to run away. He ran toward a field, chased briefly by the larger truck driver. When it was clear to the trucker that he was being outrun, he turned back to the others.

"You okay?" he asked Ben. Ben was on his feet now, swaying, still trying to catch his breath.

"I'm good. I need to get back to my truck; see if I can find him."

"You won't find him," the second trucker said. "He's fast, and he's probably got a ride somewhere nearby. Best call the cops and let them handle it from here."

Ben was seething. He walked over to Julie, letting his arm fall to her side. He pulled her close to him, wanting to protect her. *It's too late for that.*

She was sobbing, but she looked at him. "Are you okay?"

He realized what he must look like. He could feel blood draining from his nose, and he was having a hard time catching his breath. "I'm fine. What about you?"

She swallowed hard. "It hurts, but I'm okay." She turned to look at the two truck drivers. "I owe you my life. Thank you."

"Don't mention it. Isn't my first bar fight, but..." he looked at the now-empty diner. "I guess it is the first one I've broken up in a place like this. Why don't you two get inside, get something to eat?"

She shook her head. "We're fine, really. Thank you, both of you."

The first trucker spoke up. "You two need anything? A phone, a ride?" He paused. "A drink?"

Ben nodded. It was time to ditch their truck. "We could use a ride."

He knew the attacker—or someone—would be back. Whoever it was, they were going to be looking for them. They had to get away from there, and fast.

24

"What do you mean, you *failed*?" Valère asked.

He tried to steady his voice, to make it sound stronger than it was, for the other two men.

Roland and Emilio. Both were standing behind him, their meeting with Valère interrupted by this fourth man.

"I am deeply sorry, Mr. Valère," the man said. "I encountered them in a small diner, and when I —"

"Them?"

"Yes. The target was with another man. Large, built, but not much of a fighter. I was able to —"

"Then *why* is the target still alive?" Roland asked. His voice boomed out over Valère's shoulder, causing Valère to shudder. *If only I had his commanding tone,* he thought.

The man standing in front of him wasn't sure what to say. "I—I think..."

"And *that* is the problem," Emilio said. "You *think*, when we have simply asked you to *act*."

Emilio placed a hand on Valère's shoulder and leaned down, whispering.

"Your contingency is failing us, Mr. Valère. I suggest a prompt resolution to this matter."

Valère shook again and clasped his hands. His nervousness had been with him his entire life. It began as a slight tick in his boyhood years, growing into a noticeable oddity by his teens. As a young adult, Valère had learned to control it, forcing it down to a subtle, hardly noticeable level that didn't manifest itself physically.

But it was still there.

Valère was constantly reminded of his weakness. The sweating, the shuddering, the teeth-grinding. All of it was a form of nervousness, a simple reaction to *excitement*.

Whether positive or not, any exciting stimuli in Valère's life caused him to relive these moments, waiting until they passed. He dared not speak too loudly, or grow agitated, for fear that his weakness would once again wield its power over him.

He nodded. "Yes," he said, softly. "I do agree."

The man's eyes widened. "Wh—what is... what can I do..."

Valère held up a hand, and the man stopped.

"Please do not talk. You have already upset my partners, and I fear you will only upset me if you continue."

"B—but I can make it up. I *swear*. You don't need to kill me —"

"Enough!" Valère yelled, slamming his fist on the table in front of him. He felt the nervousness growing within him, quickly

superseded by the calming sensation of knowing he'd even startled his partners standing behind him.

He saw in his periphery each man take a step back.

The man—the failure—in front of him swallowed.

"Now," Valère continued. "What makes you think I am going to have you killed?"

The man turned his head slightly.

"No, my friend. I don't reward complete and utter *failure* with a swift and merciful death. It really isn't my style, anyway. The messiness of it all, it... well, it disturbs me.

"I have a better idea. SARA?"

"Yes, Monsieur Valère?"

The man's eyebrows arched when he heard the voice coming from the walls around him.

"I would like you to transport Mr. Olsen here to our facility in Brazil."

"Of course, Monsieur Valère. Is there a certain destination you have in mind?"

Valère nodded. "I do. Please alert NARATech of a possible test candidate currently preparing for stasis."

"Stasis?" Roland asked.

The man in front of them closed his eyes. "Please, Mr. Val —"

Valère shook his head, but SARA took over. *"Mr. Olsen, please refrain from additional comment. Your scheduled stasis prep will begin in exactly fifteen minutes. I have alerted security, and they are en route for escort. Please follow the green arrows I will illuminate on the walls."*

The man, resigned, left the room and slumped down the hall.

"Valère, what is *stasis?*" Roland asked again. "Emilio—what are you not telling me?"

Valère turned to his partners, scrutinizing the fat man that stood at his left. "Mr. Jefferson, I believe I have waited much too long to reassert my authority over this little project. Please —"

"*Reassert your authority?*" Roland Jefferson yelled. "What are you *talking* about, Valère? This project was given to us by —"

"No, Roland," Emilio said. "That's where you're wrong. This project was given to Mr. Valère and myself, and we brought you along because of your... *assets,* which we found valuable." Emilio turned to Valère to continue.

"Yes, Roland," Valère said. "We are excited to say that the Company no longer requires the use of these assets. Our investments elsewhere have performed admirably, and your lack of leadership so far on this project has informed our decision."

"Your... decision?" Roland Jefferson's enormous frame had moved out from behind Valère's desk, and he stood, looming, in front of him. "You can't... you can't *do* this!"

"Your investments are in nothing but corporate bonds and shady real estate, Mr. Jefferson. Most of it is drying up as we speak, thanks to the work of *our* investments. Your companies are *our* companies, and your prized real estate holdings around the globe are now being scuttled or revamped, to make way for our next phase."

"This is an outrage!" he roared, fuming.

"It is, Roland. It truly is. For you. For us—for the Company—it is a natural progression. We all eventually outlive our usefulness, and need to be *redirected.*"

"I will not be spoken to like a child! I have *not* outlived my usefulness!"

"Correct," Valère said. "SARA, are you still with us?"

"Always, sir."

"Perfect. Please arrange for Mr. Jefferson to join our friend Mr. Olsen in stasis."

"Absolutely, Monsieur Valère. And shall I arrange for his delivery to Brazil as well?"

"No, actually," Valère said. He watched Jefferson's eyes grow wide. "Please arrange for Roland's delivery to our holdings in Antarctica. He will preempt our facilities there, but our stasis research has proven to be quite effective in long-term storage."

"Very well, Monsieur Valère. Mr. Jefferson, your scheduled stasis prep will begin in exactly fifteen minutes. I have alerted security and they are en route for escort. Please follow the green arrows..."

Crack!

The sound of the rifle shot pierced the air and reverberated as it bounced over the calm, open water. Randall Brown sat up taller on the picnic table and offered advice.

"Good shot. You hit it, but it wasn't centered."

His wife grinned next to him, laughing at Randy's instruction.

His teenage son nodded, reloading the .22 caliber Remington rifle. "At least I hit it."

Randy smiled. "True. If it had been alive, it wouldn't be anymore." He took in the peaceful scene, watching the small pieces of clay disc disappear beneath the surface of the lake and the sunlight diffract over the gentle waves.

Way better than being at the office. He checked his watch. Late afternoon. He would normally be checking the server temperatures and running any final diagnostic tests, then getting ready to head home. Randall Brown had worked for the CDC for four years, moving to the Montana offices only a year ago. He'd had a brief stint in tech startups before realizing that he was considered a "dinosaur" in that world—at a mere forty-six years old. His world of IBM, mainframes, networking, and accreditations had been replaced in the past decade or so by a new world, one of sleek laptops, blogging, cloud platforms, and agile development. It wasn't that he wasn't needed, or useful; it was just that he wasn't appreciated.

No one seemed to know, or care, what kind of experience and knowledge he could provide as an IT consultant, network administrator, or general "tech guy." At the two startups he'd worked for, he was usually no more than an afterthought.

At first he didn't care. The jobs always paid well, thanks to a mix of youthful overconfidence and arrogant market predictions, but Randy knew better. He'd worked a year at a startup that was trying to bring simple image manipulation to tablets and mobile devices, only to see the writing on the wall a few months into it. The company had a long list of deep-pocketed investors who knew next to nothing about the computing world, and they had an equally impressive amount of VC funding. The trouble was, the product wasn't profitable. Worse, the college-age owners of the company didn't seem to care about the future of the company's product line.

Randy jumped ship to another company, finding many of the same problems and none of the solutions. After realizing his career would be all but over if he stayed on board, he decided to find a more stable position.

That position was found in the CDC's Threat Assessment division, as the Director of IT for a new department. It was a laid back job, never causing too much stress or overwhelming work duties. Keep email running, dust off the servers that provided intranet support through their SecuNet portal, and keep the coffee in the main office hot.

But while the job itself was decent, it was the *boss* that he couldn't stand. David Livingston. The man was more callous, abrasive, and downright rude than anyone he'd ever met.

Crack! Another rifle shot snapped Randy back to the real world. Vacation, one week, a friend's lake house. There was nothing in the past year Randy had looked forward to more than this moment.

He saw his son smiling back at him, and only then noticed the crumbling bits of clay skeet falling into the lake. All equal sizes, all the same relative shape.

"Wow—did you get it?" he asked.

His son nodded. "Right in the center."

Randy stood from the picnic table and clapped his hands, rotating them around in a large circle. A "round of applause." His wife groaned. A "dad joke," but, well, he was a dad.

"Seriously, dad?" his son asked. "You're still using that joke?"

"What? It's still funny."

"It was never funny."

"Hey," Randy said, walking toward the edge of the lake where his son stood holding the rifle. "You know what *would* be funny? If I took that thing from you and out-shot you with it."

The gun was a gift for Drew, something he'd wanted for quite some time. The three of them, Randy, his wife, Amanda, and Drew, had taken the trip to the lake house for a short vacation, and to celebrate Drew's seventeenth birthday.

"You're welcome to try, old man," Drew said. He handed the rifle to

Randy. Randy eyed the weapon, admiring the craftsmanship and build quality. Before he could lift it to his shoulder, his cell phone rang.

"Your phone works out here?" his wife asked. "Looks like it's work." She grabbed the phone from the table and walked it over to her husband.

Randy saw the number and shrugged. "Government's paying for it, so I guess they're using the best network." The number came up on the screen just below the name of the caller. Juliette Richardson. Well, at least it wasn't Livingston.

He poked at the phone to answer it. "Hello?" he handed the rifle back to Drew and walked back toward the table.

"Randy—hey, it's Julie. Sorry, I know you're on vacation. You have a minute?"

"Of course, what's up?" Unlike David Livingston, everyone liked Julie. She was fun, pretty, and adventurous, never waiting around for the red tape.

"Thanks. Listen, I don't know if you've been keeping up with the news, but something's going to break, and I'm trying to stay in front of it."

Randy *hadn't* been keeping up with the news, which was part of the family covenant of their vacation. As he was constantly bombarded by technology, industry news, and media during his job, his wife had made him promise to give it up for the week they were out of town. No TV, no internet, no computer. Just them, the lake, and peace and quiet for a week.

He glanced over at her now. She did not have a happy expression on her face, knowing that Randy's cellphone breached their covenant. He shrugged apologetically.

"Uh, yeah, okay. What's the deal?" The CDC often had something they were "trying to stay in front of," so it wasn't out of the ordinary for Julie to be asking for a work-related favor. But the fact that she'd called his cell directly seemed odd to Randy.

And her hurried tone of voice.

"Sorry, I can't explain it all right now. Can you get me access to a computer?"

"Sure—is it connected?" Randy didn't hesitate to answer. Even though it was an explicit part of his job description, he considered it to be "hacking" when he needed to gain access to another CDC machine. And he *loved* hacking.

"Uh, yeah, it is, but it's not onsite."

"What do you mean? It has SecuNet access, right?"

"No, sorry, I mean, it's *connected*, like to the internet, but..."

"Aw, geez, Julie, you're asking me to hack an outside machine?" Randy asked.

"Not hack, just... gain access. I need to get some information on—"

"That's called hacking, Julie. That's *literally* the definition of hacking."

Randy heard his wife let out an exasperated sigh from next to him on the picnic table bench. He looked at her, covering the phone's microphone with his palm. "Sorry... I... it's just something real quick."

"Hello? Randy? Hey, come on. This is a serious request. Can you help me out?"

Randy didn't know what to say. "Julie, this is... you can't. It's not legal, and I could get fired for even trying. Why can't Livingston put in a formal seizure of data request?"

"You know how long those take, Randy. And come on. Livingston? I haven't even seen him for the better part of a week."

It was true. Their boss had been enjoying a series of "work related" excursions, including golf, four-hour lunches, and strip clubs. How he managed to expense everything to the company's accounting division was beyond Randy's comprehension.

"Okay, fine. I assume you're on to something big, but I still can't—"

"It's a matter of national security, Randy."

"Seriously?" Randy almost laughed out loud. "You're going to try to guilt me into this with that line?"

"Randy, turn on the news. You can't honestly be that out of touch. After the bomb at Yellowstone, there was—"

"What? A *bomb* at Yellowstone?"

"Yes, Randy, a bomb. And it released something into the air. Some sort of virus that's killing everyone who came into the area close to the explosion. It's contagious, highly deadly, and we need to find out if anyone has anything on it."

Randy stared out at the water in shock. Never, in his year of employment with the CDC, had Julie ever seemed so... frantic. She was always calm, pleasant, and laid back, albeit in a hard-driving, get-it-done sort of way.

He wasn't sure how to respond. "I... I guess..."

"Okay, great. I need it quick, too. Can you get it, Randy?" She paused. "Randy? You there?"

Crack! Drew fired the rifle again, missing the skeet shot. He immediately prepared a second shot and launched the disc from the skeet launcher next to him.

"Sorry, yeah, I was thinking. I don't know, I have my laptop but I'm—"

"Randy, I'm sorry, but there's no time. I can't wait on this. Really. *Please.*"

Crack!

"Randy, what is that? God, it sounds like a gun."

"It is—sorry, it's fine. My son's skeet shooting—" he took the phone off his ear. "Drew! Knock it off for a second, alright? I'm on the phone!"

"Randy, you know I wouldn't ask you this unless it was serious. Trust me." Julie paused on the other end of the line.

Randy sighed. "I know. I do trust you. It's a pretty big deal, that's all. But I get it. Yeah, I think I can do it. Give me until tomorrow afternoon—"

"I have less than a day, from what I can tell. I need to get going on this before it's a media craze, and I'm waiting on more information from you now."

"Okay, okay. I can do it. I need to head into town, find a coffee shop." He thought for a moment. "It's not going to be secure, but what are you looking for? I'll email it over."

"Randy, thank you. I owe you one. Her name is Diana Torres. We need to track down anyone this person was working for, or with. I'll send you an email with her name, email address, and the company she was with. She's the only person we know who was studying the virus, and she might know what it is. Anything she found out will be on her computer, at that company."

Randy thought about the next question he was about to ask. *Did he really want to know the answer?* "Why can't you just ask her yourself?"

Julie anticipated the question and responded immediately. "We tried. She died a few hours ago, and we think her company was behind it. They sent someone to find us, too. Randy—I need this information, and I need it now."

Randy confirmed, but Julie had hung up already. Seconds after he disconnected and left the call, the phone dinged with a new email from her.

He turned off the phone's screen and placed it in his pocket, standing up from the picnic table again. "Sorry, babe, I, uh…" she glared at him. "I think I'm going to need to break the rules for a few hours."

26

The hotel was, thankfully, better appointed than The Family Diner. Situated in the suburbs of Twin Falls, Idaho, it had been purchased from an out-of-business chain and updated to reflect a lodge-like style. The street sign, front entrance, and two connected buildings that made up the hotel had a consistent wood paneled exterior.

The eighteen-wheeler and its three passengers pulled into the parking lot half an hour after the incident at the diner.

Ben shook the driver's hand before he slid down the steps of the truck. He offered the man a tip, reaching for his wallet. Their driver refused, instead asking the pair if they needed money or any more help.

"You've been more than kind," Julie answered. The man was a career truck driver, working for two main shipping companies and picking up other driving jobs in between. He had a family in Rhode Island, two kids and a wife, and was working his last year before he retired early. Ben appreciated him for another reason: he talked a lot and got along with Julie well. Their conversation had so little empty space that Ben spent most of the ride staring out the passenger window.

"Listen, here's my card," the trucker said, handing Julie a beat-up business card that he'd pulled from somewhere under the dashboard. "If there's anything else you need, you let me know."

"We will, thanks, Joe," Julie responded. She smiled and shook the man's hand, thanking him again as she hopped out of the truck. She stood next to Ben as the truck pulled away.

"Ready?"

He nodded and stepped up to the grand entrance of the lodge hotel.

"I still can't believe what happened. You sure you're okay?"

Ben nodded again. "Just tired. You?"

"Yeah, me too," she replied.

They reached the front atrium, where a young woman welcomed them from behind a chandelier-lit log desk. Everything looked warm and comforting, no doubt built and designed with those exact goals in mind.

"Do you two have a reservation?" the woman asked.

"We do," Ben replied. "I called earlier today to set it up. Sorry, we're a little late."

"No problem," the woman smiled as she grabbed the ID from Ben's outstretched hand. "Did you run into some weather? There were some thunderstorms in the area earlier."

Ben frowned, considering what to say. "No, uh, we just... got a little held up."

Julie smiled, trying to sell it as well. The woman looked them both over and grinned. "I understand. Not a problem." She winked at Ben.

Ben wasn't sure what the woman thought she understood, but he didn't press it. They hadn't called the police, though when the lady from the diner had finally come out to the parking lot, she'd offered to call for them. She may have still called after they'd left, possibly to report the truck they'd left in the diner's parking lot.

The plan was to rent a vehicle the next day and have it delivered to the hotel. After they felt certain they were no longer being followed, they'd return to the diner and pick up Julie's truck.

The woman at the counter finished typing something into her booking system and looked up again, still smiling. "I actually have you down for two full-size beds in room 201. I apologize, I can—"

"No," Ben said, interrupting her. He didn't mean to sound so forward, but it was too late. "Sorry. I know, I booked it that way on purpose. We're..."

He didn't know how to explain their relationship. He most definitely wanted them in the same room, in case something happened. They were adults after all, but there was no reason to share a bed.

"Oh." The woman seemed disappointed. "That's fine—we're good to go, then. Do you have a credit card you'd like to leave on file? I'll need one for a deposit."

"Would you take cash?" Julie asked. It was a long shot, but they weren't about to use a credit card that was linked to either of their names.

"I'm sorry, Ms. Richardson," the young woman said. "We need one in case of damages. We would accept a debit card, however."

Julie handed her a credit card. "This is my company one; it should be fine." Ben saw that the name on the card was, in fact, the name of her office at the CDC. It wasn't much, but it might provide a tiny layer of protection for them.

"Very good." The woman typed some more and handed the card back to Julie. "Thank you. Here are your keys, and will you need anything else this evening?"

Ben shook his head and took the packet of room keys.

"Do you have any wine? Red, maybe? Something, uh, sort of... romantic?" Julie asked.

Ben felt his face immediately flush a bright red. His eyes widened as he saw Julie's smile, quickly matched by the woman behind the desk. "Well, I guess we could bring something up. We actually don't have room service, but as you probably know, we have a fantastic menu at our restaurant."

The woman pointed to a hallway just off the main atrium, beneath a sign that said *Le Petit Paris—French-American Cuisine.*

"You two get situated, and I'll bring you a bottle in a few minutes." She turned back to the computer as the pair walked away, a smug look on her face.

As they neared the elevator, out of earshot from the front desk, Ben pulled a still-grinning Julie to the side. "You want to tell me what the hell that was?"

"You should have seen your face!" When she realized Ben wasn't laughing, she put on a fake-pouty look. "What? It's not like we're ever going to see her again. Besides, she seemed so disappointed when she thought we weren't together."

"We're *not* together!" Ben stormed into the open doors of the elevator, Julie trotting behind.

They rose in silence, then exited the elevator to find their room directly to the left. Ben inserted the key, then swung the door open. "I'm going to run down to the desk and pick up some toiletries. Do you need anything?"

"I have everything I need," Julie said, wheeling the suitcase she'd packed at her farmhouse into the room. "You can use my toothpaste and stuff, if you want."

He glared at her and let the door swing shut.

When he returned to the room a few minutes later, he found Julie sprawled on one of the beds, gripping a glass of red wine and wearing a pair of pajama bottoms and a worn t-shirt. She looked up as he entered, still wearing the cheesy grin. "It's good," she said, swirling the glass a bit. "You should try some."

Ben shook his head, but found that he was smiling—just a little. He threw the small bag of toiletries he'd just purchased on the bathroom counter and sat down on the empty bed. Julie had apparently done some quick cleaning up. Her hair looked like it had been combed, falling gently around her shoulders and toppling over the pillow behind her. Ben watched her drink the wine for a few seconds until she turned to look at him.

Again, he felt his face flush. *Come on, Harvey, get it together.*

Julie laughed. "What? Been awhile since you've had a girl in your room?"

It had been.

"Shut up," he said, reaching for a wine glass and the bottle of Merlot that rested on the nightstand between the beds. He poured himself a glass and took a sip. *When was the last time I had a glass of wine?* Most of his coworkers drank beer, if they drank at all. Ben preferred a glass of bourbon or whiskey, single malt on the rocks.

They looked at each other for a moment, each trying to decide what to say next. Julie lost interest first, turning back to whatever was on the television.

Ben wanted to ask her about her life. Who was she, really? Where was she from?

Was there anyone else in her life?

As someone not terribly interested in other peoples' lives, he was surprised at his train of thought.

But instead, he asked about their plans. "What's next? After tonight, I mean?"

Julie looked confused for a moment, then turned back to him. "Randy will probably get back to me soon, and he'll tell us where to go next. Whoever was working with your mother probably lives in the area, and we can track them down pretty easily from there."

Ben nodded. "Makes sense. You think Randy will get anywhere?"

"He always does. He's a genius with computers. He's pretty new at the CDC, but we get along well. He's probably not stopped working on it since I called him earlier. The real question is if Diana shared any of her findings with anyone else or not."

"No idea. I hadn't spoken to her in over a decade. She was never the secretive type, so I imagine she'd be open to working with someone else."

Julie took in the information, and both lay silent for a few minutes.

"Okay, well, I need to get some sleep," she said. "I've got my phone on, in case Randy calls. We can figure out anything we can from whoever might be around here, then I'll get us some plane tickets back to Billings for tomorrow night."

Ben shook his head. "I'll take the rental back. You go ahead."

"You won't fly?"

"No."

"Why?"

"I just won't. I don't like it."

"Come on, it's perfectly safe. It'll be much quick—"

"I'm not going to fly, Julie."

"Ben, what's the big deal? You won't —"

"Knock it off, alright? I already told you, end of story. Drop it." The words came out harsh, stressed. He regretted it, but the damage was done.

"What the hell, Bennett? Why the attitude?"

He didn't respond.

"Seriously, Ben, what's up? Why are you like this?"

"Julie…"

"No, I've had it. You barely speak to anyone, you treated me like dirt, and you've been off the grid for ten years. What is it about you that makes you so *cold*?"

Ben looked up sharply. He thought he could see Julie's eyes welling up.

He didn't know what to say. Didn't *want* to say anything. *Hell, what am I doing here?* he thought.

He stood up from the bed and walked out of the room, slamming the door behind him. Julie remained, a shocked expression on her face.

2 7

They were the only patrons in the restaurant. *Le Petit Paris* was frequented only by guests of the lodge, and this particular week was a very slow one for the hotel.

Ben and Julie sat at the corner booth, enjoying a platter of waffles, sausage, bacon, eggs, and toast. Apparently the restaurant leaned heavily on the American part of "French-American cuisine."

"Sorry about last night." Ben said the words slowly, meticulously, speaking through a mouth full of breakfast food.

"Don't worry about it," Julie said. "I went too far. I shouldn't have —"

"You didn't do anything wrong," Ben said, stopping her. "I'm uncomfortable around people, if you haven't already guessed. I don't do well with confrontation and, well, feelings in general."

Julie laughed. "You wish you were a robot?"

Ben thought for a moment and grinned. "Yeah, kinda. That would be okay."

"Really? No tasting food, no feeling joy, no, uh, *more pleasurable* emotions?"

"No feeling pain, either."

"Pain's not a bad thing, Ben. It makes the good stuff that much better."

He scoffed and grabbed another waffle. "Ever eat these with peanut butter?"

"Gross. Are you serious?"

"Oh yeah. You have no idea. It's the *only* way to eat them. My dad —"

He caught himself, choosing to take an extra-large bite instead.

"Your dad what?" Julie pressed.

"Nothing. He, just, liked it. I must have gotten it from him."

Julie swallowed. "Can I ask you something?"

Ben looked at her. "Maybe."

"What would you be doing if this bomb hadn't gone off? If there was no virus, and it was just you, at Yellowstone?"

"You mean besides hauling nuisance bears around the park?"

"Yeah, I mean *after* work. What does Harvey Bennett do in his spare time?"

Ben considered the question. "Well, I've been working on buying a place of my own, actually."

"Yeah?"

"Yeah. Some land way up in Alaska. I want to build a cabin on it someday. I'm in the last stages of the deal, but I've been waiting for the bank to finalize things."

"Wow—Alaska?"

"I've actually never even been there." He laughed. "I saw the land online, saw what they were asking for it, and called them that afternoon. It was dirt cheap because of its location. Used to be owned by a trapper who passed away a few years ago. The land went up for auction and a local bank bought it, hoping to turn a profit."

"You strike me as the kind of person who needs to be around a lot of people and live in a city, probably in a high-rise."

"Yeah?" Ben smiled. "Seems like me."

Julie paused to take a few bites, and Ben sipped his coffee. He knew what was coming next. Julie deserved the truth.

"Your mom. Diana Torres. You didn't tell me she was your mom, and you called her 'Diana Torres.' Why?"

He shrugged. "We got in a fight a long time ago. She never really forgave me. I guess we both never forgave each other."

"What happened?"

Julie wasn't one to waste time. Ben liked that about her, but it terrified him all the same.

"It was the same time I ran away from it all. Thirteen years ago, right before I started at the park. I was camping with my dad and my kid brother. He was nine at the time, and he wandered out of camp and got stuck between a bear and her cub. My dad went to get him, and the bear attacked him."

Julie covered her mouth with a hand.

"He got hit, hard, and went unconscious. My brother was pretty scraped up, but okay. My dad was airlifted out and spent a few months in a coma, then died."

"God, Ben, I'm sorry."

He waved it off. "My mom—as tough as she was—she never really forgave me. It was really Dad, though, I think she was mad at, for letting it happen. But she couldn't express that, you know? And she tried to forget about it, I think. She changed her name back to her maiden name, Torres. We sort of walked on eggshells for a while afterwards, until I gave up. I got some odd jobs, finished school, and just… left."

"I had no idea," Julie said. She was tearing up again.

"Why would you? I don't talk about it for a reason, Julie. It ain't something I'm proud of, and I don't particularly like thinking about it."

"So why Yellowstone?"

"Makes sense, for a guy like me. No education, loves being outside, and hates people. Seemed like the logical thing, really. It's a great organization, too, so I actually enjoy the people there."

Enjoyed, he thought. He looked up and saw that Julie was shaking her head.

"What is it?" he asked.

"It's—it's just that I still don't get you. I am sorry, I truly am, but you don't *really* hate people. You just said it, you know? You like those guys you work with, and you know it. You care for them, but you won't let them in. Right?"

Ben felt again, for the third time in many years, his face redden. "Yeah, I get it. Listen, Julie, here's what people like you—people who have that weird *hope* in humanity—don't get. You know what causes pain? True, *real* pain? People do. You get rid of people, you get rid of pain."

"That's stupid."

"Stop thinking that the world works some other way, Julie. Stop trying to make it work the way you want it to."

The waitress came around and refilled their coffee, while Julie and Ben sat silently at the small table. Julie held back tears as she gazed out the window. Ben simply faced straight ahead, not making eye contact with the waitress.

When he finally looked up, he found the woman staring down at him knowingly, eyeing him strangely. "Let me know if you two need anything," she whispered. Ben nodded.

"Come on, Julie, what's wrong?"

Julie turned her head. "You need to grow up, Ben."

He frowned.

"People care about you. People *love* you, and you push them away because you got hurt once. I get it, but you've got to let it go."

He stood up to leave, but she reached out and grabbed his arm. "Stop. Don't walk away again, Ben. You need to hear this, talk through it."

He wanted badly to continue, to walk out of the room. Then keep walking.

But he didn't. He wasn't sure why, but he agreed with her. He needed her to call him out. Or was it more than that?

Before he could consider an answer, Julie's phone rang. She held it up and read off the name: Randall Brown.

174

28

"Dad! Breakfast is ready!"

Randall Brown heard his son yell while sitting in his office, checking in on things at work. His wife had clearly told their son to get him for breakfast, and this was his interpretation. Seconds later he heard his wife, Amanda, yell back.

"Come on, Drew, *get* him. I could have yelled myself."

Randy smiled to himself, knowing exactly what came next:

"Then why didn't you?" Drew asked.

Randy shook his head. Knowing Amanda, Drew was risking his rifle-shooting privileges, or worse, with such a show of disrespect.

When do they grow out of it? he wondered. Drew was a good kid, but Randy was regularly surprised by the fleeting attitudes and phases of teenage boys. Drew kept them on their toes, and Randy was positive that Drew was the cause of the majority of the gray hairs on his head.

"I'll be right there!" Randy called back. Surprisingly, he didn't hear his wife reprimand their son. She must have decided it wasn't worth the trouble. Still smiling, he turned back to his cellphone and dialed Julie's number.

It rang three times before she picked up. "Hello?"

"Hey, Julie, it's me—Randy."

"Hey, Randy, good to hear from you. We're just finishing up breakfast. Anything good?"

"Might be helpful, but I don't know if it's *good*."

"We'll take anything you've got, Randy."

"By the way, who's we? You working with Stephens on this one?"

"Uh, no, a guy I met at Yellowstone actually. Stephens is back home. What did you find?"

Randy considered this for a moment. *Some guy?* Julie wasn't careless but he didn't question her. "Oh, uh, I found her—Diana's—assistant. Charlie Furmann, lives in Mud Lake, Idaho, with his parents and has an apartment in Twin Falls."

Julie paused a moment. He assumed she was taking notes. "Mud Lake? Is that a real place?"

"It is. Town of about four hundred people from what I gather. Shouldn't have much trouble finding him there."

"Ok, great. Anything else on him?"

"Not much. He was a PhD candidate in something called 'molecular modeling' and worked with Diana as a sort of work-study."

Again, a pause.

"Listen, Julie. I really need to go." He thought about his son in the dining room, waiting with Amanda to start breakfast. *Amanda.* She was already upset that he was gone for a few hours yesterday, and she wouldn't be happy with him for this, either. At the very least, he could tell her what had happened at Yellowstone and hope that it explained why he had been absent.

"Right, yeah, sorry. Randy, thanks for this. Seriously."

"No problem." He began to hang up but heard Julie's voice again from the small speaker.

"Oh, hey. Have you heard anything from Stephens?"

Randy placed the phone back up to his ear with a frown. "Stephens? No, why?"

It wasn't abnormal for Randy to not be in contact with Benjamin Stephens. Randy was the office IT specialist, not a regular team member. Most of the time he was in charge of setting up and maintaining the company's intranet server, SecuNet, and setting up email addresses and providing other IT support. In some cases, he had played a more active role by providing on-the-fly information updates and logistics, but his was mainly a hands-off job.

"I just haven't heard anything from him either," Julie explained. "He usually swamps my inbox but..."

"Weird. No, I haven't heard anything."

"Okay. Is the server up, do you know? Any major downtime?"

Randy was almost insulted. "Of course not. Why would there be? You know I've got 24/7 alerts that would get to me even if I was trapped in an Afghani cave."

"Whoa, chill. Can't hurt to ask, right?" Julie said. "I know you're on top of it. It's just weird, that's all."

"Yeah, it is. Give me a minute. I'll remote in and see if there's anything wonky going on. I'll text you in five."

"Thanks, Randy. I owe you one."

"Buy me a beer sometime, and we're even." He clicked off the phone and walked out to the dining room. He eyed his wife and son. "You know the bomb that went off at Yellowstone? Something was released into the air and it's killing people."

His wife's eyes grew wide. Drew's mouth hung open.

"We're fine here, but the CDC has people in the field, and I need to keep checking in every now and then."

His wife nodded, still taking in the horrible news.

"Okay, then. Give me five more minutes and I'll be back out."

He left the room and used the remote desktop application on his phone to access his terminal at the office.

Everything checked out—servers were up and running, intranet cabling didn't appear to have any glitches, and the inbound internet connection was functioning properly. He scanned through the list of configuration files, finding no problems.

Lastly, he clicked on the email server link and browsed the inbound and outbound connections. Through this portal, he could see every email sent and received by every member of his access group—twenty-five people in total. It was a security protocol, one that had required him to maintain a level of security clearance to remain employed. He browsed the list, reading the names of the senders and receivers of each email.

He saw names of other employees sending and receiving emails from other members of the staff regarding the current state of affairs at Yellowstone. He saw emails from Stephens sent to Julie's email address, and he saw emails to David Livingston.

Nothing out of the ordinary.

Except...

He didn't see any *received* emails with Julie's name or email address. Though Stephens had sent them, they seemingly had never reached her inbox.

Randy grimaced. This was his area, his responsibility. If there was something wrong with the mail server...

Then he saw something even more puzzling.

For every sent email from Stephens to Julie, there was a duplicate received email with Livingston's address on it.

Definitely puzzling.

He opened the configuration file for the mail server, just to see if there was anything strange going on with the routing. Everything checked out. He found nothing wrong in the name server settings, either.

There was one more place to check. Randy opened the forwarding section of the SecuNet admin portal and read down the list. Most entries were auto-responders set up for staff who were on vacation, working remotely, or otherwise wanting to receive their email through another provider's account. But one was a specific forwarding address that he recognized.

Benjamin Stephens.

Why was his address being forwarded? And where was it going?

Shocked, Randy clicked through until he found the answer. Benjamin Stephens' mail was being forwarded to *David Livingston* —*at Livingston's instruction.*

Livingston himself had set up the forward on the SecuNet server for all of Stephens' mail. Anything the man sent out was instead received by his superior.

And it was poorly done, to boot. Randy couldn't find any sort of encryption on the forwarding record, nor was the address masked in any way to a vanity email address. It was as if the man didn't care who was watching, or more likely, didn't care *why* anyone was watching.

It was certainly like Livingston to be so distrustful of his staff that he'd set up an email forward on an account, but why Stephens? And why not just ask Randy to monitor it for him?

Randy suspected why: Livingston wanted the power trip. He wanted to feel in charge; letting Randy into his little game was like inviting someone else aboard to watch him drive the train. Randy was immediately disgusted, but he was now faced with a bigger dilemma: should he remove the forward?

If he did, Livingston would know soon enough that the forward was no longer working. But if he didn't, Livingston could just log in to SecuNet and see that 'rbrown' had recently logged in and seen the forwarding page.

It was a tough decision, but he had a little time to think through his options. There was, however, one decision he'd already made.

He closed the remote desktop application on his phone and called Julie back.

29

"Seems like all we're doing is driving," Julie said from the passenger seat of her truck. The road they were on had narrowed to a two-lane highway surrounded by farmland.

"You mean all *I'm* doing is driving," Ben answered. They'd left the hotel that morning, heading toward Mud Lake, Idaho, just as soon as Julie had received the tip from her computer guy, Randy Brown.

"I told you earlier I don't mind—just let me know when you want to switch."

Ben shook it off. "It's fine, really. Enjoy the scenery."

"Yeah, I just love cornfields as far as the eye can see."

"They're soy beans."

"Really?"

"Yes."

"Huh."

They came to a cross street and turned right onto a farm-to-market road that apparently led farther into the great expanse of fields and farms. According to Ben's map, they were about ten minutes from Mud Lake. Julie had chided him for almost an hour about the map—a Rand McNalley road atlas he'd purchased at the hotel's gift shop—but if he were in a laughing mood, he would have gotten the last one now.

Never one to trust technology, Ben had purchased the map "just in case," having a hunch that neither of their cellphones would pull a decent enough data connection to get them to Mud Lake, and then to Charlie Furmann's parents' place outside of town. As of about thirty minutes ago, he was proven correct.

"You'd like the CDC. They hate flying too, since it happens to be one of the most efficient ways to spread airborne diseases."

"I'm not *afraid* of flying," Ben shot back. "I just don't... prefer it."

"Oh, right. Just like I don't *prefer* spiders."

"That's different. I just don't like feeling so... helpless."

Julie thought for a moment, looking out the window. "I get that. Makes sense—all those tons of metal, breaking the laws of physics—"

"Hey, I don't need to be reminded of it."

"You *are* afraid of flying! I can't even mention flying without you getting all bent out of shape."

"You're relentless, you know that?" Ben said.

"I do. How much longer?"

"Ten minutes, I think. Check the map." Julie grabbed the open atlas spread out on the center console and looked it over for a few seconds.

"What? Haven't had to go tech-free in a while?"

"Shut up. I can use it. I just need to get my bearings."

"North is up."

"Be quiet."

"I literally outlined the route we're on. Just look at the red line—we're toward the end of it."

Julie contemplated the map for a few more seconds, then threw it back down and looked back out the window.

"Well?" Ben asked.

"Yeah, about ten minutes."

Ten minutes later, they saw a lone silo stretching up over a field of deep green, leafy plants. As the silo grew larger, they could see a few smaller buildings spread out over the expanse of soy fields, including a yellow farmhouse. But it was the vehicles in front of the farmhouse that made Ben's skin crawl.

"Are those police cars?" Julie asked.

"Yeah. Four of them."

"Oh, man, this just keeps getting better."

Ben navigated down the road a little farther until he saw a dirt road leading to the farmstead. He started to slow the vehicle, preparing to turn, but Julie stopped him.

"Don't. They're not going to let us just walk around there, and if something did happen, we're not helping ourselves by showing up on the doorstep."

Ben knew she was right.

"Besides, the police aren't going to give us anything until they've figured it out. Especially if there was a crime. Let's head back into town and see if anyone knows what's going on."

Ben sped up again and grabbed the atlas. "This road intersects with another farm road that runs parallel to the main highway. Should take us back toward Mud Lake."

They found their road in another minute, and ten minutes after that, they were on the outskirts of town.

Town, however, was too strong a word. Mud Lake, Idaho, seemed like not much more than a rest stop on the way to something bigger. A few stoplights, a general store with a few gas pumps, and a large industrial facility of some sort was all the small town's main street offered.

Ben pulled the F450 into the small lot in front of the general store and parked.

"Is it open?" Julie asked.

"No idea. Let's find out." They got out and walked to the front door. Ben grabbed the handle and was surprised when it gave easily. A series of dings sounded from a group of bells hanging on a string attached to the door let the owner know they'd arrived.

"One minute!" a voice called out from somewhere in the back. They waited at the counter for a moment before a short, rotund man with reddened cheeks and wispy white hair appeared from around a corner. He shuffled along, appearing almost weightless as his upper body hardly moved. He wore an impressive smile, aided by his large, jolly eyes, and his overall impression told the couple they'd found the right place to ask for help.

"How may I help you?" the man asked. His voice matched his appearance in every way. Crisp, light, and nuanced in a way that only an older man with years of communication experience could portray. His demeanor was disarming.

"We're looking for some information. About someone who lives here," Julie said.

The man nodded slowly, eyeing each of them for a brief moment. "It's a small town, as you've no doubt gathered," he said cheerfully. "We do tend to know one another quite well."

Ben sensed a bit of hesitation in the man. *Maybe this was a bad idea...*

"His name's Charlie Furmann," Julie said. "I think he lives here with his parents, just outside of town—"

The man held up a hand, halting Julie. Ben watched as the man's expression and stature changed almost instantaneously, going from a peaceful, inviting shop owner to a ruffled, bothered old man. "Get out. Now." He pointed to the door. "Please leave."

"Sir—we're just—"

"No. Out."

Ben clenched his teeth and tried to interpret what had just happened. The man clearly knew Charlie or knew *of* him. *Maybe he knows his parents?*

"Sir, we're sorry to intrude. Really. But we're with the CDC... the Centers for Disease Control." The man's face softened slightly, but he still looked about three seconds away from grabbing a broom handle and shooing them out of the store. Ben said. "There's been an outbreak of something, and we're trying to figure out what it is. We think Charlie might know something about it—"

"It doesn't matter what he *knew*," the shopkeeper said.

"Wait," Julie said. "*Knew? As in past tense…?*"

The man nodded.

"My God," she said. "We're so sorry. We drove by his parents' farm and saw the police cars… How?"

The man sighed, realizing that he wasn't going to get rid of these patrons as easily as he once thought. "He was found in his apartment, in Twin Falls. Had that rash on him—the one that's been going around east of here."

Julie nodded, taking it all in.

"Terrible thing. You people know anything about that rash?"

"That's what we're working on now," Julie explained.

Ben added. "It's killed a lot of people who were around that blast in Yellowstone. We think it's related, that Yellowstone was the epicenter."

The storeowner's faced drained. "I sure hope not, son. Seems like this country's already gone to hell in a handbasket. Kid hadn't been home in something like five years, too. All focused on his work in the city. The Furmanns are beside themselves."

Ben and Julie thanked the man and left. They walked in silence back to the parking lot and the truck. Ben slid into the driver's seat.

Julie waited until the truck was on the main road through town before she spoke. "Twin Falls is outside the blast radius by *hundreds* of miles. And the virus is not technically an *outbreak* yet—it's not contained, but it hasn't been spreading outside of Wyoming. *Much* slower than a tradional epidemic."

"Right," Ben said. "My mom wasn't anywhere near it either. Whoever got to her also must have paid Charlie a visit..."

They both let that information sink in. What it meant, what it *might* mean, was even more terrifying. Someone had brought the virus to them intentionally.

30

Julie decided it would be best to check in with her office and see if they had anything new. As they drove in silence, she checked her phone again to see if she had service.

"Anything?" Ben asked.

"Not yet," she said. "I think I had bars outside Twin Falls."

"We're only a few miles out. Keep checking."

Soon enough, a single bar of service grew to two, then three. Then her phone vibrated. She had a waiting voicemail from Randall Brown. She played it over the phone's speaker so Ben could listen in.

"Hey Julie, it's Randy again. I checked SecuNet. Everything's working properly, but I did find something odd. Livingston put a mail forward on Stephens' email account—anything he's sent in the past forty-eight hours went straight to him. That's probably why you haven't heard anything."

Julie looked up at Ben, shocked.

"Anyway, I didn't delete the forward. Livingston would know that I was in there right away if he stopped getting Stephens' updates. Still, if he decides to log in to SecuNet again, he'll see my timestamp there. I'm kinda between a rock and a hard place on this one, Julie, so let me know what you want me to do."

"You've got to be kidding me," Julie said.

"What's your boss paranoid about?" Ben asked.

"—Everything and anything, but this crosses the line. To prevent the flow of information like this during an active investigation..." She shook her head, staring down at the phone.

"What do you think he's up to?" Ben asked.

"He's always had a problem with me, but this is weird even for him."

Julie looked out the window. The sign for Twin Falls read: *135 miles.*

"How far are we from Idaho Falls?"

"I'd guess about an hour, maybe less. We're coming up to Highway 26, which goes back that direction. Why?"

"There's a regional airport there. I can hitch a ride on one of the smaller jets if there are any going out today." Julie started. She caught Ben's eyes. "Don't worry. I'll fly back to Billings and get things straightened out at the office, and you can drive the truck back."

Ben kept one eye on her as he continued driving down the highway.

"Only if you ask me nicely."

She rolled her eyes. "Would you *please* drive the truck back for me?"

He sighed. "Sure. What's another five hours of driving, anyway?"

"Actually, six. You'll want to go around Yellowstone."

Just then, her phone rang. *Stephens.* She answered it, again placing the phone on speaker.

"Stephens?"

"Yeah, hey Julie, how is everything going?" The muffled voice asked.

"Good, I guess. Have you been getting my emails?"

"I have. Are you getting mine?" he asked.

She hesitated. "Uh, no, I actually haven't had time to check." It was a poor lie, but it would buy her time. Stephens paused on the other end.

"Okay, right. Hey, how did that last contact work out? Any information?"

Julie had emailed her itinerary to Stephens before they visited Mud Lake, and in it she'd included the information Randy Brown sent along.

"It was... not fruitful." She changed the subject. "We're still working on where to go next, but I think I'm heading back to the office later today."

He paused. *"Okay, sounds good. Uh, listen, we got some news I wanted to call about."*

Julie exchanged a glance with Ben. "Okay."

"Livingston and some higher-ups at the CDC and the Department of Homeland Security called in a team of excavators to check out the area beneath Yellowstone Lake and the West Thumb areas, at the park."

"Where the bomb went off?"

"Right. They know there are a few caves that run around that area, though none of them are very long or deep. But they checked them all out just in case."

Ben scratched his arm while he listened.

"What did they find?" Julie asked.

"A tunnel, cut into a wall of one of the caves."

"Manmade?"

"Yeah. Cut recently, too," Stephens said.

Ben scratched his arm again. Julie looked like she'd seen a ghost.

"What's their thinking? That's where the bomb was placed?" she asked.

"No, or it would have collapsed the tunnel."

"But it could have been a staging area," Ben cut in. "Away from prying eyes."

"Correct." Then the realization that he wasn't talking to just Julie must have sunk in. *"Wait—Julie, was that Ben? That guy from Yellowstone?"* Stephens said.

"Yes, don't worry about that," Julie said.

Ben grew increasingly annoyed with the itch in his arm. *What is that?* He finally looked down at his forearm. A red rash had begun to spread down and over his hands.

His breath caught in his throat. *"Julie,"* he whispered.

Julie didn't hear him.

He began yanking his sleeves down to cover his arms. Reached into his jacket pocket and pulled out a pair of leather works gloves without running off the road.

"What do they think is going on, then?" She continued. "Do they know?"

"They don't know," Stephens replied. *"But they have an idea. They're thinking the first bomb was a warning, to get our attention."*

Julie tried to take it all in. "From who? Wait. What do you mean the *first* bomb?"

"Julie." Ben said her name louder, hoping she'd look over at him. Instead, she held up her pointer finger. *Wait.*

"They think there's a second bomb," Stephens said. *"Bigger than the first. It may or may not have a viral payload this time, but regardless, if it detonates..."*

"Julie!" Ben barked. His voice easily filled the truck's cab, and she jumped.

—Her eyes widened as she saw what Ben had grown so frantic about. His hands and forearms were covered, but he wasn't looking at his own arms. Instead, he was pointing at hers.

She dropped the phone on her lap and stuck her arms out in front of her.

A rash was blossoming across her skin.

3 1

Ben gunned it, pointing the large gray F450 down the narrow highway that twisted through Billings, Montana. An alarmed family in the car next to him swerved out of harm's way.

Ben didn't care. The rash had spread and was continuing to do so. He could feel it creeping up to just below his shoulders, though it was still only visible on his hands and arms. It was moving much more slowly than he'd seen back at Yellowstone, but it was definitely moving. He could only hope that Julie's own rash was moving even slower.

He sped ahead of another eighteen-wheeler, this one carrying a load of brand-new vehicles to some dealership. The driver flipped him off. Ben hit the gas in response. He had to get to the hospital. To Julie.

When they'd reached the regional airport in Idaho Falls, she'd nearly convinced him to keep driving, terrified of what might happen to everyone around her while she carried such an extremely contagious disease.

The argument, however, was settled for her when Livingston called. The very man who had been intercepting her communications with Stephens. He voiced surprise when he heard her news but had a plan in action within minutes.

"I'll have a private plane waiting for you," he'd said. It turned out to be owned by a business tycoon who golfed with Livingston often. It was ready to leave as soon as they'd arrived—they could even drive directly onto the tarmac to save time. Julie was overjoyed, thanking Livingston profusely and promising she'd pay him back someday.

They tried to get Ben to go too, as a precaution, just in case he'd caught it. Ben refused to reveal that he *did*, in fact, have a rash, silently convincing himself that Julie's was worse. He'd rolled his sleeves down and spoke as little as possible.

"He doesn't like to fly," Julie kept telling the team. It was the only excuse they had, and besides, there was technically nothing they could do to force him to. So, they'd given him a card and asked him to call if he experienced any symptoms, and they warned him to limit his interactions with other people as much as possible.

Ben told them he would, stuffed the card into a back pocket of his jeans, and was on the highway toward Montana before they could send someone to tail him.

He didn't trust a single one of them.

His phone had buzzed about an hour ago, the number an unknown caller. When he'd answered it and heard Benjamin Stephens' voice on the other end, he knew it could only mean bad news.

"Julie's here," Stephens reported.

"What?" Ben said. "Why is she at the office? She got the virus thing, and —"

"She's not," Stephens said.

Ben breathed a sigh of relief, then remembered his own rash. It had grown a bit, but it hadn't gotten any itchier. He took that as a good sign. "Okay. Where is she now?"

"Quarantined at a local hospital that's converted a wing for the virus outbreak. She's sedated now and being fully monitored."

"How is she?" Ben had demanded. "Don't bullshit me."

"The rash has spread. It's up to her neck and is beginning to cover her torso. It's still in its early stages, from what the doctors can tell, but it's not stopping," Stephens said.

Ben swallowed hard. *Shit.*

"Okay, I'm coming there. Where is the—"

"You can't, Ben. The hospital wing is completely off-limits, and—"

"Where is the hospital?" he yelled into the phone.

Stephens paused, and Ben could hear him sigh on the other end. *"Listen, I'm only doing this because she told me to call you."* He gave Ben the address of the hospital, then added one more thought. *"If the staff catches you in there, Ben, hell's going to break loose. This is a completely unknown force we're dealing with, and you'd better believe there are going to be suits from every branch there, trying to figure out what the deal is. It isn't just the CDC anymore."*

Ben understood his meaning. *If you aren't careful, you might get thrown in jail. Or worse.*

"I understand."

Ben hung up and an hour later he was pulling up to the parking lot in front of the hospital. The small, early 1900's building sat on an acre of green manicured lawns. A tall iron fence with brick towers at the corners ringed the property. Picnic tables were sprinkled here and there, each shaded by massive, centuries-old oak trees. The hospital itself featured a grand entrance and lobby, adjoined on each side by two five-story hospital wings.

He parked in a visitor parking spot and looked at the clock. It was getting late, but he knew there would still be a night staff. The problem was, he didn't know what time the switch would happen; when most of the day staff would go home for the night. He took a few deep breaths to relax himself and surveyed the surrounding area.

He saw a few unmarked vehicles parked together in a clump behind his truck. Each had deeply tinted windows and seemed to be brand new. He assumed they were government, but he had no idea what department. He couldn't tell if they were unoccupied.

He watched the pedestrian traffic in front of the old hospital. An elderly couple walked through the grounds, the woman holding onto and supporting her husband as he shakily moved down the sidewalk. Another couple, younger, sat beneath one of the oak trees, laughing.

A few people wearing scrubs walked into the building using a side entrance. He watched them swipe a card and enter, the door slamming shut behind them. *That's it.* If he could gain access to one of their cards, he could get in without drawing too much attention to himself.

It would never work. What was he supposed to do, beat up some poor old doctor and steal their ID card? He almost laughed out loud. *This is ridiculous. I'm trying to break into a hospital.*

He knew he couldn't pull that off—he was a park ranger.

Instead, he opened the car door and walked purposefully toward the entrance. If the government suits were, in fact, watching him from their recon vehicles, he needed to look like a visitor. He walked up to the front entrance and opened one of the doors.

"Good evening, sir," a young man at the front desk announced. "How may I help you?"

Ben panicked. *What do I do?* His thoughts became mush. "Uh, hi, yes. I'm here to see someone I, uh, know."

The man's smile faded a little. "Okay, sure. Visiting hours are actually over, but—"

"That's okay, thanks anyway." Ben started to sweat. He turned quickly and walked back toward the front door. *You fool.*

As he neared the exit, he stole a quick glance over his shoulder. The receptionist was on the phone, hunched over his workstation. A few other nurses and doctors walked across the expansive lobby, but none seemed to notice him. He saw a skinny door against the wall, wallpapered to look like the lobby's striped two-tone wall, and he reached for the knob.

It twisted fully, and he pushed it open. He closed the door behind him and looked around. A small orange bulb hanging from the ceiling illuminated the room enough to give him what he needed: it was a small janitorial closet, filled with mop buckets, brooms, and cleaning chemicals. He found an upside down five-gallon bucket against the wall. Sitting down on it, he recapped his plan.

There wasn't much to recap: *enter lobby, find a place to hide.*

Wait.

Wait for what?

He had no idea. He knew he needed to see Julie, to make sure she was okay, but he was in over his head. He was a large, lumbering park ranger, not a spry little covert operative.

He waited for a few minutes, trying to gauge the activity outside the little closet. He couldn't hear much. Footsteps here and there, telling him nothing other than the general location of the person on the other side of the door.

Another five minutes passed, and he heard footsteps again making their way past his closet.

No, they're not moving past.

They were moving toward him.

Ben waited, praying the footsteps would recede into the distance.

The footsteps stopped. Someone was directly outside the door now.

Please go away.

The handle turned, and he reached for something—anything—to use as a weapon. There was nothing but a bucket of mops sitting within arm's reach. He grabbed one and untwisted the handle from its base.

A second later, the door slid open. Light pierced the dim room.

Ben raised the mop handle, wincing.

A man's frame was silhouetted in the doorway, but he didn't step into the room.

"You must be Harvey Bennett. Ben, I believe?"

3 2

"Who are you?" Ben growled.

The man took a step forward, and Ben raised the mop handle higher.

The man raised a hand. "Whoa, there, son. I'm not going to hurt you." He paused, taking another step into the closet. He looked at the mop handle. "Works better than you might think, too."

Ben frowned but didn't release his grip on the weapon.

The man was now fully in the room, and the light from the lobby was enough to give Ben some idea of who had entered.

A janitor.

Dressed in crisp blue overalls and a matching blue cap, the man was older than Ben, but about as tall and built similarly. Wisps of whitish hair fell from around the cap, and Ben could see he was not exactly smiling, but close enough.

An ironed-on name badge stared back at Ben from the man's chest pocket.

Roger.

"You—you're a janitor?" Ben asked.

The man nodded. "We prefer 'sanitation engineer,' but yeah, janitor works too."

"How do you know who I am?" Ben asked.

"I saw you run in here after your *harrowing* encounter with Junior."

Junior must be the kid from the front desk.

"That still doesn't explain how you know who I am."

"Right. There's more to it than this, obviously, but Julie filled me in."

The mention of Julie's name sent a chill down Ben's spine. "Is she okay?"

"She's fine. In the quarantined ward, but they've got her on some sort of sedative that dulls pain and slows her blood flow. It's not enough to, uh, stop the virus, but it'll help."

Ben was growing more and more confused by the second. Standing in front of him was a man—a *janitor*—who knew who he was, who Julie was, and apparently what sort of outbreak was going on in the hospital's quarantine.

"She told me you'd be coming here. Gave a pretty good description too. I was in there when they brought her in. There's a hazmat chamber set up just outside the entrance, but only staff and facilities, like me, can go in."

Ben shook his head. "Listen, that's great. I need to get to her. Can you help me or not?"

"Slow down, slow down," the man said. "We'll get in there. Mind dropping that mop handle, though?"

Ben didn't realize he was still poised for an attack. He relaxed a bit and dropped the wooden stick.

"So… you were just cleaning in there, and happened to start talking to her?"

The man's half-smile disappeared, and Ben could see him grow serious. "Oh, no. You don't understand. I've been working on this for quite some time. It is certainly a coincidence that fate brought her here, but it's not fate at all that did the same for me."

Ben had no idea what he was talking about. "Working on *what?*"

"The virus. Trying to figure out what it is. I've been studying it—as much as I can, anyway, for months. This hospital *has* to be involved, somehow, but I'm not sure exactly how. I was starting to lose hope, but then a few days ago they transformed the first floor of the east wing into the quarantine, and I heard whispers that they were helping with the Yellowstone Virus."

Ben thought about that for a moment. *The Yellowstone Virus.* He hadn't tuned in to what the media was touting, but he was sure the moniker owed its existence to some marketing-minded news editor.

"As the virus spreads there are bound to be other hospitals in the area gearing up for similar quarantine efforts, too, right?" Ben reasoned.

The man shook a finger at him. "But this one is different."

"How different?"

"This hospital is part-owned by a company called Rainbaucher's, which itself is mostly owned by another company, Dragonstone Corp. There are also two pharmaceutical companies, one in Norway, called Drage Medisinsk, and one here in Canada called Drache Global."

All Ben could picture was a crazy guy in his basement, Beautiful Minding bits of red string all over a map.

"Dragonstone is the organization behind these attacks," the man said.

That got Ben's attention. "There's a *company* behind this?"

The man nodded. "I am just following the breadcrumbs."

Ben thought for a moment. "How'd you know where to start? How did you even find out this information?"

"The smaller companies, like this hospital, have to file public financial statements. They're obviously convoluted and circuitous enough to be nothing short of useless, but it at least gave me a glimpse into what other companies were behind them. I had enough prior knowledge about all of this to know where to start looking."

Ben didn't know what that meant, but right now he didn't care. "If you know where to look, help me get to Julie."

The man nodded and held out his hand. "I'm glad I found you, son. You two can help stop this thing."

Ben reached out to shake the man's hand, before having second thoughts. *The rash.* Even with gloves on he was still infected.

The janitor, Roger, laughed and grabbed Ben's hand anyway. "Don't worry about that. Doesn't matter anymore. Nice to meet you."

Ben frowned. "Good to meet you as well, uh... Roger."

The man laughed. "Ha! I forgot I had this on." He flicked at the small patch on his overalls. "I had to sort of go 'undercover' a bit when I started here. You can call me Malcolm."

"Malcolm?"

"Dr. Malcolm Fischer. Professor of Archaeology."

33

There was a crawlspace-like attic above the corridor close to where Julie was being kept, supported by a metal catwalk. Used for electrical conduit, plumbing for the upper floors, and the modernized HVAC system, it was primarily intended to house cables and pipes, not people. When Malcolm showed Ben the small space he wanted them to squeeze into, Ben thought he was joking.

"You can't be serious."

"If I can do it, you can," was Malcolm's reply.

Ben wasn't claustrophobic, but this was cutting it close. The space measured about a foot tall by three feet wide. Enough for a dog or small animal to pass through easily, but a large male human? It would be tight.

"I'll go first, you follow behind. There will be an air vent directly above her room, but we'll need to reopen it. The CDC crew that was in here sealed up all the airflow points and redirected them so they could keep everything contained."

"Right." Ben was still eyeing the small crawlspace. "Lead the way."

Malcolm squeezed himself up and into the space, surprising Ben with the older man's strength and speed. He followed behind, catching a face full of shoe rubber when he entered the shaft.

"Might want to wait until I get a little bit ahead."

"Yeah, I got that," Ben said.

They slid slowly through the shaft, crawling over lines of electrical and networking cables, PVC pipes, and other forgotten infrastructure. It was hot inside the tunnel, and they quickly worked up a sweat. "How much longer?" Ben asked.

"Not much farther. We can pop in and out of her room without anyone seeing us. Worth it."

Malcolm stopped over a grate. "This is it. I'll unscrew the panel, but I need you to hold it up. We can't let it fall on her."

Ben followed his instruction and slid up next to Malcolm's legs. The man's upper body was contorted and twisted back around, allowing him the freedom to work a small screwdriver while giving Ben room to squeeze up next to him.

Ben felt the grate pop with the last screw and held it in place. It was heavier than it looked, but it didn't fall. Together, the two men turned the grate on its side and pulled it up through the ceiling. When it had cleared the hole, Malcolm pushed it up above his prone body, farther into the shaft.

A cool wash of air hit Ben, and he breathed it in. It made his skin itch, especially the area around his neckline, chest, and arms, right where the rash covered his skin. He popped his head through the open hole in the ceiling and looked into the room.

Julie.

She was there, eyes closed, on a bed in the center of the room. A few IV lines ran into her arms, and Ben could see the purplish rash on her skin, but she seemed otherwise unharmed. No one else was in the room.

He sighed in relief and looked back at Malcolm. "Give me a hand when you're down there, I'm not built for this."

Malcolm nodded and swung his feet down and through the hole. He dropped gracefully from the ceiling catwalk and into the room. "Ready," he called up.

Ben dropped through the hole until he felt pressure on his feet. He lowered himself slowly, letting Malcolm help him down. When his feet hit the hospital room floor, Julie's eyes fluttered open.

"Ben?"

"Julie! Hey, how are you feeling?" He rushed to her side.

"I—I'm good, I think," she said. "A little groggy, but I'm okay. It's mostly the drugs. The rash—is it gone?"

Ben looked at her. She had been changed into a light blue hospital gown and placed under a bed sheet, but her neck and arms were outside the blanket. The rash was now purple, deepening into the start of boils and blisters just under the surface of her skin.

"Uh, yeah. You look great," he said, smiling.

"You're a jerk," she said. Her voice was shaky, but she seemed to be more alert. "Get me out of here."

"Julie, we can't. I'm sorry—you're not strong enough…"

"Knock it off. Look at you. If you can get in here, I can get back out." She sat up a little and started pulling at the IV lines in her arms. "What are these, anyway?"

Malcolm stepped forward. "They're keeping you sedated," he said.

She frowned, trying to remember where she'd seen him.

He reached out a hand and placed it on her shoulder. "My name is Dr. Malcolm Fischer, remember? We met when you were brought here."

She nodded, slowly.

"I met your friend here a few moments ago in a janitor's closet."

She raised an eyebrow. "Finally came out of the closet, eh, Ben?"

"Really? Right now?"

She laughed, turning again to the IV lines. "Well I appreciate your grand plan to come see me, but you honestly thought you'd just waltz in here, say 'hi,' then leave?"

He was stumped. What *was* his plan?

"You're the one who wanted Livingston's help," Ben said.

"Not like this," Julie replied. "They started treatment on the plane, but... it seemed wrong. As if they were testing something else, not actually trying to heal me."

"But you're alive," Ben said.

"For now. Get me out of this hospital, take me somewhere we can talk, and you," she pointed at Malcolm, "tell me what you know."

Malcolm smiled. "I like a girl with spunk." He nudged Ben and winked. "Sounds like a plan."

Julie pulled out the two needles from her arm and sat up higher in the bed. Ben hoisted Malcolm up and into the ceiling vent hole and turned to help Julie. She was standing now, gaining her balance. Her hair was a tangled mess, and her eyes were sunken.

She ran a hand through her hair in vain, then gave up and turned back to Ben.

She stepped in front of him, her bare feet lining up directly in front of his shoes. Standing there with no shoes on, a head shorter than Ben, wearing only a hospital gown, he noticed just how *small* she seemed. She looked up at him with her big brown eyes.

"What are you waiting for, ranger?" she asked. "Let's do this."

She grabbed his hands and placed them on her sides. He felt his face flush.

"You got a crush on me, ranger? Stop freaking out. This isn't your middle school dance. Lift me up." She cocked her head to the side, waiting.

He swallowed hard. "That gown doesn't cover much. I'm going to get a real good look."

She blinked, bit her lower lip and stared at him, letting him stew in his own embarrassment for a few seconds.

He tightened his grip on her sides, preparing to launch her upwards, and…

She leaned forward and *kissed* him. Long and slow, the type of kiss he'd never experienced.

His ears suddenly felt hot. She pulled her head back slightly but slid her body closer to his. Then she leaned in, close to his hot ears, and whispered.

"Enjoy the show."

34

As Ben withdrew his foot from the hole in the ceiling and went to replace the air vent panel, he heard someone open the door to Julie's room.

"Code zero! We've got a breach in the quarantined sector!"

No one needed to speak paramedic to crack that code. The whole place would be on lockdown now. They needed another escape plan.

"They'll figure out where she went pretty quickly," Ben whispered. "It's not like *Die Hard* is a secret. Malcolm, is there any other way out?"

"Sure, but we'll have to unscrew the grate again, like we did for Julie's room."

"Do it."

Malcolm didn't stop shimmying moving forward until he'd reached a ceiling grate over another hospital room. Julie slid up next to him to help, but when Malcolm had unscrewed two of the four screws holding the grate in place, he apparently changed his mind.

"Slide back a little. I'm going to do this the fast way." He slid forward, over the grate, letting his shoes come to rest directly over it. He lifted his foot as high as it would go in the small space and slammed it down.

Ben could see the grate twist and fall through the hole, one of the remaining screws having popped under the force. The fourth and final screw was all that was holding the grate in place, but Malcolm bent it out of the way and hopped down into the room.

Julie and Ben followed.

"They're going to search each room, but they'll probably be slow since they need to put on the suits and keep things contained," Julie said. "They won't take that chance."

The two men nodded and looked around. They were in another hospital room, as small as Julie's, but this one had two beds—both empty. Apparently, 'quarantine containment' didn't mean the same thing as 'luxury quarters' to the hospital staff.

Ben rushed to the door and opened it a crack. "There's no one out there yet."

"They'll be coming, though," Malcolm said.

They followed Malcolm out into the hall. A set of double doors stood at the end of the long hallway. They sprung open and three men in containment suits and two others wearing tighter, clear protective suits over their normal clothes came bursting through.

They were armed.

"Stop, or we'll shoot!" one of them yelled.

Julie immediately turned and ran the other direction. Malcolm and Ben had no choice but to follow. Ben waited for bullets to slam into their backs, but they didn't come. Instead, he heard heavy footsteps as they ran after them.

"Sir, should we engage?" one of the men asked.

"Negative. Only if there's danger of a breach," another answered.

Julie ran for the single door at the opposite end of the hallway. Malcolm pressed the horizontal bar to open it. It pushed in, but the door wouldn't budge.

"Of *course* it's locked," he said, cursing.

"In here!" Julie shouted from the right. Ben turned to see where she was and found her inside a large office room, full of cubicles and computer stations. The men followed her in, and she closed the door behind them.

"It was cleared out when they quarantined this whole area," Malcolm explained. "There's another entrance a little ways back. We'll need to block that door, too."

Julie ran to the other end of the room and Ben came over to help her. While they slid a couple of the tall filing cabinets against the door, Malcolm did the same at the entrance they came through.

"What about this door?" Ben asked, pointing to a third exit.

"No idea," Malcolm said.

Ben didn't wait around. Marching over, he hammered on the horizontal bar. Locked. "Well, there goes that option."

From a speaker on one of the desks a soft, reassuring voice, sounding like Alexa's long-lost cousin, suddenly announced, *"Nine, Nine, Two, Eight, Five. Black. Nine, Nine, Two, Eight, Five. Black."*

"It doesn't matter, now," Julie said. She slumped down into an office chair that had rolled into the gap between two cubicles.

99285. Black.

"What does that mean?" Ben asked, frantic.

"It means we've defaulted to another protocol."

"'What other protocol?" Ben said.

99285. Black.

"It means they're operating according to CDC Threat Assessment standards. If there's a possible breach in a contained facility—like this one—they move to contain the threat. If they can't, or they believe the threat to be 'imminently plausible,' as it's written, they move to *eliminate* the threat. Since these doors probably lead outside, they'll move to close down our escape routes." Julie explained, exhausted.

"In other words, those guys are going to start shooting us as soon as they get these doors open?" Ben asked.

As if on cue, a pounding bounced through the small office.

"Yes," Julie said. "I'm a threat. And now you two are risk vectors."

It was a tough reality to accept. Ben suddenly took a serious interest in their defensible position. "There has to be *something* in here we can use as a weapon." He looked around but couldn't find anything worth trying. *Computer mice, keyboards, monitors...*

"Okay," Malcolm noted. "They'll probably split up—five in all, three armed. So expect one, maybe two guys with guns to come through each door."

99285. Black.

The pounding intensified, now coming from behind each of the two hallway doors. Ben stationed himself near one door, with Malcolm and Julie close to the other. Julie reached up and flicked the light switch, plunging the room into almost complete darkness.

When his eyes adjusted, Ben saw his door bow and buckle. The filing cabinets edged back until—

The door crashed open and one of the men in hazmat suits fell through.

He didn't see Ben.

That's my edge, Ben thought.

The man's suit blocked most of his peripheral vision.

Ben snuck around the filing cabinets, stopping when he was almost behind the open door. The man recovered his balance and brought his gun up, searching for a target as he stepped through…

…Just as Ben smashed the door forward as hard as he could with a solid kick. The door rocketed back, catching the man in the hazmat suit in the back of the head. The man grunted, dropping his gun and falling to the floor.

A second armed man lunged forward, but Ben had the drop on him. He stood up just as Ben pointed his gun back at him.

"Stay there, sir. I will shoot you."

The man's eyes were visible through the suit, and Ben focused on them. He steeled himself, not daring to flinch. The man finally relented, dropping his gun on the floor and raising his hands above his head. Ben heard another crash behind him—the third gunman had broken into the room.

The man in front of Ben flicked his eyes up and away from Ben, then back.

Shit.

Ben anticipated the shots, not a moment too soon. He dove toward the unarmed man in front of him and fell to the side, just as two shots rang out behind him.

"Ben!" he heard Julie yell from the other side of the room.

He was on the ground, groping around in the dark, looking for the gun he'd felt slip out of his hands. The second man was on him in a heartbeat, wrestling Ben to the ground.

Helpless, Ben felt like a turtle on his shell. The man on top of him was larger, heavier. He wrestled Ben's hands behind his back and grabbed a fistful of Ben's hair.

Another gunshot.

Ben flinched, but the man's hand released his head, and he felt the weight lifted off his back.

He rolled over, raising his arms to defend a blow he knew would come, but instead he heard another gunshot.

This time, a cry rang out from the third gunman who'd entered, and he watched as the man fell to the ground. A third and fourth gunshot sent Ben's wrestling partner into the filing cabinets against the wall.

Ben looked up to see Julie standing over the third gunman's body, her jaw clenched in rage, holding a gun.

"You okay, ranger?" she asked.

He did a mental check of his muscles and bones. Finding

everything to be in working order, he sat up and nodded. "Yeah, I'm good. Thanks."

"No, thank *you*," she said. "And thanks for throwing the gun my way. Good thinking."

He stood. "Uh, yeah. No problem. Where's Malcolm?"

"The door hit him when that guy busted it open. I think he just got knocked out."

"Same thing happened to this guy. He's probably going to wake up soon, though. We'd better get out of here before he does." Ben counted the bodies sprawled on the floor. "I count three. What happened to the other two?"

"We have to go after them," Julie said.

"Are you crazy? We're leaving. Now."

"Didn't you see who they were?"

"No. I didn't. Let's go."

"Ben," Julie snapped, enraged. "It was Livingston. *And* Stephens."

35

They checked into a hotel near the hospital under the name 'Roger Ebert' and paid cash.

It was Malcom's idea and elicited only a shrug from him. "I always thought his reviews were terrible anyway," he said.

Their plan was to stay there until they formulated a better plan.

Malcolm and Ben stared across the table at Julie.

"We need to get a bomb crew out to Yellowstone," Malcolm said.

"Whatever other departments are on this have most likely already done it, so it would be a waste of time to try to call it in and set one up ourselves," Ben said. "Julie can call and make sure on the way."

"On the way where?" she asked.

"We need to get you help. Obviously, we can't go back to that hospital, but there has to be somewhere else that's set up a quarantine." He rubbed his forehead. "And someone is going to have to come here and hose this room down now too, I'm guessing."

"You need help too," she said, flatly.

Ben thought about feigning ignorance, but what was the point? He pulled his shirt sleeve back and scratched his forearm. "How did you know?"

"It's crawling up your neck." Julie looked at Malcolm. "Hey, what about you?"

Malcolm blinked. "What about me?"

"You're fine. No virus, no rash. Why?"

Malcolm sighed. "Yes, you are correct, Ms. Richardson. I have no rash, and I won't get it. I believe the virus, while highly contagious, is non-recurring."

"Non-recurring?"

"It means it won't come back," Julie said. "Like chickenpox."

Ben rolled his eyes. "I know what it means. I want to know *how...*"

"I've already *had* the virus," Malcolm explained. "I believe I was subjected to the virus a year ago. I believe I contracted it and they used me to test a treatment. I'm not sure they succeeded, but I did overhear them say the virus had 'run its course through my system,' and that I was immune."

Julie was bewildered. "What are you talking about? Yellowstone only just happened."

"Well," Malcolm began, "about a year ago, I was on a research trip with some students from my university, up in the Northwest Territory—"

"You're *that* professor!" Julie said. "Those students that went missing…"

"Yes. The team disappeared, and news agencies rode the media wave for months after we disappeared, but no one from the expedition was ever found, as you recall."

Julie's eyes were wide as Malcolm continued. "It wasn't an innocent accident, like many thought. We didn't fall through a frozen lake or get eaten by bears. My students were murdered."

This revelation took Ben by surprise. Apalled, he asked, "Murdered? Why?"

Malcolm swallowed, trying to summon the words. "We made a discovery. An important one. I've since come to believe that one of the students may have been working against me. They must have alerted these *murderers* to our location. A helicopter came. It was… horrific."

"What did you find?" Julie urged.

Malcolm tensed as he recalled the archaeological site. "Some kind of shrine. A place of some religious significance. There were offerings. Coins. Strange coins we'd never seen before. My guess is that they were tokens of some sort given to the indigenous tribe from that area, likely the same people who created the powder. The powder," Malcolm added, "was the *real* discovery. White. Sandy. We assumed it was some medicinal herb offered to a god of some kind." Malcolm looked her directly in the eye. "It was no such thing."

"What was it?" Julie asked.

"The remnants of a native plant, dried leaves that had been left to decay before being ground in a pestle to form this powder. After so many years undisturbed, I believe it served as an incubator…"

"You think it's somehow related to the virus?"

"I believe it *is* the virus, or at least the medium in which the virus was able to grow," Malcolm said.

Ben recalled the news stories as well, vaguely. "No one mentioned a dig site on the news. They said you went looking and wound up lost."

"Yes, because whatever company massacred my team did a good job or cleaning up after themselves. They staged our tents and equipment miles away at a different location. They left nothing that would have pointed to any suspicious activity."

"But the whole thing *was* suspicious," Julie said. "It was a big deal. Every news outlet in the country was reporting on it, and there were conspiracy theories about it too."

"I know, I know. But like I said, the company did their job well."

"You keep mentioning a company," Ben said. "How do you know?"

Malcolm nodded. "They took me somewhere that had state-of-the-art medical facilities and questioned me. They didn't torture me, as I doubt they thought I would ever leave the facility, but they weren't satisfied that I knew next to nothing about this powder. They put me in a medically-induced coma, only bringing me out of it after months of being under."

"My God," Julie whispered.

"I did have plenty of time to think—it was odd, being in that state. I could sort of form thoughts and run through the things that I could remember, though it was a slower process than if I had been lucid. But it was when I was awake, or at least mostly awake, that I tried to piece together the information. The doctors working in my room each wore the same logo on their coats, and they worked in regular shifts—a large operation. Eventually, I caught a glimpse of the company's name. 'Drache Global.'"

"Drache?"

"Yes," Malcolm said. "Drache Global. A pharmaceutical company based in Canada. I'd never heard of them, but I promised myself that I would get out of there and figure out who they were. I had plenty of time, remember, as I was lying on a hospital bed for months. I formulated a plan, and I got out one night." Malcolm looked at the wall, examining the lattice-shaped wallpaper.

Ben could tell there was more to the story behind the man's escape, but he didn't press him about it.

"I got out, and I ran. I ran for my life. I wanted to hide, but I wanted more than anything to right the wrongs done to my students and their families. I had to figure out what Drache Global was."

"What did you find?" Julie asked. Ben noticed she had placed a hand on Malcolm's forearm on the table.

"That this hospital you were brought to, Julie, is part of it. Drache Global, like the hospital, is owned by a group of shareholders. It's a corporate conglomerate. Publicly listed, but not easy to piece together who the *real* owners are. I researched and cross-referenced as many of their board members as I could manage, but found very few promising leads.

"I spent many hours in the depths of libraries and scouring the web, and all I was able to figure out was that they're semi-legitimate, at least on the surface. They've worked on countless grant proposals, major nonprofit medical research projects, and more public goodwill campaigns than a politician. But I think there's a simple thread connecting them to some other organizations with bipolar personalities."

"What thread is that?" Julie asked.

"They have the same names," Ben said.

"Yes," Malcolm said, smiling. "Very good. Dragonstone, Drache Global, Drage Medisinsk. They are all very similar, using different languages that all mean 'dragon.'"

"Why would they broadcast that? If they were trying to operate under the radar, why share a common name?" Julie asked.

"Plenty of companies borrow that name. It's not particularly unique, even within the medical and pharmaceutical research industries. And I believe it's more like a calling card. A *brand*, if you will."

"So, you think this 'dragon' company is working across its sister organizations to create some worldwide virus?" Ben asked. He scratched his forearms. While still somewhat itchy, it did in fact seem like the virus had slowed to a halt. *Weird.*

"No," Malcolm answered. "I believe it's the work of a handful of people, not a worldwide corporate effort. Secretive or not, I cannot believe something that large-scale could go unnoticed by world governments. I also believe they aren't targeting the entire world, but the United States. Through the spreading virus, the bomb at Yellowstone."

"For what purpose?" Julie asked. "It doesn't make any sense."

It made sense to Ben. "To sell a cure."

"By using a bomb at Yellowstone as a delivery method for the disease? That's insane," Julie objected.

Yet there *was* virus. And there *had been* an explosion. Those were indisputable facts.

Ben shrugged. "Yet here we are."

Malcolm nodded. "I think it's worse than we're contemplating."

"What do you mean?"

"Yellowstone is the largest *active* volcano in the entire world."

"He's right," Ben agreed. "The Yellowstone caldera lies directly underneath the park. That's a fact. It's a supervolcano. We've been arguing about is exactly when it's scheduled to erupt again for years. If there were a bomb placed at just the right spot, underground, anywhere in that area, and it went off…"

Julie thought about this for a moment. "What would the blast radius be?"

"The last time it blew, it shot ash about twenty miles into the air, and was around 1,000 times more powerful than Mt. St. Helens. It would instantly wipe out half of the United States. Followed by a volcanic winter for years afterwards."

Julie went pale. "Total destruction."

Ben nodded. "*Total* destruction."

Julie whistled. "So, we've got a mystery organization trying to blow up Yellowstone and half the United States, while *also* working on spreading a virus to the *rest* of the United States."

She had summed it up pretty well. Malcolm nodded. "It's the destruction of an entire nation, within the span of mere days. Possibly the collapse of society as we know it."

"And you think Stephens and Livingston are somehow involved?" Ben asked.

"I don't know. They were just following protocol back there. Trying to keep it contained. But Livingston's actions from earlier —blocking Stephens' emails from getting through, preventing me from getting them altogether—*that* doesn't sit well with me."

"You did say he's a bit paranoid." Ben said.

"He is," Julie answered, "but he's not *crazy*."

The two men shared a glance. "Julie, how well do you know him, really?" Malcolm asked.

Again, she paused before speaking. When she did, her jaw was set and her eyes steady. "Not well enough, I guess."

Her phone vibrated on the table in front of her. *Unknown.* She frowned but answered it anyway.

"Hello?"

She waited.

"Randy! My God, are you okay? I've been trying—"

She turned on the phone's speaker function so Malcolm and Ben could hear.

"*—Fine. I didn't want to call on my phone in case it's being tracked. I saw an email thread between Livingston and Stephens. They said you were in a hospital. Are you okay?*"

"I'm okay. It's the virus, but it seems to have slowed down for the moment. I'm with Ben..." she wasn't sure how to explain Malcolm's presence, so she moved on. "Listen, Randy, I—I don't know for sure, but I think Livingston might be involved in all of this somehow."

No response.

"I know you're already under fire for this, but I really need eyes on him. And keep sending me anything you find on Diana Torres and what she was working on."

"Got it."

"I owe you one."

"You owe me more than one."

She hung up.

36

David Livingston flicked off the 95-inch curved television in his living room. Brand new and still priced like the novelty it was, the Samsung was his pride and joy, at least for this month.

He had satellite and cable television, Netflix, and an action movie collection of over one-thousand titles, and he still couldn't find something to watch. He tossed the remote control to the other side of the couch. Unsure of how to satiate his desire for entertainment, Livingston sat in silence for a minute.

Juliette's involved in this, he thought. He *knew* it. It was stronger than the standard pang of paranoia that constantly plagued him about each of his employees; this was *real*. He had proof.

Stephens believed him. Both men had been at the hospital, planning to interrogate her after she'd failed to turn over the information she'd acquired during her "stint" in the field. And after Livingston had discovered that Randall Brown, his own IT technician, had *helped* Julie, it was enough for Livingston to convict her.

He didn't know exactly how, or why, but he knew Juliette Richardson was involved in this mess. He'd spent enough time in government to know that careers were made or broken by the men who went the extra mile to prevent mutiny within their ranks.

And his career would be *made*. He just needed a little more proof, and a motive wouldn't hurt, either. He had ordered Randall Brown to record and send over to him any conversations Julie had with him, but he'd also placed a few IT bugs of his own on Brown's network. Any calls the IT tech made or received would be immediately recorded and emailed to Livingston.

It was these types of plays that Livingston knew would eventually get him noticed in Washington. He wasn't naive enough to think that those in power got there by cashing in on their good deeds.

He rose from the couch, pacing before heading to his office. The foyer of his house was immaculate, smaller than he would have liked but impressive nonetheless. He paid a few hundred dollars a month to a maid service to keep the place clean enough to meet his standards, and another couple hundred on the side to the maid herself for "on the side"-type activities. It had taken a few months to find a woman agreeable to his terms, but as he'd discovered in his own career, a little cash went a long way. The companionship did nothing to satiate his loneliness, but it helped make his large house feel more like home.

He entered the great office at the front of his house, admiring his decorating job. A huge bust of an elk or moose—he wasn't sure which, and he hadn't shot it anyway—smiled down at him from the far wall, hanging directly above a large fireplace with an ancient-looking mantle. He'd placed a few picture frames, the stock photos still inside, on the mantle and around the room on floating shelves.

But his prize possession, the *pièce de résistance*, was the huge Scottish coat of arms hanging above his desk. The placard was enormous, stretching almost four feet across and six feet tall. It was red, yellow, and green, and didn't match anything else in his house. But it was *him*. His history, his name, his origins.

It represented him, and all that he stood for, and he stood a moment in front of it, admiring the wooden shield.

He walked behind his desk, grabbing the decanter of whiskey and pouring himself a glass. He stood face-to-face with the coat of arms for another moment, enjoying the warm liquid. Finally, he sat.

And saw a man standing in the center of the room, staring at him.

Recognition washed quickly over Livingston, but he was angered that the man had caught him by surprise.

"Oh—my God," Livingston said, nearly dropping his glass of liquor. "You scared the shit out of me. What are you doing here?"

He made a mental note to call his security company to set up perimeter alarms. The HD motion cameras were enough to turn over footage to the police after a break-in, but they obviously weren't meant as an early-warning system. He grunted and sipped on his whiskey.

The man continued staring.

"Well, what do you need? You seemed to enjoy sneaking up on me. What is it?"

The man finally looked Livingston up and down and shook his head. Livingston sat down behind the desk, acting preoccupied with a stack of papers. As he picked up the stack and began to rummage through them, he heard a clunk on the desk.

At the edge of the desk, Livingston saw a small, compact 9mm revolver. His visitor had placed the gun there, and now stepped back from the desk to the middle of the room once again.

Livingston felt his blood run cold. His nostrils flared, and anger flashed through his body. Still, he was calm. He took another sip of whiskey, this time deeper, letting the heat sting the back of his throat.

"Trying to intimidate me?" he asked.

"Is it working?"

Livingston snorted through a mouthful of liquor. He swallowed and blew out a breath of alcohol-laced air.

"This is a waste of time," Livingston said. "I don't know anything, or anyone."

"I didn't say you did," the man replied immediately.

"You want answers, talk to Julie, or that thug she's running around with."

"I don't need to."

Livingston's anger grew. "What the hell are you here for, then?"

The man blinked.

Livingston looked down at the pistol, then up at the man, catching his eye. He looked to the large bust of the moose-elk, across the mantel at the pictures of someone else's family, and then back down at the gun again. He picked it up slowly, delicately.

He'd actually never held a gun before.

It was heavier than he'd imagined, surprising for its compact size.

He examined it. The barrel, trigger, and hammer—*is that what the back thing is called?*

He felt its weight beneath his fingers. The man didn't say a word as Livingston pressed the safety release back and forth, locking and unlocking the gun's firing pin.

Livingston wasn't going to let himself be intimidated. He wouldn't be humiliated, especially not in his own home. He felt his lip turn upward into a slight sneer. *This asshole.*

He stood up, gaining confidence. "Get out." The words were cold.

The man didn't move.

"*Get out,*" he said again. He lifted the gun quickly and pointed it at the man's chest. "Don't make me repeat it."

Still, the man didn't speak. His expression was stoic, but Livingston could see a glint of something—amusement?—in the man's eyes.

He felt his right arm shaking, and he tried to force it to stop. He aimed the revolver and closed his eyes just as he pulled the trigger.

He heard a tiny *click*.

That wasn't right.

He tried again.

Click.

Shit.

He looked down at the gun, as if silently arguing with the metal contraption, but nothing happened. When he looked up, the man standing in front of him was shaking his head.

"You're too predictable, Livingston. Always have been. All of you."

Livingston frowned, but the man was already moving. He closed the distance between them in less than a second, and Livingston saw him pull his arm back.

He smashed his fist into Livingston's face. Livingston felt his hands open, dropping the empty gun and the glass of whiskey. They both tumbled and fell to the top of the desk. The glass shattered, whiskey and shards of crystal exploding around him. He was immediately in a daze, his mouth opening and closing as his brain tried to offer some sort of help.

The man, however, didn't stop to wait for Livingston to recover. He grabbed a wad of Livingston's thick, dyed hair and yanked up on it. He met Livingston's eyes for a brief moment, then slammed Livingston's head down on the top of the desk. Hard.

Livingston's face and ears exploded in pain, only to be followed by a much more penetrating ringing pain that lanced through the inside of his mind. He felt as if his entire head had been lit on fire from the inside out.

He flailed his arms wildly, but the man was still in control. Once again, he brought Livingston's head up, held tightly by the tufts of hair, then smashed it back down on the desk.

Livingston groaned, and his body went slack. His eyes were blurry, but he was still conscious. He felt a trickle of drool escape the corner of his mouth, but he made no motion to wipe it away.

He collapsed downward, his rear end somehow finding the chair as his torso and upper body sprawled forward onto the desk. He lay still, wondering why he hadn't already blacked out.

"You've been a cancer to this organization for years, Livingston," the man said. Livingston heard a scrape and felt the desk vibrate slightly. He turned his face to the side, trying to will his eyes to focus.

The man had picked up the gun and was now reaching into his jacket pocket. He withdrew something—something small, shiny.

A bullet.

Livingston was unable to panic, or perform any other voluntary function, but alarm sirens erupted in his brain. Or was it still the pain? He was unsure—everything was blurred together, one giant smear of pain and confusion.

"You're predictable, useless, and spineless. I can't think of a greater waste of air than the breath you breathe."

Livingston was surprised to discover he was still capable of feeling anger. He relished the anger, though he was unable to act on it. He grunted again.

The man loaded the bullet into the chamber and Livingston heard a succession of clicks.

"This has been a long time coming, Livingston. Sorry it had to be this way, but like I said—you're predictable."

Livingston didn't hear the explosion of the bullet as it raced out of the barrel and found its target.

37

Julie was adamant. "Go! Stop being ridiculous—I'll be fine!"

Ben shook his head, planning to stage a resistance. Malcolm grabbed Ben's arm and pulled him out of the hotel room. "It's fine. We'll only be gone for a few minutes."

She had insisted that the two men go pick up some supplies and takeout Chinese for the three of them. After a few minutes of arguing back and forth, Julie had prevailed, and the two men left for the F450 parked outside.

When they were gone, Julie opened her laptop. She initiated a few searches, first inside the SecuNet database and the rest of the private CDC intranet, then through Google. She tried numerous combinations. *Livingston CDC, David Livingston, David Livingston CDC,* and more, but each result was merely a bare-bones biographical entry that was obviously written by Livingston himself.

David Foster Livingston is a successful leader and proven manager in many corporate settings. He is currently head of the Biological Threat

Research division of the Centers for Disease Control. A growing list of Livingston's accomplishments include successfully restructuring the BTR division for efficiency and efficacy, increasing employee retention, and streamlining data systems for cost effectiveness at BetaMark, Inc., where he was previously employed. He has one daughter and resides in Minnesota.

Julie saw the same paragraph pasted onto every page that referenced Livingston. Each of the surrounding articles only mentioned the man, too. A project he co-sponsored, a few articles written by a team Livingston had served on, and a few shots of the man on a company softball team years ago. Livingston was certainly paranoid, as the verbatim biography on each site suggested that he'd been successful in forcing each of the article's writers to update his information with the same paragraph.

She shook her head and reached for her phone.

"Hey Randy, it's me again. Anything yet?"

"Julie, it's been like ten minutes. Are you serious?"

"I know. I'm getting a little antsy."

"I get it. What do you want now?"

"I'm trying to find something on Livingston—just in case."

"Don't bother," Randy said. *"I already tried. It's pointless. The man's got the PR team of a celebrity."*

Julie laughed as she read the first line of the Livingston biography. "David Foster Livingston is a successful leader and proven..."

"...Manager in many corporate settings," Randy finished. *"Ugh. You've got to be kidding me. What a joke."*

"Okay, well, thanks for checking. Let me know if you come up with anything else."

"Will do—."

"Hey, one more thing," Julie said into the phone.

"What's that?"

Julie paused. "Uh, don't worry about it, actually. Let me see if I can dig something up first."

She hung up the phone and woke up her computer's screen. She started a new search and began browsing through the results.

Eventually one result jumped out at her.

Teenaged Hero Rescues Father and Brother was the headline.

She clicked the listing and waited for the slow hotel Wi-Fi connection to load the advertisement-riddled page. It was a newspaper article that had been scanned and transcribed for the news site's archives, dated thirteen years ago.

"...The Bennett men were camping in a southern region of Glacier National Park when the youngest Bennett, nine-year-old Zachary, wandered to a clearing where he accidentally stumbled between a mother grizzly bear and her cub...

"Johnson Bennett ran to his son's aid, but the mother grizzly struck Johnson, knocking the man unconscious...

"...Shooting the larger bear first with two rounds from the father's rifle and scaring away the cub. Harvey pursued the smaller animal and eventually shot it, bringing it down with one round..."

Julie covered her mouth as she read the account.

"...Zachary and Johnson Bennett were rushed to St. Andrews Memorial

Hospital, where they were both treated for severe trauma, and the elder Bennett for a concussion. Zachary Bennett is expected to make a full recovery. Johnson Bennett is currently comatose in a stable condition, however, doctors are unsure of the possibility of recovery..."

The door to the hotel room opened, and Julie quickly slammed the laptop shut.

"Julie!"

It was Ben.

Startled, Julie nearly tripped over the chair as she stood and turned toward the door. Malcolm Fischer entered the room just behind Ben, breathing heavily.

"Julie, I got an email from Randy. Just now."

Julie looked at him. "Randall Brown? My IT guy?"

"Yeah, he wanted to send it over directly, since he thought there might be an issue with your emails or something. But you should have gotten it too."

She started to check her email but stopped herself. "Okay, well what did he say?"

"It was a forward of my mother's email draft. She must have tried to send it, but it never went out."

Julie's eyes widened.

"It has information in it, Julie, about the virus. The night... the night she died, she must have been writing it. It's got everything she was working on, and everything she and her assistant discovered. For one, it's not a virus."

Julie narrowed her eyes. "Go on."

"My mother's research seems to prove that the virus is a mutated bacteria—"

"No, that's not possible. The contagious spread, the outbreak pattern, the—"

"It's a virus *inside* a mutated bacterial infection."

Julie's head snapped up. "Come again?"

"That's right, Julie," Malcolm explained. "Dr. Torres is postulating that the reason this strain has been so difficult to model is due to its uncharacteristic qualities. Map it as a virion, and it fails many of the chemical application tests. Map it as a bacteria and it doesn't appear to be *living*—immediately disqualifying it from the ranks of bacteriophages."

"Did she figure out a way to combat it?" Julie asked, hopeful.

Malcolm and Ben shared a knowing glance.

"No," Ben said.

"But," Malcolm added. "She did find that the infection will naturally die out, after running its course. It reaches a certain point and just *vanishes*."

"Not until after it kills its host," Julie said.

"We're not dead yet," Malcolm said. "And I'm still here." He stepped forward, his voice calm and steady, "We need to get to a research lab. If there's any way you can find out exactly why none of us in this room are dead, you *must*."

Julie started pacing. "We're not going back to the CDC. Livingston and Stephens might be there."

"What about the bomb back at the park?" Ben added.

"Can't you call someone there? Someone who might—"

"Julie." Ben's voice was firm, but he looked her right in the eyes until she understood. *"There's no one else."*

She hesitated, thinking through it. "You're right. There's no one there who can help anymore. The government agencies involved are going to wait until they know it's not dangerous to their staff. It's what I'm supposed to do—wait until someone presents some compelling research as to why it's safe for us to go in, then send a bomb squad in hazmat suits to find anything unusual."

"That will take much too long," Malcolm said.

"It will," Ben answered. "But there's a lab at the park—it's not much, but it'll have to do. I'm going back there, to figure this out."

As if remembering the dire situation they were all in, Ben looked down at his hands and arms.

"Does it hurt?" Julie asked.

"No. It hasn't really done much at all, and it's not itching at the moment."

"Neither is mine," Julie said, examining her own arms.

"So," Malcolm said, calling them to attention. "I guess it's just us, then?"

"Dr. Fischer, you don't need to come along," Julie said. "If what we're saying is true, we're going into an infected quarantine, looking for a massive bomb hidden below the surface somewhere. It's not exactly a risk-free project."

Malcolm lifted his chin. "Julie, I understand that you are concerned. And you are right to assume that this is extremely

237

dangerous. But I will not sit idly by and do nothing to right the wrongs done to me, or my students."

His monologue over, he tensed his jaw and waited for the others' response.

Ben looked over and shrugged. "I feel you, Doc. I wouldn't make you sit on the sidelines."

Julie smiled.

"Let's get to Yellowstone."

They sat down at the table in the small hotel room, ready to plan their trip back to Yellowstone, when Julie's phone rang again. She grabbed it before it rang a second time.

"Randy—what's up?"

As she listened, the muscles in her face tightened and her back became rigid. She swallowed a few times, her mouth suddenly dry.

When she hung up, Ben and Malcolm were perched in their chairs, awaiting the news.

She blinked a few times, as though suddenly embarrassed that she might cry.

"—Livingston," she said. "He's dead."

"Monsieur Valère, the conference is now available," the voice said. It sounded metallic and hollow, detached, yet it was the most lifelike computerized voice system Francis Valère had ever heard.

"Merci," Valère responded. He waited for the computer system to check the Ethernet connection, test internet speed, and finally ping the waiting room of the online web conferencing service. Within seconds, the voice emanated from the walls of Valère's office again.

"Connection speeds are exceptional, Monsieur." The voice had an eerily attractive component to it, Valère realized, as he waited for the two other participants' faces to appear in front of him. She had also been upgraded to a human-like level of what they were calling "AI hyperbole," which was, as far as Valère could tell, just a library of phrases that replaced the usual metric and clinically precise statements that plagued most artificial voice systems.

SARA—Simulated Artificial Response Array—was the Company's latest alpha release they were testing in their offices. At this point, it was nothing more than a computerized artificial intelligence, more advanced than anything on the market, but far from deployment-ready.

The plan was, Valère had been told, to get SARA to beta and then release the code and sound sample library, alone more than ten terabytes of information, to a few universities for further development and testing. Eventually, they would either use the application for internal purposes or sell the final design schematics to the highest black market bidder. As SARA's development was about as removed from Valère's professional expertise as possible, he wasn't entirely sure what she would finally become. But if the previous applications their affiliates had released were any measure, SARA would be nothing short of miraculous.

Valère was involved in a number of startup tech and pharmaceutical businesses. He was independently wealthy, thanks to the benefit of a long line of rich relatives who'd left a startlingly large inheritance, as well as his own knack for choosing investment opportunities. A few had bombed, but he had invested far and wide, amassing a fortune of interests in just about every sector related to computer intelligence and medical advancement.

"Francis, are you with us?" a man's voice spoke from inside his computer screen.

Valère cleared his throat. "*Oui*, I am here. I apologize for my tardiness—I have been following the latest developments in the United States."

"As have I," the second voice answered. The man's face in front of Valère was enlarged on the gigantic screen. The sound emanated from the walls themselves. Audio-Enhanced Surfacing, if Valère remembered correctly. The walls of his Quebec office space were essentially made of thousands of speakers, each implanted with a computer chip that made them "intelligent"—allowing them to emulate a natural sound environment. He could play music that followed him throughout the room, providing a sonically perfect artificial surround-sound in an acoustically exceptional environment.

For now, the man's voice, in crisp and clear stereo, was all Valère cared about. The man inside the window continued. "It appears as though our initial plan has been delayed. After your dismissal of Mr. Jefferson—"

"Nonsense," Valère said. "Our placements were sound. Each of the departments is operating smoothly, according to their protocols, and taking no unnecessary risks or making any rash decisions."

"Francis," the first man, Emilio Vasquez, said, "while I admit our infiltrated agencies are doing exactly as we had hoped; you cannot deny the existence of a few rogue operatives. The CDC's department head has been removed, but it still seems as though a few members of its lower ranks are curious."

Valère thought about this for a moment. "Do you honestly believe they have become a threat?"

"Hardly," Emilio responded. "It is merely in our best interests to ensure that these possible threats stay just that."

"And how exactly do we ensure that?" Valère asked.

The other man paused for a moment. "I believe it's time for the contingency plan."

"I—we—don't need a contingency plan," Valère responded. "This plan is sound—it always has been."

"I'm not saying it hasn't been, Valère. But there's always room for improvement."

"But these rogue operatives have been working *outside* of our target organizations. They are no more a threat to us than the local police."

"But you're wrong, Valère. They are *far* more of a threat to us, especially now. They are mobile, and we are still unsure of their capabilities. Borders mean nothing to them, nor do their organization's standards. We've worked far too long on this project to lose the investment entirely."

Emilio's face was growing slightly red, though his voice betrayed no raise of emotions. Valère knew the man was moments away from growing indignant, but the man stopped himself just short.

Valère sighed. "These deaths are unnecessary," he said. "They are inevitable, but must they come from our hands?"

"Valère," Emilio said. "As you know, these deaths are *nothing* when measured against what we will accomplish."

"I agree, but—"

"And their deaths will not be 'by our hand,' as you say. Far from it."

Valère nodded.

"Let us see this through to the end, Valère. Let us complete our mission."

He nodded again.

No one spoke at first. Finally, SARA's voice boomed through the walls. *"We will need your verbal commitment, Monsieur Valère. Please provide verbal confirmation of your agreement to the chosen contingency."*

Good Lord, she was remarkable. SARA had parsed, compiled, and transcribed the conversation, as she had been instructed, but she had also extrapolated from the silence that the other man was waiting for Valère's confirmation, as per the contract, as well as the fact that he didn't want to specifically ask for it.

Technology. Incroyable.

"Yes," he stammered. "Yes, I confirm. We shall commence with a contingency that merely supports our overall direction, as discussed in previous communications. SARA, please transcribe, encrypt, and archive this discussion into your database, and remove all references therein."

"Oui, Monsieur Valère," SARA said. As Valère stood from his computer desk, the woman's computerized voice followed the location of his head with pinpoint accuracy, causing Valère to feel as though she were *inside* his head, not just talking to it. *"I will alert you of any updates."*

He nodded, knowing SARA could see that, too.

39

"We're almost at the park border. Lab's about another half hour," Ben explained.

Julie sat with her feet up on the dash of her F450, focused again on her laptop. Malcolm sat in the back seat, reading a stack of papers Julie had printed at the hotel's business center, all on infectious diseases, viral outbreaks, and bacterial infections—internal CDC documentation and reference material.

Malcolm was specifically looking for research into anthrax-type infections, where the originating material was powdery, dry, or airborne. A fast reader, he had almost made it through the entire stack when they finally reached the gates of Yellowstone's northeast entrance, with nothing intriguing to show for his efforts.

Outside, the wooden Welcome to Yellowstone National Park sign drifted by, sitting atop a log display, surrounded by a freshly manicured garden of flowers, shrubs, and small trees. Behind it, the sprawling wilderness that drew three-million-plus visitors a year.

Except today.

The road narrowed, pointing them toward a service building where police officers and park rangers were operating a road blocking and turning tourists away. A white tent had been erected off to the side and Julie could see that it was meant for hazmat teams from her own organization for the mobile treatment of any infected individuals found inside the park.

"If they see we're infected they're going to pounce on us," Julie warned.

"They may have been advised to watch for us anyway," Malcolm remarked.

"Ten Most Wanted?" Ben said. "Great. That's a comfort." He fished his wallet out and held it up. "Well I'm still a ranger here. They better have a damn good reason to detain me."

Ahead, one of the police officers had spotted their truck approaching and had walked into the road, standing in front of his police vehicle. He held up his arms and waved them down.

"They may not need a reason," Julie muttered under her breath.

Ben slowed the truck to a stop and rolled down the window.

The police officer almost had to stand on his toes to see into the truck's high window, but he removed his sunglasses and spoke loudly over the rumble of the engine. "Park's closed," he said. "No access in or out."

Ben displayed his ID badge from his wallet. "I work here—"

"Doesn't matter." The police officer cut him off, curtly. "No one in or out. You can turn around right here, then head back on this road..." His voice trailed off as he pointed in the direction from which they'd come.

245

"Officer, I'm going to need to get into the park. We've got information on this virus, and—"

"Son, I'm not going to ask you again. Park access is *prohibited.* Go home, stay inside, and keep watching the news."

Ben gritted his teeth and revved the engine. As the officer stepped backward, Ben spun the truck around him and accelerated onto the north-bound side of the road.

"At least he didn't arrest us," Julie said.

Malcolm called up from the back of the truck. "Now what?"

Ben didn't answer. He drove another mile and turned left onto a dirt road leading back to the southwest, and sped up again. They bounced over the uneven, rocky road and swerved between trees that jutted out over their heads.

"Where are we going?" Julies, said, alarmed.

"Private access road," he snapped.

"Won't they still find us? There are probably hazmat and outbreak teams from every branch of government and local police forces inside the park."

"Probably."

"It doesn't matter," Malcolm answered. "They'll know soon enough that we're here, but if we don't get to that lab and figure out what makes this thing stop, it will be too late anyway."

As a confirmation, Ben poked at the radio until he found a news station. It didn't take long—one station was playing a prerecorded commercial, but the second he tried was broadcasting a nationwide message. He turned the volume up as an anchor's voice solemnly read the latest update.

"...Reports are in that the viral outbreak has extended as far south as Albuquerque, New Mexico, and as far east as Wichita, Kansas. Experts from the CDC and other sources suggest that if the outbreak can be contained, the death toll will rise to around 10,000 people, but if not, that number could skyrocket to more than a million. Estimates predict that number to be far too conservative, especially if the trajectory of the disease places it anywhere near the western seaboard.

"As a reminder, please stay inside, try not to interact with anyone outside of your immediate family, and stay tuned to news and radio updates."

The anchor signed off, promising another update in an hour, and went to a commercial break. Ben punched the power button.

None of them said anything for a while.

The truck bounced over ditches and through a stream until, taking the short cut to another dirt road. Once on level ground, Ben smashed the gas pedal, sending the already fast-moving truck hurtling over potholes and bumps as if they were no more than pebbles on the road.

Minutes later, they reached the lab facility. A brownstone building, painted to blend into the surrounding forest and not stick out to any vacationers camped nearby. Ben pulled the truck into a spot outside the main entrance. The windows were dark. It appeared unoccupied.

Julie's phone rang before they could get inside.

"Stephens? You want to explain to me what the *hell* happened back—"

"Julie, listen. I'm sorry. That was Livingston's decision, not mine. Just ask him."

But she couldn't ask him. Had Stephens heard the news? It didn't sound like it.

"Where are you now?"

"We're at Yellowstone. We're trying to—" She felt a hand rest on her arm. Ben was shaking his head.

"Trying to what, Julie? What are you up to? You need to get away from there, before this gets out of hand."

Julie dithered, but Ben was insistent. Again, slowly, he shook his head.

"Sorry—Benjamin, I can't. We're close. I can't give you an update right now, but I—"

"Julie! You can't afford to keep gallivanting around. If Livingston finds out..."

The words tumbled from her mouth before she could control them. "Stephens, where have you been? What are you doing?"

There was a pause.

"I'm—I'm... working on this, too, Julie. What do you mean?"

She waited a moment, then said. "Don't worry about Livingston. Listen, I need to go. I'll check in tonight, after we leave."

"Okay..." the voice was shaky, uncertain. *"Okay, you're right. Keep at it, Julie. Let me know what you need."*

She thanked him and hung up, then looked at the other two passengers in the truck.

"He doesn't know already?" Malcolm asked.

"I… I guess not."

Ben put the truck in park and opened his door, still shaking his head. When he caught sight of his hand on the door handle looked up sharply and caught Julie's attention.

"What is it?" she asked.

"Look," Ben said. He held out his left arm and pulled his sleeve up. The rash had disappeared from his exposed hand, and his arm looked almost completely normal, replaced by his natural skin tone. His right arm looked similar. Julie checked out her own rash and found the same to be true.

"It's gone," she said.

"Almost. Come on, we need to get in there. Whatever's left of the virus in our systems is the only hope we have left to figure out what this is."

"But why's it going away? I feel fine, too."

Malcolm jumped out to take a closer look too. "It appears to have naturally run its course. I think it's dying out on its own."

"Is that what happened to you?" Julie asked.

"No," he replied. "I don't know if I had a rash. I was sedated —comatose."

Hurriedly, they head into the laboratory building.

40

"They built this place back in the '80s for onsite research," Ben explained. "No one uses it much now. It's not much of a lab but it's all we've got."

"Looks very, um, 'high school,'" Malcolm noted.

"That's why no one uses it much. It's not specific enough to be considered a chemistry lab or a biology one. It's also not quite big enough to be helpful for our geologists, geographers, or animal scientists. So, it's a backup."

Malcolm muttered something under his breath and continued exploring the small room.

Julie zeroed in on a collection of microscopes and immediately began preparing one, searching the drawers for glass slides. "It'll have to do," she said, setting up the standard issue compound light microscope on a table in the corner of the room. "Damn."

"What's wrong?" Ben asked.

""This is a compound scope, and there's no way there's enough power to magnify anything smaller than a bug. I wish there was a transmission-electron in here. Even an LVEM or something would be fine."

Ben simply stared back at her.

"This will have to work," she said. "It's not going to get us all the way there, but it might be enough to measure chemical reactions and test for an antidote. Come here."

Ben stepped forward, and she reached for his arm. He pulled back, reacting involuntarily.

"Chill. I'm not going to bite." She rolled up his sleeve. "Dr. Fischer, would you mind helping me?"

Malcolm came over as Julie whipped out a strand of latex she'd found amongst the assortment of scientific equipment. She handed Ben's arm to Malcolm, who held it precariously in front of him. As he held it, she tied the latex band around Ben's upper arm, causing the veins to bulge as the blood became restricted.

Taking a small syringe, she poked it into one of the veins. The chamber began to fill with a deep crimson color.

"Geez," Ben said. "You didn't test it for rabies or anything."

"Rabies is the least of your worries," Julie answered, focusing on holding the syringe straight. "Besides, I doubt that would be the problem with these needles. God knows how long they've been here." As a sort of flourish, she blew on the latex band and the syringe that was plunged into the vein. A thin veil of dust sprung from their surfaces, causing all three to blink and look away.

"Ah, right. Seems perfectly safe."

She shushed him, and withdrew the syringe slowly from his arm.

"How much do you need? Seems like overkill," Malcolm said.

"I don't know how many units are left inside the bloodstream or if we'll be able to see it at all. Plus, the virus is wearing off, as we saw earlier. I may not have time to extract more later, since the units might be working their way out."

She placed the cap on the syringe chamber and loaded another. This one, she stuck into her own arm, not bothering to check for a vein or tie off her upper arm.

"Units?" Ben asked.

"Like chickenpox," she answered.

Malcolm and Ben still didn't understand.

"I'm developing a hypothesis about it, but it's pretty simple. Imagine a kid has chickenpox—the *varicella zoster* virus—and has a birthday party. Some kid comes to the birthday party and gives the birthday boy one unit of the virus. That unit multiplies—as viruses do—to a certain point, until the virus has physically manifested itself in the host's body."

"Little red bumps all over his skin."

"Yes, exactly. But that's it. It doesn't ever really get worse than the bumps, though as you might remember, those bumps are bad enough. The virus has reached its 'critical mass' in the kid's system. The units have reached their maximum exposure ratio, and they won't—can't—proliferate any more. But he's still very contagious, too. Since the virus is at critical mass, every kid who comes over will probably get it, right?"

"Unless they've already had it," Malcolm said.

"And then they'll do the oatmeal baths and stuff and eventually the virus goes away," Ben added.

Julie nodded, removed the full syringe from her arm, and continued. "Well, this virus-bacteria is a bit different. Let's say the kid was infected with a unit of this... *stuff*. Whatever it is. That one unit would reproduce and multiply into ten units, become contagious, and spread to other people, just like the chickenpox. They'd all get infected, it would grow to ten units in each of them, and they'd all be contagious—but still alive."

"So far, so good," Ben said. "Except for the life-threatening rash."

"But, if the kid is infected with *more* than ten units initially, it's over. He's quarantined, but the effect is devastating—the virus is too much for the body to handle and will begin to shut down."

"The body can't handle more than ten units?" Malcolm asked.

"Well, ten is an arbitrary number, but in this scenario, yes. Whatever number of units our virus needs to reach critical mass is the amount of virus that can 'safely' infect a person. Anything over that, and the host dies. Below that—"

"And it reproduces itself up to that number but doesn't go over," Ben finished.

Julie nodded. "That's my hypothesis. After that, the virus naturally works its way out of the host's system, rendering them immune to further attack."

Ben and Malcolm thought about this a moment. It made sense—hypothetical or not—and both men nodded their approval.

"I'm guessing that whenever we were exposed to the disease, it was only a small amount," Ben said. "Less than critical mass. It's run its course and is now working its way out."

They heard the laboratory door slam shut, and all three turned to look. A tall, thin man stepped into view, smiling. "That's exactly right, Mr. Bennett. What a precise deduction."

"Stephens?" Julie asked, jumping up from her perch near the table and microscope. "What—how are you here?"

Benjamin Stephens drew closer. "I was already on the way," he replied. "When I called, I was already in the area. I thought I'd check in with you in person, since our tech communication seems to be consistently ineffective."

Julie didn't respond.

"Don't worry, Julie. Ben—" he turned to look at the third man in the room, hesitated for a split second, and frowned. "Mr.—I'm sorry, I don't believe we've met." Stephens walked over to Malcolm and stretched out his hand.

"Dr., actually. Dr. Malcolm Fischer."

"Right. *Dr.* Fischer. My apologies." Stephens had the room completely focused on him, and he savored the moment. "Sorry for my intrusion. As I mentioned, I merely came to help. Julie, what can I do?"

Julie thought about it for a few seconds. "You agreed with Ben when you walked in. Why? What do you know about the virus?"

"Well, for starters, as I'm sure you've already discovered, it's not actually a *virus*. Or, to be specific, it's not *only* a virus."

"We're past that already, Stephens," Julie said. "How do you know that?"

"Julie, my job is to collate and organize information. Every disease prevention authority in the country is working on the same thing you are. I saw a report yesterday that confirmed your theory of a viral-bacterial strain."

Stephens had stopped in front of a square table in the center of the room. He pulled out a folding chair from beneath it and sat down. He placed his arms on top of the table as he spoke. *Trying to appear submissive,* Ben noticed.

"I also found out where the strain originated."

At these words, Malcolm stepped toward him, before stopping himself.

"The virus is the byproduct of an ancient extinct plant that was found inside Native American baskets in a Canadian cave. An unlucky Russian expedition found it and thus became the virus's first modern casualties."

"Who told you that?" Malcolm asked, his voice low, almost a whisper. Ben reached out and held the man's shoulder.

"Again, it's just some of the information that's come across my desk." Stephens turned and looked directly at Julie. "Julie, that's why I'm here. I've been sending this stuff to you for days, but I know you haven't been getting it."

She shook her head.

"I sent it up to a lab, and they've been processing it with the CDC as well. From what we can tell, someone found that original strain, put some sort of protective 'shell' around it, and created the 'super virus' we're now dealing with."

Stephens stood up, and Julie saw Ben cross his arms.

"But like I said, I couldn't get through to you. It seems like Brown found some sort of redirect on my account, but he didn't set it up. Maybe Livingston—"

"Livingston's dead," Julie said.

Stephens was about to continue, but Julie's words stopped him in his tracks. "Excuse me?"

"Livingston," Julie repeated. "He's dead."

"But..."

"They found him at his home, in his office. Suicide."

Stephens' face seemed to scrunch a bit around the eyes, for the briefest amount of time. But as soon as Julie noticed it, it disappeared. She must have taken him by surprise.

"You—you can't be serious," he said.

"Why would I joke about this?" She watched Ben and Malcolm react. Both men stood still, stoically gazing toward Stephens. They were watching his reaction, she realized.

Stephens seemed to falter a bit, taking a step back. He grabbed the corner of a table and steadied himself. "But... but that..." his voice trailed off.

"Stephens." Julie's voice was strained, but she tried to pull him back in. "Benjamin. I know it's insane, but we *have* to keep moving forward."

He nodded.

"Can you tell us the rest? What else do you know about the virus?"

He swallowed, but began to speak. "Well, as you already know, our organization isn't exactly swift when it comes to handling crises, but there have been a few departments that have had a little success modeling the strain and calculating its progression." He walked back to the chair and sat back down at the table. Julie found a bottle of water and brought it over to him.

"They found out that the agent works by infecting the

bloodstream, but also the air around its host. It sort of 'festers' inside the host, releasing particulates through the skin—likely the reason we see a physical manifestation in the outer epidermis."

"The rashes and boils," Julie said.

"Yes. It's airborne—it doesn't need direct contact with blood or fluids, just time and close proximity. Once it's in the bloodstream, it moves to the internal organs, where it proliferates and reaches viral titre for contagion."

"What's viral titre?" Malcolm asked.

"Viral load. It's like a concentration of the actual virus. The point at which the virus will infect enough cells to become contagious."

"The critical mass," Julie added, explaining it to the two men standing next to her.

"Exactly. The lab reported that anything below around 8,000 copies per milliliter of the virus is considered below the danger line. Above it, the host can't contain the virus in its own body, and the strain tries to jump to another host within range. If it doesn't jump and proliferate there, the initial host's systems will shut down. If it *can* jump, it will, causing the titre to drop by half in both hosts."

"Does proliferation continue from there?" Julie asked.

"It does, but only to that magic line of viral load—somewhere around 8,000 copies. If the load is higher than 16,000 when it jumps, though, both hosts have a concentration of higher than 8,000 cpm. The virus will continue to spread inside their systems, consuming cells and antibodies mainly, but also overloading vital organs."

"So the answer is to find a *third* host?" Malcolm asked. Ben was nodding along, trying to piece it together as Stephens explained.

"Right. And then a fourth, fifth, and so on, until the virus has equally spread through these hosts and the titre count drops below 8,000 in each."

"What happens then?"

"We don't know," Stephens said. "Initial tests have shown that it starts to clear up within a day or two, and works its way completely out an infected host within a week."

"Ok, so we don't have an antidote for it, yet. *But* we know that it goes away on its own?"

Stephens nodded. "It does, but like I said, only when the concentration in the host is low enough. Under load, it will increase to the point of becoming contagious to others, but then stop, immunizing the host." His eyes flicked to Malcolm. "*Over* the viral load, however, and it will completely destroy the host's internal system."

"That's good news, Stephens," Ben said. "But we're running out of time. This thing's spreading around the country, and it's not slowing down. Plus—"

"The bomb," Julie finished.

"Right," Stephens said, nodding. "The bomb. Any ideas as to where it is?"

"No, not yet."

"Okay, well I can help. Julie, why don't you and I—"

"You're not going anywhere with her," Ben said, stepping forward.

"Excuse me?"

"You're not leaving." Ben said again.

"Ben," Julie said, coming up alongside him. "What's the deal?"

Stephens stood up from the chair again, frowning. He looked at Ben, scrutinizing him.

Before he could react, Ben took another step forward and punched Stephens in the gut, hard. Stephens doubled over, trying to catch his breath.

"Ben!" Malcolm ran toward him, but Ben held up his arm to halt his approach.

"Stop—let me deal with this." He turned back to Stephens. "What else do you do, Stephens?"

"Wh—what are you talking about?"

"You know exactly what I'm talking about. Who are you working with?"

Julie panicked, her attention shifting between the two men standing in front of her. "Ben, wait, just—"

Ben grabbed Stephens under the chin and hoisted him up straight. He delivered another blow to the man's side. "It's not just that you were suspicious of me from the beginning," he said. "You came in here, somehow finding the road without, apparently, outside help. These back roads aren't on *any* map, and we've specifically removed them from GPS data feeds to make sure wandering tourists don't end up finding a back entrance to the park."

Julie watched the exchange, mouth agape.

"I—it was the IT… Randall. He got me here. He helped me find—"

"That's not true," Julie said. Ben looked at her, surprised. "Randy didn't even know we were coming here. I didn't tell him where we

259

were going, and even if he tried to track me through my phone somehow, he wouldn't be able to do in time to send you our coordinates until we were *here*. You showed up *minutes* after we arrived."

Stephens' eyes grew wide. "Seriously? You don't think—"

"Explain how you know so much about this virus," Ben said. "You're a research assistant, right? You collect research and deliver it to Julie?"

Stephens' nostrils flared, and he gritted his teeth.

"*And* I saw the way you looked at Dr. Fischer when you mentioned 'immunization.' How did you know that he was immune?"

"I didn't!"

"Of course you did. I saw it in your eyes. You knew exactly who he was the moment you walked in here, didn't you? You've seen him before!"

Stephens' eyes darted back and forth from Julie to Ben to Malcolm. Ben grabbed him again and started to swing his arm back. A slight smile escaped the side of Stephens' mouth, and just as quickly, it vanished.

Ben stopped, shocked. "You *do* know something, don't you?"

A look of anger washed over Stephens' face. He spat.

Ben punched him in the jaw, sending the man's head hurtling backward as it absorbed the blow. Ben winced in pain, opening and closing his fist.

Stephens didn't react. He stared coldly back at Ben.

Ben hit him again. Julie ran forward and grabbed his arm, trying to stop the attack.

When Stephens' head came back up this time, Julie saw a trickle blood dripping just next to his mouth.

His *smiling* mouth.

Stephens spat out a mouthful of blood. "You just couldn't figure it out, could you?"

Julie was stunned. "What are you talking about?"

He laughed. A chuckle, slowly rolling out of his bleeding mouth. "It's too late anyway. Too late."

Ben looked at Julie, silently asking her what to do. She shook her head, and Ben dropped his hand.

"It's too late. Too late—"

"Too late for what?" she yelled at Stephens.

"You can't save them. *Couldn't* save them. Diana Torres, Charlie Furmann, David Livingston. And the others. You can't save them now."

Ben took a step back. Stephens. It was him—the man who had killed them all.

Including his mother.

41

Julie couldn't believe what she was hearing. Not just *what* Stephens was confessing to, but the unbelievable *scope* of what Stephens claimed he'd done. Following Julie's threads of evidence and research to Diana Torres' door, then to Charlie Furmann and Livingston. Anyone who'd gotten in his way had paid the ultimate price.

Not to mention however many others they *didn't* know about.

Julie was beside herself. She'd worked with Stephens long enough to trust him, to even grow fond of him. He was a smart kid, and he worked hard.

But he'd betrayed her.

He'd betrayed them all.

She didn't know how to respond. Malcolm was also shocked, still recovering from Ben's attack on Stephens. He slumped in the corner, leaning on the table Julie had been using as a lab table.

Ben, however, *did* know how to respond. Julie watched him as he laid into Stephens, landing punches as fast as his arms would allow. They weren't targeted well, and many brushed Stephens' head and shoulders. Ben lacked control, and he wasn't putting much force into the blows. It was an emotional reaction; one Julie and Malcolm were both astonished to see.

But it made sense.

The man in front of her had killed Ben's mother. He had been the cause of her infection and eventual death, all while Stephens led them through a dead-end maze.

But why?

The question nagged at her. She hadn't noticed it the first time, focused instead on overcoming the initial shock of Ben's accusation, and the subsequent revelation that he'd been right.

Still, the question was there, and she had to know the answer.

"Why?" she asked, softly. Then again, louder. "Why, Stephens?"

He looked up at her. Ben stopped swinging.

"Why?"

Ben stepped back, his breathing labored from the exertion. He looked at Julie.

Waiting for the answer.

But Stephens only laughed, gurgling blood that had filled his mouth. He spat, a wry smile on his face. "It's too late," he said.

"You mentioned that already. But I'll make that decision for myself," Ben said. "Where's the bomb, Stephens? I know it's in the park somewhere. In the caves, like you said on the phone?"

"You'll never find it," he replied.

"Stephens, please," Julie said. Stephens just shook his head.

"Like I said," Stephens said, looking at each of them in turn. "It's too late. America isn't united enough to save itself."

Julie cocked her head. Where had she heard that before?

"This country values freedom, but you and I both know that 'freedom' is a joke. We're somewhere between a third-world country with a corrupt government and an overbearing corporation on the scale of how free we really are. Americans now hold on to every scrap of 'freedom' they can find, including their own individuality—"

Ben stepped forward and punched Stephens again. *"Where's the bomb?"* he yelled.

Stephens staggered backward, nearly losing his balance. He seemed dizzy, but remained standing. Then he looked up sharply. He started to laugh as he withdrew something from his coat pocket.

A small glass cylinder filled with a liquid of some sort, and a large hypodermic needle. They glinted in the fluorescent light of the lab room.

Without warning, Stephens shoved the syringe into his own arm.

His eyes rolled back into his head, before eventually returning to their proper position. He sniffed, like a drug addict. "As I said, Harvey, it's too late. America is not united enough to save itself. It doesn't matter now, whether you find your bomb or not." His mouth began to leak saliva, foaming around the edges. "I would leave, if I were you," he continued. "This is a highly concentrated specimen of the strain, and I estimate there is less than a minute before I'm contagious."

Julie winced as the virus visibly tore through the man's body, ripping it apart at the cellular level.

Highly concentrated specimen.

Ben lunged forward, throwing Stephens' back against the far wall. Even with the virus destroying the man's body, he still didn't fall.

"We're immune, Stephens," Ben said. "Remember?" He pulled the sleeve of his left arm up and held it up to Stephens' face. "You took too long. The virus has already died out of our systems. We're inoculated. And Dr. Fischer—" Ben nodded toward the professor. "He's *been* immune, but you already knew that, didn't you?"

Julie watched the exchange, piecing everything together. She thought through Stephens' explanations; she considered the specific words he'd used.

"Ben…" she tried to coax him backward, but Ben wasn't listening.

"You led us here, to our deaths, for what? For your amusement?"

Stephens was smiling again. He reached back into his pocket. "No," he whispered.

Ben frowned.

"It was an experiment. *My* experiment. I told them no one would be able to figure it out, and that it was an embarrassment on our part to accomplish something so miraculous and not have the satisfaction of watching it unfold. Up close."

"So you let us figure it out?" Ben asked.

"There will be nothing left," he said. "America will be a barren wasteland, Harvey. The end is justified, but what about the *means*? What about my reward, knowing that my role has been fulfilled?" The man's voice began rising, his face showing more and more emotion. "I was groomed—*born*—for this role," he continued. "And I must get the satisfaction of knowing it was foolproof. I had to finish it here, to watch you die, just like the rest will."

Julie's eyes widened as Stephens' hand came out of his coat.

"And no one is immune from death," Stephens said, holding a gun up to Ben's chest. He flicked off the safety, staring into Ben's eyes the entire time. "You've performed your role admirably, Mr. Bennett. Now let me perform mine."

He pulled the trigger.

Everything became a blur. Julie felt herself brutally shoved aside as a dark form rushed past her. She stared, helpless, as Ben's body flew sideways toward the tables in the center of the room. Nothing made sense. Instinctively, she screamed, rushing Stephens as he aimed the second shot directly at her.

She collided with Stephens headfirst, sending her forehead into the man's sternum. She felt his lungs expand rapidly, involuntarily gasping for air. She kept moving forward, now back on her feet. She ran full-speed *through* the man's slender body, lifting it off the floor and smashing it into the wall. Glass vials and beakers, along with a stack of neatly filed papers, exploded from their location along the back table and down onto the hard floor. The sound of breaking glass and chaos almost blocked out the sound of her own screaming.

Almost.

She reared back with her fists and pummeled Stephens, who was lying haphazardly across the table. She aimed for the same spot Ben had hit him earlier—just below his eye where a gaping wound was forming. She punched, again and again, and he eventually stopped moving.

She took a step back, breathing heavily. Benjamin Stephens' skin had begun to stretch and rise, as if being filled with water like a balloon. She knew that the virus had moved completely through his body, but she was astonished at how quickly he'd reacted to it.

There must have been a very *heavy concentration of the virus inside that vial.* The realization terrified her.

Purplish welts formed on his exposed skin. Rapidly changing hue within seconds from from a purplish tint to a lighter red, until finally she noticed that his breathing had stopped. She waited another few moments and then checked his vitals.

Dead.

4 2

Ben heard Julie say his name from somewhere behind him.

"Ben..." it was forceful, yet hesitant. *A warning.*

Ben plowed forward anyway. He hadn't felt emotions like these for over a decade, ever since his dad had been taken.

"You led us here, to our deaths, for what? For your amusement?" he asked the questions pointedly, as if he already knew the answer. *Did he?*

Stephens smiled. "No. It was an experiment. *My* experiment. I told them no one would be able to figure it out, and that it was an embarrassment on our part to accomplish something so miraculous and not have the satisfaction of watching it unfold. Up close."

Ben asked the next question carefully. He wanted to get closer, to try to subdue Stephens. "So you let us figure it out?" He took a step forward. *Careful.* He treated the situation like his many encounters with wild animals. *Don't approach directly when possible, but don't move too quickly.*

Another step.

Stephens kept talking, but Ben had already tuned him out. He was focusing on the hunt, trying to sneak his way into Stephens' personal space. He knew Stephens wasn't an animal, but that was to Ben's benefit. Stephens was acting emotionally, based not on animal instinct but human perception. Ben could rely on a slower reaction time from him because of that.

But as he planned his move, he caught sight of Stephens' arm. It swung upward, cradling a weapon.

"You've performed your role admirably, Mr. Bennett," he heard Stephens say. "Now let me perform mine."

Ben tried to lunge forward, but he couldn't get his mind to form the direction and send it out to his body. It was all happening so glacially, as if he were watching a movie in slow motion. He felt his feet move, imperceptibly at first, then more quickly.

But not quickly enough.

He'd never make it to Stephens in time. The gun rose a little more, now pointing at Ben's chest.

He thought he saw the muzzle of the pistol flash, a small bristle of fire lancing from its barrel, but his vision suddenly went white. He felt something too, a crashing pain that hit him from his side, knocking him off his feet.

He was flying. Blinded and in pain, but he recognized the sensation of vertigo. He tried to reach his arms out to stop the fall, but he had no idea if his arms had registered the order or not.

Then he heard the explosion from the gun. It was louder than he thought it would be—he'd almost always been on the sending end of a gun barrel. It deafened him.

Blind, in pain, and now deaf.

And still falling.

Ben hit the ground hard.

He felt another pain, similar to the first, shoot through on his arm and shoulder, and into his hip and leg.

This can't be right.

It was a point-blank shot—how could Stephens have missed? Ben should have felt something in his chest.

Right?

He tried to blink, trying to convince his senses to return.

Nothing but pain.

A dull pain, admittedly—throbbing, but manageable. *What happened?*

He breathed, now realizing he'd been holding his breath. His lungs struggled with the weight, trying to push it off.

Why was there a weight on top of him?

His vision returned. Narrowly at first. The lights of the lab creeped into his periphery, followed by a darker shadow.

A man's face.

Malcolm Fischer's face.

The professor was lying on top of him.

Ben gasped, pushing upward with his throbbing hands, trying to heave the weight of the man's body off to the side. He struggled until he was free.

Ben sat up, blinking.

When his vision fully returned, he found Malcolm's body lying next to his in a crimson pool of blood.

No...

Ben reached out and felt behind the professor's neck.

Come on, he willed. *Wake up.*

He noticed the professor's brown coat, wrapped around the older man, a ragged hole almost dead center in the man's back.

The exit wound.

Ben heard sobbing. In a daze, he looked up. Julie stood over him, tears falling from her face.

"B—Ben," she muttered. "I thought you..."

Her voice trailed off as she finally saw Malcolm lying next to him.

"Oh my God," she whispered. "He—he saved you."

Ben simply nodded. "Where's Stephens?" Anger flashed behind his eyes, and he stood.

He saw Stephens lying across a table against the wall, unmoving.

"I have his blood on me," she said.

Ben didn't care. He stepped over Malcolm's body and gently reached for Julie, pulling her close. He wrapped a hand around the back of her head and slowly pressed her to his shoulder. He stroked her hair while she sobbed.

The truck bounced over another pothole in the dirt road.

Julie again in the passenger seat, staring out the window, holding back tears that she knew would eventually come.

They'd left the lab a mess—two dead bodies, one extremely contagious, and both bleeding onto the white tiled floor.

Julie couldn't decide what had been worse. The true extent of Stephens' double-crossing, or the hard realization that nobody came to help. Gunshots had rung out in Yellowstone and the reaction had been silence.

They were alone.

Chaotic as it was, Stephen's execution to this point had been flawless. From the initial blast to the spreading virus, down to Stephens' own arrogant desire to watch it unfold from a front-row seat.

He'd told them everything. It was cryptic and difficult to understand, at best, but it was complete.

He'd wanted it that way—to watch them suffer through the pain of searching, only to see their helpless eyes as he unleashed his weapon.

His final move.

Checkmate.

She looked at Ben as he drove. "I can't believe he *knew*, Ben. The whole time."

Ben nodded slowly. She saw his knuckles turn white as he gripped the wheel. "I know," he said softly. "But there's still something I don't understand. The syringe—why'd he do it? I mean, inject himself with the stuff? He could have just shot us."

"No, that's just it." She said. "I figured it out right before he tried to shoot you."

"Really?"

"Yeah. Ben—*he's* the endgame. He's the final piece."

"I know. He orchestrated the whole thing, and—"

"No, Ben—he is part of the bomb."

Ben didn't understand. "Say that again...?"

"Stephens had to make sure he was in the park because he's supposed to be the final piece of the puzzle. Remember what happened when the first bomb went off? It sent a payload of the virus into the air, which contaminated a lot of the area. But this *second* bomb can't carry that payload—it'll be too big. And if it's going to go off anywhere around that caldera—"

"Then the eruption from the volcano beneath us will more than eradicate the strain."

"Right," she said. "A bomb too small won't destroy the underground structure enough to cause an eruption, but a bomb too big will just incinerate the payload."

"So," Ben said, thinking aloud. "To make sure you get both the volcanic eruption *and* the virus to be spread, you have to place the viral payload far enough away from the initial blast that it's safe from that explosion, but close enough to the caldera that the resulting eruption will send the payload into the atmosphere.

"And Stephens *is* the viral payload."

Julie sighed. "Like I said, he's part of the bomb."

"Then *I* need to find that bomb," Ben said, "and you need to get out of the park." He pushed the accelerator to the floor, and the truck swerved, barely missing a deep hole in the road.

She looked over at him. "Excuse me?"

"You heard me. I'm not letting you get anywhere near that eruption."

Julie stiffened her jaw, annoyed.

"Ben, listen to yourself," she said. "You're not making any sense. You explained it to me, remember? If that bomb goes off, it starts a chain reaction. There's no place in *two hundred miles* that's safe."

Ben shrugged. "Still—"

"No, Ben. Stop. Forget it. Where are you going to drop me off? Ten miles from here? Twenty? How much time are you going to waste trying to get me away from the blast zone? And how long do you think you have before the bomb actually goes off?"

Ben wanted to answer but flipped the radio on instead. The news report was already in progress. He upped the volume. It was a computerized message, reading a pre-written response.

"...Local police and SWAT teams on high-alert for riot activity, including looting. Please stay indoors, and remain out of contact with anyone outside of immediate family. Contaminated areas include as a southern border Las Cruces, New Mexico. Western border, Kansas City. Eastern border Reno, Nevada. CDC and FEMA have prepared quarantine stations at many metropolitan areas. Please visit www..."

He yanked the volume down again as Julie spoke.

"It's not true," she said.

"What?"

"The report. The CDC can't mobilize that many quarantines that fast. They're just not set up for it. And FEMA... There's just no way."

"At least they're doing something," Ben said.

"What? What could they possibly be doing?" Julie asked, her voice growing emotional. "Stephens kept me in the dark the entire time, and he murdered the man who's supposed to be at the front of this thing, keeping the investigation moving forward."

"Okay, well what do you want to do, then?" Ben asked. He tapped the brakes.

Julie thought for a moment. "We're it, Ben. We're the *only* people close enough to do anything about it. We have to find that bomb, and fast. And don't get any ideas about ditching me on the side of the road somewhere."

Ben looked at her for a minute, considering the offer. He nodded, then sped up again.

4 4

Julie checked for updates on the spreading virus, and sent a few emails up the chain of command at the CDC.

It was a long shot, the CDC was already doing everything they could to stop the spread of the virus, and their ability to provide research support had been extremely stifled by Stephens' handiwork, but their options were limited. After a few minutes of clicking around, she closed the computer.

"Try calling again," Ben said.

"There's no point," she replied. "Anyone there is already deployed at a waypoint or helping with disaster relief. We need to get to an actual location—"

"Julie, we've talked about this," Ben said. "We don't have the time to drive all the way there. We have to get others involved *somehow*."

"I know, I know!" Julie snapped, exasperated.

"Think," Ben said, talking as much to himself as to Julie. "Where would he put a bomb that size and not be noticed."

"This is Yellowstone," Julie remarked. "All he has to do is zip it up in the right gear and looks like any other camper."

Ben shook his head. "Not camp grounds. No one just leaves their stuff behind."

"Not even a cooler?"

"Only if there was an accident and it fell of a boat into the—"

Julie squirmed in her seat. "In the lake?"

"Under the lake," Ben answered, his voice confident. As he said the words, a sign flew past on the right side of the road with the words *Yellowstone Lake– 1 Mile* printed on it.

"Ben, Livingston's already checked there. Remember? He sent a team of geologists and excavators through most of the caves in the region, and found that tunnel. If there was something there, he would have—"

"Julie, Livingston didn't tell you that."

"He did! He called, an —" she suddenly remembered what Ben was getting at.

Livingston hadn't called—*Stephens* had.

She bolted upright in the seat. "Stephens called, not Livingston. He only *said* Livingston had sent the team in, and he didn't have any reason to be communicating with Livingston, which means..." She thought for a moment. "Which means he was lying. Ben, if he was lying, we could be heading in the wrong direction."

"But we're not. We're going exactly where Stephens told us to go. So far he's double-crossed us at every step, but it's been his information that's gotten us this far. He even told us *why*—he wanted to watch us try to figure it out." Ben looked at Julie. "If that bomb is actually somewhere in Yellowstone, we're going to find it exactly where Stephens told us to look."

Julie knew he was right—it *had* to be right. "Yeah, why *wouldn't* he just tell us exactly where it is? As insane as he was, he believed it was too late to do anything about it."

She hoped Stephens wasn't right about that.

"So where is this cave, anyway?" she asked.

Ben shook his head. "I don't know. But there's only one cave I can think of that's long and deep enough to be a good spot. It has to be close enough to the surface that an explosion would penetrate, but deep enough to affect the magma area below the caldera. It's a few miles around the lake, once we get there, but the cave isn't terribly long."

"But he cut a tunnel into the side of it, right?"

"Right, and we have no way of knowing how deep *that* is. It's wide enough that we can crouch or slide most of the way through, and there aren't any major forks. We'll know right away if we see a manmade tunnel."

Ben pulled the truck to the left as the road took a dogleg turn, then he sped up again. This section of the road was considerably better than the one they'd been on, with a gravel base and fewer potholes and bumps. As he aimed the vehicle down the center of the one-lane drive, he couldn't help but notice the immense beauty of the surrounding country.

This land had been his only home for over a decade. Diana—his mother—had tried for years to bring him and his brother together again under one roof, but she'd failed.

Or, rather, he'd failed *her*.

After his father died, Ben did the only thing that felt right. He ran away. At the time it hadn't felt like running *away*, though, as much as it felt like running *toward* something. This something was staring down at him as he drove through it.

The trees, pine and spruce, scraping at the ceiling of the sky, their tops ripping into the vast blue and white. The forest floor, which had acted as his bed for so many nights he couldn't count them, and the soft prickle of the needles that littered the ground and crunched when he walked.

And the *smell*.

That forest, deep-green, fresh, *alive* smell.

The smell was the biggest reason he'd settled here, and he swore he'd never live another day without it. Whether it was a mountaintop in Colorado, the sweeping forests of Yellowstone, or his secluded cabin in Alaska, as long as that smell was there when he arrived, he could live anywhere.

And now this madman, dead as he was, wanted to take all that away?

This was his home and he was going to defend it.

Home.

He looked again at Julie and saw her gazing back at him.

Something's missing...

The question rose again.

What's missing?

He silently tried to answer it, to make it go away. But it didn't—it wouldn't. He tried again, and failed.

Ben suddenly realized it wasn't a question he as asking about his own life—that question had already been answered. Instead, this question was about the task at hand.

What was missing?

As he posed the question again, emphasizing different beats, different syllables of each word, the answer struck him at once.

The reason.

He turned his head sideways, chewing on that answer. *The* reason *was missing.*

The reason Stephens had done it. He wasn't being paid—he'd given his life for the cause. It couldn't have been about money, at least not for him. And he wasn't just a murderer, a basket case with a chip on his shoulder.

There was something more.

Something, Ben realized, they should have already figured out.

A chill came down the back of Ben's neck as he gripped the steering wheel tightly, all of the possible solutions to the problem suddenly pouring through his mind.

The plan was, Ben had to admit, all but perfect. If Stephens hadn't fed them every scrap of information they currently knew, they'd be no better off than the CDC and the rest of the population. They'd be lost, looking for a needle in a haystack.

No, they wouldn't even know to look—Stephens was the one who'd told them there was a second bomb. Why had he gone through all the trouble to stage a massive terrorist plot against an entire nation, to then simply die alone?

Even if he *was* working with a larger organization, as Malcolm had suggested, why make it a point to have witnesses for his suicidal last stand?

To simply die alone?

"Shit," he whispered. He whipped the truck around, barely coming to a stop. Gravel flew out from the truck's tires, spraying the trees and bushes growing next to the road and sending birds clamoring out of the way.

The computer on Julie's lap slammed against the car door as she shrieked and grasped at the ceiling-mounted handle.

"What the hell?" she shouted, trying to fight the centrifugal force of the truck's rotation. "Ben, what's going on?"

To die alone.

That was the reason. That had always been the reason.

No, the answer.

That had always been the answer.

Stephens was talking to him, communicating to them still, from beyond the grave.

"Ben?"

He wanted them to feel his pain—the very real, human, pain. Isolated, gripping, terrifying pain.

Alone.

"The lithosphere of the Earth, consisting of the Earth's crust and upper mantle, is normally just under one hundred miles thick. The outer shell of crust makes up what our entire planet lives on, either on land, in the air, or beneath the sea."

The Indian man's voice crackled through the station's tube TV, the color long since faded. Officer Darryl Wardley wondered why no one had bothered to change it out, or at least have it fixed.

Could you even fix tube TVs anymore?

He thought about the question, finding it genuinely more interesting than this Dr. Ramachandran fella with his thick black glasses and even thicker accent, droning on about stuff Wardley hadn't thought about since high school. He'd pulled the desk shift this evening, but with the mass hysteria keeping everyone insanely busy lately, it was a welcome rest. He blinked, once again concentrating on the TV.

"This shell is typically between three and five miles thick beneath the Earth's surface, and closer to thirty-five miles thick on land.

"The crust section of the lithosphere below the Yellowstone caldera in Yellowstone National Park is less than two miles thick, meaning that the upper mantle, full of molten rock and magma, is extremely close to the surface. This 'hotspot' is one of only a dozen on Earth, and means that the extreme temperatures found within the Earth are much closer to the surface."

Again, boring. He wondered if there was a game on—maybe baseball, since they always played. If not, there might be a decent hockey game rerun on ESPN, but he'd have to get up to change the channel. *Why can't we afford a Universal Remote Control?* He'd been around long enough to know that it wasn't anyone's job, so it had probably just never gotten done. He made a mental note to pick one up at Walmart the next time he was there.

"The last time this caldera erupted was over 640,000 years ago, and the blast was large enough to send ash as far away as the Pacific coast, some of the plains states, and even the Gulf of Mexico." As the professor spoke, the station had superimposed a slide showing a map of the western United States, covered by a red oblong shape—the volcano—and a lighter shaded section labeled "Ash Zone."

"Yellowstone has experienced a massive volcanic eruption just about every 600,000 years, and the prior eruptions—1.3 million and 2.1 million years ago, respectively—were even larger. Actually, because of this fantastically large land area, the Yellowstone supervolcano is considered to be the largest active volcano in the world."

Officer Wardley frowned. *Volcanoes were huge smoking mountains,* he thought. But as he considered the park's many geologic features, including geysers, hot springs, and smoking fissures in the ground, he changed his mind. *Maybe there was a volcano under there after all.* His family—wife and three kids—and he had spent many summer vacations there, since it was so close. Only a few hours away, and they'd had numerous friends over the years to travel with.

Dr. Ramachandran continued explaining the seismic activity that could be found at the park. *"It was extremely lucky that this bomb went off where it did, and not closer to the caldera's center, and that it was not larger. The right explosion could do more damage than a simple blast—it could potentially fracture the already delicate infrastructure of the plates holding the magma below at bay. In fact, since many scientists believe that Yellowstone is due for an eruption, a blast of a certain size could jumpstart this timeline."*

Wardley sat up in his chair, no longer daydreaming. He saw for the first time another person on the television, this time a woman in a red dress, obviously the interviewer. She asked a few questions, which the man answered one at a time.

"To put in perspective how large this volcanic eruption will be, consider the Mt. St. Helens eruption in 1980, which we no doubt all remember. Yellowstone's volcano would be on a force magnitude of 2,500 times that size. It would send ash more than thirty miles straight up into the atmosphere, blocking out the sun and most likely causing the planet's global temperature to plummet.

"But this ash would be a long-term problem. For the people within five to six hundred miles of the actual eruption, all life will be either incinerated instantaneously or consumed by pyroclastic lava flows that move at high speeds. The western half of the United States might simply cease to exist, but the effects to the global economy and that of humanity in general will be devastating."

The woman made a remark about the man's dire explanation, calling into question the confidence he had in his prediction.

"This is not speculation, mind you. It is scientific fact. Volcanologists and

geologists have long been hard at work predicting not if *this eruption will take place, but* when. *There is a strong possibility that we will be without an eruption for the next 1,000 years, and even 10,000 years, but there is no definitive way to understand the dynamics at play beneath the surface of the Earth."*

The woman turned away from the man and spoke to the camera.

"You heard it yourself. Dr. Ramachandran is an esteemed volcanologist and the author of numerous books on the subject. With the increased interest surrounding the explosion at Yellowstone National Park only days ago, and of course the terrible virus that is spreading throughout the United States that is believed to have been initiated by that same explosion, we wanted to bring you a special edition feature for tonight's newscast that examined the Yellowstone caldera.

"In a moment, we will return to your regularly scheduled programming after a brief update from our disaster relief team regarding the Yellowstone Virus."

The show cut to a square-jawed cliché in his mid-fifties, with perfectly combed salt-and-pepper hair. He was smiling, but Officer Wardley had worked with people long enough to know the man on the television was holding onto a certain amount of fear. Maybe even panic.

"The Yellowstone Virus is still eluding the nation's best researchers, though we are told that a breakthrough is imminent. As you have no doubt already heard, please stay indoors, lock your house, and do not venture out for any reason. Stay isolated, and do not physically interact with anyone other than your immediate family..."

Wardley scoffed at the guy on TV. The anchor was stuck at work, just like him. How many others were out there, stuck at their jobs, explaining their own demise to the rest of their species? Wardley had already fielded calls from three of his fellow officers—two accounts of looting and one small riot gang making its way up and down the main street of town. Even for a small city, the crazies somehow seemed to be the majority.

He got up to refill his coffee—he'd need another pot of it before the night was over—when the phone rang.

He growled and sat back down. "Officer Wardley, Sheridon County Police, how may I assist you?"

He frowned as he heard the explanation on the other end of the line. "Excuse me, you're going to need to slow down. You said you're *in* Yellowstone right now?"

The voice yammered on. "Son," Wardley said, his voice stern. "You need to get out of the park. There's a virus—"

But the voice continued. Wardley's heartbeat rose slightly. He was not fond of being yelled at, especially by a civilian. "Listen, Bennett, I don't care if you're a park ranger or not—you need to get out of that area."

He started to explain their protocol regarding a refugee from a disease-infected area as he pulled out a regional map that had the quarantine checkpoints and stations marked in highlighter, but the man on the phone interrupted him again.

He was starting to get *really* angry.

"Bennett, I'm not going to ask you—"

He paused.

"Sorry, *what?*"

Bennett spoke again.

"There's *another* bomb?" He listened to Bennett explain, for the third time, what he wanted Wardley to do. "And you're sure about that?"

Yes, apparently Bennett was decidedly sure, before he slammed the phone down onto the receiver.

46

Officer Darryl Wardley's police cruiser, a decade-old Dodge Charger, raced down the highway at ninety miles an hour. He would have gone faster if it wasn't for the handful of stray vehicles disobeying the now government-mandated house arrest for every citizen spread out on the open road.

Wardley's comm squawked out just about every excuse in the book as he'd listened in on his fellow officers' 11-95s. Most of the civilians were panic buying last-minute supplies, or checking in on family and friends who hadn't responded to their phone calls. One deranged individual even admitted he was on a joyride; he'd never seen so little traffic on the highway, and he wanted to take advantage of it.

Most civilians, with the exception of the wannabe racecar driver, were let off with nothing but a warning and a stern reminder that they were supposed to be inside. The federal government, after all, hadn't issued a formalized process notice explaining what the local officers were supposed to *do* with 11-95s out and about against mandate. Wardley's comrades were driving blind, simply pulling people over, asking them for their license and registration—nothing but a formality these days, anyway—and then letting them go after they heard the driver's excuse.

Wardley was glad he wasn't on patrol duty tonight. Nothing but a bunch of crazies and nut jobs taking advantage of the fact that most of the United States government was busy trying to figure out this virus.

Still, driving ninety miles an hour down an almost-abandoned highway felt an awful lot like being on duty—holy crap he looked tired.

Catching sight of his own deep-set brown eyes, and eyebrows that could use a trim, in the rearview mirror took him by surprise. Whose face was that staring back at him? He looked so exhausted. And old. So old. He'd slept just before his shift, no more than five hours ago. But he felt physically, emotionally, and mentally drained.

He adjusted the mirror to remove his face.

After the call from Bennett at Yellowstone, he'd called a his superiors at the station, including two that were out on patrol already. He told them what he'd learned from Bennett, explaining that he had no proof that any of it was true, then waited for the inevitable tongue-lashing as his commanding officers showed him all of the reasons why the madman in the park was just looking to start a fight, and there was no bomb.

Surprisingly, Wardley met little resistance. It seemed as though the officers wanted to do something other than drive around the area, looking for idiot grocery shoppers and insane joyriders. They all agreed to meet him at the park, and one told him to place a general wide-band call to ask for even more backup.

It must be the solitude, Wardley thought. The virus was all anyone was talking about lately, and they all knew that driving around the area just outside the infection zone was the equivalent to suicide, whether it was part of their job description or not. Maybe playing a more active role in figuring out all of this mess helped assuage their fears.

Or maybe it was just their ego, their testosterone-laden desire to do *something,* even if that something was guided by a guy they never met, begging for help at a park they had no jurisdiction entering.

Five miles later, Wardley was entering that exact park. He slowed the cruiser a bit and caught up to another officer in his department, rolling down his window as he pulled up.

"Think we'll get sick going in here?" Hector Garcia asked, before Wardley even stopped.

"If we were, we'd have gotten it thirty miles ago. The radius is growing, even this far north."

"Yeah, so I heard. Crazy stuff, man. I hope this Bennett guy isn't messing around."

Wardley looked down the road at the park, wondering if Bennett was right. It could be that easy. Wardley realized that an easy answer was probably the real reason his fellow police officers had jumped at the opportunity to get their hands dirty. They'd all signed on for different reasons, but one they all had in common was the simple desire to right wrongs.

And finding the viral payload delivered by a second bomb was certainly in the category of "righting wrongs."

"I don't think he is," Wardley said. "I had Jones pull a background check on anyone matching the ID he gave, along with his job title at the park. It's a long shot, but if the match he found is, in fact, our guy, he's clean as a whistle. Pretty much off the grid as long as he's been alive."

"Yeah, I don't see what could be in it for him, if there's something else going on. I'd bet he's telling the truth."

"Let's get inside, then. As crazy as it sounds, if what he said is true, we need to get moving."

"Roger that. I'll keep the radio open in case we get some more volunteers." Officer Garcia paused, then met Wardley's gaze. "If I don't see you on the other side, man, take care."

Wardley knew what he meant, but he corrected him anyway. "If we go anywhere, we'll be on the *same* side, Garcia."

Garcia chuckled. "Hopefully it's the good side, then."

Wardley rolled his window back up and accelerated. Out of the corner of his eye, he saw Garcia do a quick cross sign with his fingertips, then pull out to follow on behind.

He hoped Bennett was right.

They needed him to be right.

4 7

"Ben, what are we looking for?" Julie asked. They'd now been in the truck for almost two hours, first heading toward the massive lake that made up the central area of Yellowstone National Park, then back toward the edge of the park where a string of campsites sat.

Julie's back hurt. She shifted in the seat and tried, in vain, to get comfortable. She felt like she'd never spent so many hours in one place, much less in a vehicle. Every passing minute was excruciating.

She almost wanted the bomb to go off just relieve—

No. That wasn't true. A little discomfort in exchange for fixing this terrible massacre.

It was a fair trade, she decided.

She watched Ben drive. That severe look on his face. What had gotten into him?

"Ben," she said again. "What's up?"

He finally glanced over, but only for a brief instant before the rough terrain forced him to focus on the road.

"Sorry," he said. "I—It's just..." His mood seemed to darken.

"What?"

"Nothing... I mean, I don't know yet. I have a theory, but I need to check some of these campsites first."

"I thought you ruled campsites out?"

"I know."

He said the words flatly, almost commanding, as if he felt the conversation was over.

Julie felt the opposite. Why did they need to find a campsite? What was the theory? And why was it important enough to abandon their plan to find the bomb?

She didn't ask any more questions. She'd never seen Ben focus so intently on his goal, and she didn't want to distract him. She examined the man sitting next to her. His forehead glistened with sweat, bloodied knuckles over the steering wheel. As they drove, Ben pulled up an internal list of registered campers who'd booked a campsite for that week, using his phone. He scrolled through a few pages and clicked off the screen when he was satisfied.

They reached the first of the line of campsites spread around both sides of the road, each marked with a short driveway and a wooden sign with a number painted on it. These sites, Julie realized, were meant for glamping. People who thought roughing it meant sleeping in a pop-up trailer or RV, spending the evenings by a controlled fire inside a ring of rocks, with running water piped in through the park's small but reliable water supply. Many of these sites even had electricity, meant to plug the RVs into a power source that didn't need to run on batteries.

Julie wasn't much of a camper, and it looked like it would have been rough enough for her, even with the RVs and pop-ups. Ben wasn't like most people. He would have been happy sleeping on a bed of pine needles.

Ben slammed on the brakes in front of the first site and hopped out of the truck. The tree cover cast shadows over the road and campsites, making it nearly impossible to see far into the sites. He ran to the fire ring, spinning in a circle as he searched for whatever he was looking for.

Julie opened the door to help, but Ben was already running across the street to check the second site.

"Ben, what are you looking for?" she asked. She knew better than to expect an answer, but was surprised when he yelled back to her.

"Anything. I'm looking for anything that doesn't belong. In these first three sites."

She shrugged and ran to the third site. *I can find that.*

The third site differed from the first two, and she noticed it right away. Here, the driveway had tire tracks in it from a large vehicle. She wasn't nearly good enough to tell what kind of vehicle, but she could easily see that the car or truck had exited the driveway quickly. The tracks widened as they hit the street, a sign that the vehicle had slid on the loose gravel as it sped up and turned. She turned to the rest of the site.

The ring of rocks at the center were a deep black, as if smoke had blackened them as a fire inside died out. There were no coals or bits of wood, but she thought she could smell the faint scent of charred ash from a recent fire. She walked over to it, examining everything in sight.

There.

"Ben," she called out. She stepped around the ring and walked toward a picnic table that sat at the far side of the campsite, right where the site ended and the line of thick pines began again.

She heard footsteps behind her and turned to see Ben running toward her. She pointed at the picnic table.

He nodded, continuing past her, and stopped at the bench of the table. Sitting atop the two planks of wood was a small picnic cooler.

"Were you able to talk to Randy?" he asked.

She was surprised by the question—they were searching for something in the campsites, and he wanted to know about Randall Brown? She'd called just after they left the lake and left a message.

"Yes, he sent me a text a few minutes ago. He said he's fifteen minutes from here, and he's got the maps."

Ben whipped around to look at her. "What? He's here?"

She nodded. "I guess he wanted to help..."

He stiffened a bit but didn't say anything. Julie guessed the thoughts that were going through his mind—they were the same ones that she had been struggling with when she got the text. *Why are you coming to a highly contagious outbreak area, risking your life to find something we don't even understand? Not to mention the bomb...*

But she knew Randy well enough to know that he couldn't sit back and watch as the world came down around him. He'd stepped up before for far less important cases. Julie knew his wife would be beyond upset with his rash actions, but she also knew Randy wouldn't take no for an answer.

If he said he was coming to help, they'd better be ready for him to help.

"You did say people would notice if someone left something behind like a cooler," Julie remarked. "Well, I noticed."

Focused on the cooler, Ben did not reply. Slowly approaching it, his chest rose and fell. His breathing sounded labored. Julie wondered if all the action had finally gotten to him.

"Ben," she said, then stopped. What was she going to say? "Be careful?" What did she expect to find in the cooler? A bomb?

He ignored her. The cooler was like one of the small six-pack coolers that Julie owned, with a zippered lid and a few pockets around the sides.

Slowly, he unzipped the lid.

"It's placed right where it needs to be," Ben whispered.

Julie stared at him.

"Far enough away from the blast, but still close enough to be affected by the eruption."

Julie looked down at the top of the cooler as Ben pulled it open.

He stepped back as a cloud of white powder rushed out of the vessel, filling the airspace in front of their heads.

"Shit," she said. The powder—no doubt the contagion mechanism itself—packed inside the cooler, filling it halfway to the top. The dusty substance crept up out of the container, like smoke from yesterday's fire.

"Yeah," Ben said, closing the lid again. He stepped back another step and turned to Julie. "That's what I thought. I'd bet there are more—a *lot* more."

"Dotted around the other campsites…" she realized.

He nodded. "All around the lake, not to mention miles of open land for backpackers and survivalists to set up camp. I don't know how much of this stuff they planned to release into the air, but I'd guess you'd want more than a half-cooler full to get the job done right."

"And it's far enough away from the bomb's blast out here?"

"That's my guess—leave the cooler here when you leave the campsite for the evacuation and…" He stopped to look back toward the road. "You can't see it from the road, meaning my crew would have just driven past, not looking for anything but people and vehicles that stayed behind. You only found it, because we were looking for it."

The picnic table would be all but invisible from the camp road, and even if you were looking for manmade objects like the cooler, it would be sheer luck to see it perched on the bench from the inside of a moving vehicle.

"I'm guessing when the bomb blows out the bottom of the lake and the top of the caldera, the eruption will pick up the coolers and spread the virus that way," Ben said.

"Maybe," Julie replied. "But a large enough eruption will incinerate anything within miles."

"I agree. That's why they packed it cooler insulation, Just enough to keep the payload safe through the blast." He picked up the cooler and zipped the lid shut.

Ben marched back to the truck, and Julie followed. "What now?"

"Tell the cops what to look for and make sure they don't open the containers when they get here."

Julie thought about their own situation. The virus had fully run its course through their bodies, rendering them both immune to its effects. But the police officers weren't as lucky. They knew what they were getting into, and that it was likely a one-way trip for them.

4 8

They all met at the road that stretched between the lake and the campsites where Ben and Julie had found the first cooler. Five officers, Ben, Julie, and Randy. As they gathered, Ben introduced himself.

"Thank you all for being here. I won't take any time to explain the dire situation, as I know you all are fully aware." Nods all around. "Second, this is likely the end of the road for us. I'm not much of a speech guy, so I'll just leave it at that. Feel free to turn around and head back the way you came."

No one moved.

"Okay, then, here's the deal," Ben continued. "We found a cooler containing about two pounds of powdered viral agent under a picnic table at a campsite 17. Not far from here."

Ben went on explain why they believed it was placed where it was, and why he thought there would be more around the park. "We're dealing with a literal ticking time bomb, literally, and the largest outbreak of a deadly disease since the Spanish Flu. If you have anyone you can call for support, *get them here*. We need bodies, and we need them fast."

Some of the officers were nodding in approval, and others were already taking their phones out of their pockets and preparing a string of text messages to their groups.

"Start with the list I emailed to Officer Wardley. It's a list of the registered single campers and their designated sites. Julie and Randy will split up with two of you," Ben said, ignoring Julie's surprised and upset expression. "I'm going to find that bomb."

Two officers spoke at once, suspicious. "You know where it is?"

"Nope. But I have an idea," Ben answered. "Randy brought me some maps he pulled from our staff web access point of the underground cave systems below Yellowstone Lake and the surrounding area. Most aren't very big, if I remember correctly, but a few could be deep enough and long enough to be a good spot to set up a bomb."

"You know anything about bomb disposal?" Wardley asked.

"No."

"So you're just going to walk in there and switch it off?"

"No."

"Then I think we need to go with you, don't you, sir?"

Ben turned it around. "Do *you* know anything about bomb disposal?"

"No," Wardley admitted. "But we're trained for this sort of thing."

"But not bomb disposal."

"No."

"Look," Ben said. "I'm not here to disarm it. I'm not even going to touch. I'm going to find. *You're* going to get someone here who knows how to take care of it. And in the meantime we need all hands on deck identifying these caches around the park. It's a lot of land to cover—over one hundred individual sites, and I have no idea how much time we have left. If I can't get to the bomb in time, this place turns into a lava field within seconds. We have to make sure that that's all it is—not a contagious spawn point for a massive disease as well."

Again, some of the officers nodded. "What do we do with the caches?"

Julie stepped in. "Don't touch them. Keep your distance. Just call them in and mark them on GPS—"

Ben disagreed. "No."

'What, do you work for the CDC now?"

"Dump them in the lake," Ben insisted.

"But that's ground zero."

"Exactly," Ben said. "If we can't get this thing diffused, the least I can do is bring it up to the surface and drive it into the lake. That alone will lessen the impact and vaporize the viral agent."

Julie stepped back, suddenly realizing the full extent of Ben's plan. "That's suicide."

"Okay, that's it. Keep your radios on and check in when you can," Wardley said. Someone threw Ben a walkie-talkie, and he set it to their designated channel. "Let's go!"

Immediately, the small crowd dispersed, each heading back to their vehicles. Randy tagged along with a short, portly officer and stepped into the man's passenger seat.

"Ben, I'm going with you," Julie said.

Ben was already walking the other direction, trying to ignore her. Her stubborn nature immediately sprang into life.

"Ben! I'm going with you," she said again.

"You're not."

"I *am*. And if you try to stop me, I'll—"

"What?" Ben yelled, whirling around to face her. His face was red, his eyes bloodshot. He looked a mess, and it stopped Julie in her tracks.

"I…" she started again.

Ben's nostrils flared as he tried to control his emotions. He looked at Julie, a few inches shorter, standing in front of him. "What?" he said. His voice wavered slightly.

She didn't speak.

Ben grabbed her by the arms and pulled her toward him. He leaned down and kissed her, not letting go. She stood dead still for a few seconds, taken by surprise, then gently fell into him.

She tried to say something, but he pressed his lips harder to hers. She felt warmth crawling up her spine, taking over the steel resolve she'd felt moments ago. He released her arms, and she quickly entangled them around his waist, hugging him tightly.

Finally, he pulled back and looked into her eyes. She saw tears forming in his, and he blinked them back.

"You're coming back, Ben," she said. "Understand? You're coming back."

He took one last look at Julie, then jumped in the truck. He revved the engine and drove away, leaving Julie standing in the road.

In the rearview mirror, he saw a police cruiser pull up beside her and wait for her to open the passenger door. As she got into the vehicle, she looked once more at the trail of dust behind her truck as it disappeared over the rise.

49

Ben reached the first cave on his list in record time. He wasn't sure anyone had ever driven that fast over the weathered roads crisscrossing the park. He sure hadn't. It was all he could do to keep the truck on the center of the road, hoping that no wildlife jumped in front of the moving battering ram.

The cave was off to his left, and he could easily see the markers from the road. A few stakes in the ground with brightly colored plastic strands marked the location as one of the park's future tourist attractions. It hadn't been fully excavated yet, nor had it been assessed by the park's surveying crews.

Ben didn't care about any of that. He needed to find the actual cave, get inside, and find that bomb.

What would it even look like? He wasn't sure he'd ever even seen a bomb in real life. And it certainly wouldn't look anything like they did in the movies. Would it? As he exited the vehicle, he grabbed a heavy flashlight he'd borrowed from one of the cops and tested it.

He found the entrance behind a large bush, and he brushed the prickly stems from his face as he crouched down and lowered himself into hole below the rocks. It was a tight fit. His large frame was going to have a difficult time navigating the cramped space, not to mention the sharp protrusions of rock he felt jutting out of the walls.

He sighed. *Julie would fit.*

He forced the thought out of his mind and slid through the entrance.

It was much tighter than he'd initially thought. His shoulders scraped against the rocks as he sucked in his gut and slid farther. He breathed in slowly, feeling the space narrow. When he exhaled, he slid once more, gaining another six inches.

This could take a while.

He repeated the inhale-exhale-slide process another a couple dozen times and suddenly found himself in a larger hole. Still small, but he now had room to maneuver through the cavern. Still, he found it hard to believe someone could cram a body *and* a bomb through this tunnel, but it didn't matter. He had to find it. If it could even possibly be in this cave, he would search the entire thing.

A few more feet and the space opened up again, this time large enough for him to crouch. He crawled forward on his hands and knees, careful to dodge the small rocks and sticks that had collected on the cave floor, ready to stab his knees as he slid past.

For an eternity, he slid, crawled, and hunched his way through the tunnel, hoping there were more than an eternity on its countdown clock.

"Har— nett." The radio he'd clipped to the back of his belt crackled to life. *"—Ennett. Do—read, over."*

He stopped, grabbed the radio and tried to send a response. "This is Bennett. You're breaking up, but I read you, over."

He waited for a response, but none came. Ben checked the radio for battery—less than a quarter remaining, but enough to receive and send a signal—and the antenna. Everything seemed to be in working order, so he clipped it back onto his belt and continued on down the gently sloping decline of the cave.

If it's important enough, I'll hear it when I get back to the surface. We have to find this bomb.

But another ten minutes of slowly moving downward proved to be useless. Eventually, the cave narrowed to a funnel shape, and he found forward motion growing more and more impossible.

Shit, he thought. *This can't be it.*

He'd wasted thirty minutes, at least, searching for this cave and diving down it headfirst. There was nothing in front of him suggesting that the roof had fallen in, nor was there any sign of prior human contact with the rocks and walls of the cavern. For all he knew, he was the first person ever to set foot in the place.

He shimmied backward, painstakingly moving uphill feet-first, waiting until the cave widened enough for him to turn around and exit.

It had been a massive waste of time. But worse than that, there would never be enough time to spend thirty minutes in each of the caves.

He couldn't hail the rest of the team and pull any of them off their search, either. If the bomb detonated, he had to hope the contagion would be close enough to the lake to be incinerated by the blast.

50

It took longer climbing back out of the tunnel, than it did going down into it. Ben was exhausted, frustrated, and—a new feeling now began to wash over him—fear.

Fear of not getting to the bomb in time.

Afraid for the officers and volunteers racing throughout the park to find the virus caches.

Fear of losing Julie.

It was a thought that rattled through his mind like a run away train.

There was something between them, but didn't know what to call it.

They were attracted to each other, obviously. But it felt deeper somehow. More important than lust.

Did she feel the same way? How could he ask her if he ever got the chance?

He'd had a few flings here and there, mostly with other park staff, many of whom were seasonal and changed every summer. None were serious, and none made him feel the same way Julie did.

And what way is that? he asked himself.

The shaft of sunlight leading to the surface beckoned up ahead. Pushing up off the rock floor he shimmied, trying to move faster. The radio broke his concentration—

"—Bennett, report —Hear me?"

Ben pulled the radio from its clip and answered. "Hey, I'm here— just finished exploring the first cave, and nothing." He took a breath. "Over."

"You're cut— out..." then, *"We've—three caches in about—sites."* Ben resorted to interpretation. *They found three virus caches?* It was a start. More importantly, he was right about there being more of them in single-camper sites. This was no wild goose chase—they were on track.

Now, to find that bomb and clean up this mess.

He peered up at the lip of the hole and the surface beyond. Just a few more feet.

"Ben, do you copy?" It was Julie.

He immediately brought the walkie-talkie back up to his mouth. "I read you."

"Hey, I have an idea."

"I'm all ears," he replied. They'd quickly abandoned the radio protocol of saying 'over' every time, and Ben didn't miss it.

"Listen—I need to get with Randy to figure it out. Randy, if you're on this frequency, let me know..."

309

"Right here, Julie. What's up?" Randy's voice sounded hollow on the police radio, and Ben wasn't sure if he was farther away from them or if the police officer was holding it up to him in the car.

"Guys, I need to get out of this hole. My battery's going down on this radio, too." To be sure, he checked it. There was a light next to the battery charge symbol, and it was now flashing. *That can't be good,* he thought. "I'm going offline for a few, but I'll jump back on when I'm out. Try calling me on my cell if you can't reach me."

"Roger that, Ben. Stand by."

Ben spent the last few feet scraping his head and back against the jutting rocks until he was able to haul himself out of the hole. He rolled onto his back, sucking in a lungful of fresh air.

He checked the radio. The battery low indicator light was still blinking away. No telling how long he had left. He should have checked it before he set out. He clicked it on, just in time to hear a broadcast from Julie.

"—Back on? Ben, can you hear me?"

"I'm here," he said, winded. He stood, stretching to his full height for the first time in over an hour. He could feel the deep muscle pain in his lower back already beginning to creep over the area, and he made a mental note to himself to work out more often.

"Okay, great. I've got something for you. Check out the cave on the northeastern side of the lake. There are a few, but the one farthest north should be right."

Ben reached the truck, simultaneously fumbling with the ignition and rifling through the maps spread on the passenger seat. The western side of the lake, with a few caves—including the one he'd just emerged from—No, not that one. He threw it back and grabbed the second map.

There. The blown-up view of the northern and northeastern sides of the lake, a dozen or so winding caves traced over. Larger lines extended into the body of water itself, signifying that at least a portion of the cave traveled below the lake.

"Got it," he said as he put the truck into gear and sped up onto the road. He could already see the lake glistening back at him, catching light and bouncing it back into his eyes. He took a quick look back down at the map to confirm. "I'm looking at it. Seems to be one of the only ones that goes under the actual lake, and not just stop before it gets there." He waited for a response, but none came. "How'd you find this one?" he asked.

Still nothing.

He held the radio up to examine it. No blinking lights. It was completely dead.

Crap.

He hoped Julie was right.

51

This cave was significantly larger than the last one. Thank God. Hopefully he wouldn't need to crawl around on his hands and knees this time.

He parked the truck, left the keys on the seat, and jumped down. He unclipped the radio and left it on the stack of maps on the passenger seat too—. It was dead weight now.

The cavern ceiling ran high enough that he had more than enough headroom as he followed its twisting curves. It descended much slower than the first, but he was able to almost jog through it, making up for lost time.

He kept the beam of the flashlight in front of him, avoiding pitfalls, rocks, and branches as he went. Yet still he completely missed the sudden step that almost swept his foot out from under him. His foot hit the ground hard and he almost bit his tongue.

"Goddamnit."

He swept the flashlight over it. How had he missed that? He quickly moved on.

As the tunnel bottomed out, it grew wider, into a main artery large enough for two or three people to walk side-by-side, until it took a steep drop and the *real* descent began, forcing Ben to slow to a walk.

He calculated that this shelf must be the point where the cave twisted beneath the lake's bottom, a cavity carved from millions of years of water dripping through cracks and fissures in the ground.

The precarious drop shallowed a bit as he descended, and he was able to pick up the pace once again. After a while, he came to a fork, but barely slowed as he chose the left passage. It was arbitrary but there was no time to dither.

The right side was larger and seemed to continue beneath the surface of the lake, while the left was a bit smaller and had a shallower decline. But it was the way the tunnel had been *cut* that made it the obvious choice.

Instead of being smooth from years of water and weather, the left tunnel had an unnatural sheen to it, along with a rugged, scratchy look.

As if it had dynamited out like an old railroad tunnel.

All along the trail, he could see the slight hint of depressions in the rock, small half-cylinder horizontal pathways, dead straight and spaced out about two feet apart, up the wall and over his head. The spots where they'd placed the sticks of Nobel's fortune.

It would have been a low-grade explosive, with enough in each channel to blow the rock to bits and allow it to be cleared, but weak enough that it wouldn't cave in on itself.

Still, it was a massive amount of work, and Ben grew livid as he walked. *They did this right under our noses.*

Whoever "they" were, they had done a fantastic job, too. The lines were straight; the tunnel was well-defined and appeared stable. There were no support beams.

They had brought in their tools, dug this place out, cleared the mess, and no one knew about it.

Ben couldn't remember the specifics of the numerous park restoration and construction contracts he'd heard about over the years, but this one had to have been one of them. Most likely, this one had been part of a larger operation, masked as a standard safety excavation and then piled with paperwork to become lost in a bureaucratic mess.

Still, it had been done, and it had taken a long time—perhaps started before Ben was even hired on.

He stifled his anger, focusing instead on reaching the end of this manmade nightmare.

The tunnel bent to the right and down, and suddenly came to a stop. There, in the dim light of the flashlight's glow, Ben saw it.

The bomb.

It was… not what he expected. Then again, he had no idea what to expect. Not really. He remembered the newscasters explaining that the first bomb had been a… hyperbaric bomb? *Something like that. Is this the same kind?*

The device looked strangely like a beer keg, the kind he'd seen at a few of the park's staff parties at the end of their summer seasons. It was silver, and stood in the middle of the room. The sides bulged out, rounded, but the top and bottom were flat, perfect circles. It wasn't huge, maybe rising to his waist.

On top of it sat a tablet computer hardwired into the top of the barrel, a mess of cabling that Ben wasn't about to try and fiddle with.

He stared at the cold metal object, wondering what to do next.

I don't really have a plan for this part, he realized. He'd just assumed he'd find the bomb, take it back up with him, and throw it in the lake.

Or, he had secretly hoped it would be like an old western—a single fuse, lit and burning its way down the cable until it reached the payload. A simple *snip* with a knife or a deadeye shot with a six-shooter would have taken care of that.

But this wasn't the wild west, and Ben stood motionless for a few moments. *What now, genius?*

He stepped closer to examine the cables. All of them were black—no guessing "blue" or "red" and pulling one of them out. They were wrapped in a thick bundle with electrical tape after protruding from two sides of the tablet, and spread out again at the other end, before heading into the large metal canister.

As he examined the device, a plan began to form. It was primitive, but it was something.

The bomb is cylindrical. Which means it can be rolled.

He had no idea how heavy it was, or how delicate. But he was beyond waiting around for something else to happen—it was just him, a bomb, and not much time left.

Did it have a mention sensor? Would it blow if he moved it?

Only one way to find out.

He gently grasped the top lip of the barrel-like container and rocked it back and forth. It seemed heavy, which made sense, but not completely stationary.

It didn't blow. He was still here.

This might work.

He rocked a little harder, testing both for weight and, as he suddenly realized, to simply see if could get it to explode.

If I get out of this, there's no way anyone's ever hiring me to be part of a bomb squad.

Trial and error didn't seem to be a factor in examining an explosive device, but then again, there was nothing else he could do.

Thankfully, no fiery blast wave ripped him to shreds as he played with the bomb-keg, so he continued with the plan.

Rock gently. Rock a little harder. A little harder... harder —

He lost his grip on the barrel, and the whole mess crashed to the floor. It clanged as it bumped on the hard rock and began to roll down the slightly sloping cavern until it smashed into the wall at the bottom of the chamber.

Instinctively, Ben cowered when it fell, as if holding his head in his hands back would have saved him.

Yet it still didn't exploded, and though he wouldn't purposefully repeat the experiment, he now knew that a little tumbling around wouldn't be enough to detonate it.

Ben calmed his nerves, breathing in and out a few times before stepping back up to the bomb and noticing a dim bluish light emanating from the barrel's top. He pointed the flashlight away and saw that the dim light remained.

What the —

The top of the barrel, now on its side, faced away from him. The light was casting shadows in the room, fighting with the beam of his flashlight. He walked around the device and saw the cause of the blue glow.

The screen.

The tablet computer was on, with nothing but a blue screen and white text scrolling around. It was code, no doubt some sort of computer program that the creators of this device had installed on it.

But at the top right of the little screen appeared a few strings of numbers as well, and it didn't take a genius to figure out what they represented.

A countdown.

Ben read the numbers, afraid of finally learning the truth. There were four two-digit spaces, and he assumed what each meant. Days, hours, minutes, seconds.

He felt a chill run down his spine as he saw that the first two places held only zeroes.

00:00:52:37.

52 minutes, 37 seconds.

52

52 minutes, 36 seconds.

If crawling out of the first cave had been exhausting, it was a piece of cake compared to this.

Like Sisyphus pushing his rock up the mountain, Ben rolled the heavy device with everything he had. Shallower parts of the cave floor were hard enough, but the steep sections were nearly impossible. Sweat dripped for him every pore, making his hands slippery and only adding to the challenge.

This thing had a weight a hundred pounds, easily. Maybe more.

Every bend and change in grade only exacerbated the agony. Ben couldn't help but wish that he'd taken someone—anyone —with him.

Why was I trying to be such a hero?

He knew it had been the smart thing to do at the time. Mitigate risk, spread out, stretch their resources to their capacity, and get as many people away from ground zero as possible.

But now, struggling to roll a tin can up a cave floor with wet hands, all while running out of energy and time, he was having second thoughts.

Maybe I can leave it here, call for help, and then wait for someone to come by.

He shook his head, reminding himself of his dead radio. Even his cellphone was worthless down here. He'd never had great service in the park, and certainly not in this area. The closest tower was near the ranger station and base areas, a small pocket of civilization in an otherwise vast—and remote—wilderness.

He'd found the blasted thing and he couldn't tell anyone!

So he kept pushing, rolling the device up and over sticks and rocks. Many of them were small enough that he could push the object over them without hesitating. Larger rocks forced him to hold the bomb still with a knee while he grabbed the obstacle and threw it to the side.

In this way, he'd covered most of the ascent. It was slow going, but he was making decent time.

Until he reached the step.

He'd forgotten about the step—the rock lip in the cave floor that almost wiped him out when he first entered the cave.

The first thought he had was that he was close to the exit. But that wasn't what mattered to him right now.

The cylinder bumped into the rock, and Ben crouched behind it, stuck, both supporting himself and trying to hold the weight of the rolling explosive device from plummeting back down the cavern.

So far he'd been able to work in the dark, keeping the flashlight in his back pocket. But now he needed a better plan. He reached around and grabbed the light, flicking it on and examining his predicament.

The ledge wasn't large, just as he remembered it, but it presented an extremely frustrating problem—the bomb would need to be lifted completely up and over the lip, then set back down on the cave floor above it, all without losing control of it.

There was no way around it, literally or figuratively.

Ben stuck his knee behind the bomb and flashed the light in a full circle around him just in case he'd missed something, his heavy breathing calming slightly as his body took advantage of the short break.

As he brought the flashlight back to his right hand and prepared to put it away, he felt his knee sliding sideways.

"Nononono—"

He shrieked at the metal cylinder, but still it rolled backwards. Ben fell on his rear, then on his side, panic suddenly setting in. His hands were no use, covered in sweat and sliding as easily on the smooth cave floor as they did on the metal surface of the bomb's casing.

This is not good.

The bomb rolled faster, and Ben knew it was going to roll right past him.

It gained speed, and he did the only thing he could think of.

He stuck his leg out and shoved it in front of the runaway cylinder, praying it wouldn't bounce right over and keep going. As it approached, Ben slid his upper body around quickly so that it was downhill, right in the path of the bomb's getaway.

The heavy object rolled over his foot, and he felt its weight slam down on his shin. He roared in agony and instinctively tried to pull his foot back, but the bomb was already up to his knee. He could feel the pressure exerted by the weight, crushing as it sailed over him.

It slowed, the angle of Ben's leg stalling it, and it rolled backwards. It bounced a little and then came to rest on his left foot, a crunching sound in his ankle causing Ben to gasp and almost pass out.

The initial impact of the device and the final crushing blow as it bounced and stopped on his foot rendered Ben completely immobile. He lay upside down, his head farther down the path and lower than his feet, one of which was pinned beneath the metal cylinder.

He groaned, pain lancing up his leg, as he tried to wriggle his foot free. He sat forward, resting on his elbows, so he could examine the situation. Every time he even thought about moving his foot, his brain seemed determined to disobey the order. Still, he struggled against it and tried to force the foot free.

It was no use. The pain was too much to bear, and the device wouldn't budge.

He fell back.

53

37 minutes, 13 seconds.

This is it. It's over. I'm going to die in a hole in the ground, waiting to blow up.

Ben's foot was on fire. The pain had grown worse, surprisingly, and he was now nearly hyperventilating as he tried to breathe in and out, focusing his mind on other thoughts.

But the thoughts that came weren't helpful.

I failed. I let everyone down, and I let Julie down.

I lost her.

He tried again to force his mind to other thoughts, but the only other thing that came to mind was to check the time on the bomb. The screen hadn't shut off and as he slid sideways a bit he caught a glimpse of the countdown clock.

36 minutes...

He watched every second tick down, the display mesmerizing him, calming him.

35 minutes...

This really is it, he thought. The seconds ticked by, and all he could think about was the bomb, the countdown timer, and Julie.

Julie, I'm sorry.

He wished he had the radio and that it had a little battery left. Not to call for help, but to hear her voice again.

Just one more time.

"Ben!"

He shook his head. Great time to start hallucinating.

"Ben?!"

Not, that was real. As real as the screaming pain in his leg. He fell back to the floor, but managed a weak response. "I—I'm here!?" he cried.

"Oh my God, Ben! We're almost there! Don't go anywhere!" she called again.

It really was her. She was some ways off, probably at the mouth of the cave, but she was here.

"Wasn't planning on it," he said, trying not to burst into tears. Christ this hurt.

He could see a flickering light now dancing above him, casting shadows on the walls around him.

"I'm coming down—are you hurt?"

He didn't answer, instead waiting for her face to appear. *How do you explain an idiot move like this?*

"Ben! What happened?"

He wanted to yell *what do you think happened?* But he was just thankful to be found. "I got attacked by a barrel. Came out of nowhere. Like an ambush."

Julie did not look amused. "You think you're funny?"

"Funnier than you," he replied, the sarcastic twinge of his voice downplayed by the obvious pain he was feeling.

"Let's get this thing off of you." She examined the bomb, noticing the countdown timer, but not saying anything about it. "Hang on a minute."

Ben's eyes grew wide as Julie turned and ran back up the cave, leaving him and the bomb in complete darkness. "Hey!"

No response. Ben waited impatiently. A minute ticked by, then another. He wished he didn't have a way to tell exactly how much time had passed, but he did.

Three minutes, on the dot.

"I'm here," he heard her say. He saw the light again, and she raced around the corner and over the step, this time holding a large stick.

"It's not going to be strong enough to lift it all the way over—"

"It doesn't need to be," she responded, cutting him off. "Shut up and hold that thing steady."

He did as he was told, and Julie propped the end of the stick underneath its bulk, careful to keep it away from Ben's foot. She wiggled it deeper, pushing it around until it cracked a little. She met Ben's gaze. "Let's hope that was just the very end of it," she said. "Ready?" She reached behind her and grabbed a sizable stone lying next to the cave wall. She jammed it beneath the stick, right in front of the bomb, forming a lever.

Ben nodded, and Julie heaved downwards with all of her bodyweight. A strained noise escaped her mouth, and Ben couldn't help but notice how *cute* it sounded. Of all the the things to rush through his brain at a time like this—

He snapped his attention back to the situation at hand and placed his hands on the bomb's casing. He held it steady as Julie pushed again. The metal canister shifted a little, and Ben felt the immediate sensation of freedom. He ripped his leg back, the terror of having his foot crushed greater than the pain of moving it that quickly.

He put more weight on the bomb, and nodded. Julie took a well-earned breath and released the lever. The bomb slid back a little but stopped as it hit the rock and the force from Ben's hands.

"Okay, now what?" she asked.

Ben looked up at her. "You didn't think to bring any of those cops down with you?"

She shook her head unapologetically. "I didn't tell them I was leaving. A few of us met up, and I, uh, sort of borrowed one of the cars."

"You stole a police car?" Ben asked incredulously.

"You stole mine," she responded.

He almost smiled. "Whatever. I guess you get to help me with this. Here—" He moved his hands over to the side of the device, and she crouched down to help him, placing her hands on the right side. "My bum leg is going to slow me down," he warned.

"We can do this," she said, and started lifting.

Ben felt the bomb move a few inches up toward the shelf, and he struggled to keep up. He added his strength, and together the pair lifted the metal tube up the side of the short rock step, using the vertical section of rock as support.

With a final push, they lifted the barrel over the edge and onto the flatter section of cave above.

"Whew, how the hell did you get it this far," Julie said.

"I figured I'd go out on a limb," Ben said.

Together, they moved it along, hand over hand, inch by inch.

"That was funny," she said, breathless. "A real dad joke."

"I do my best work in caves" Ben shot back.

"Now I know why you don't talk much," she said, a smirk forming at the side of her mouth.

"You know I don't know what hurts more, the pain in my foot, or the pain in my a—"

"Uh-Uh. Don't go there. I can you leave you behind."

Ben laughed, forgetting momentarily not to but all his weight on his bad foot. "Jesus Christ!" he yelped.

"Probably a hairline fracture," Julie surmised. "In my expert medical opinion."

They reached the end of the cave and rolled the device over the grassy land between the cave and the truck. They stopped when they reached the road, letting the bomb come to a rest in front of the truck's high tailgate. Ben sat down on the grass, letting his leg relax.

"Hey," he said. He wasn't looking at Julie, but instead up at the sky, which was growing darker as the sun prepared to set.

"What's up?"

"Thanks for coming back for me." He finally looked back down, turning his head to catch Julie's eye.

"You knew I would," she said, smiling, as she stood up. "Now let's get this thing out to the lake."

5 4

18 minutes, 28 seconds.

Ben sad he was shocked Julie even knew how to drive; she'd done so little of it. Julie told him to shut up and get his keys out. She drove the Dodge Charger police cruiser that she'd "borrowed" from the officer earlier, leaving Ben to drive her F450. He tested his leg, finding it in pain but not broken, and he walked in a few circles outside of the cave before continuing.

Together, they'd lifted the bomb up and over the tailgate of the truck and slid it against the cab, opting to stand it up on its base rather than leave it to roll around. Julie didn't have any tie-downs or rope in the truck, so Ben asked her to follow behind and make sure the bomb didn't fall over. If it did, and Ben couldn't hear or feel it himself, she'd agreed to flash her headlights a few times to let him know.

In the end, it didn't matter much. The road around the lake was paved and almost entirely free from potholes.

The plan was to find a spot to dump the bomb into the lake, trying to get it as far out onto the water as possible, and that meant they'd get to higher ground and find a hill or raised location from which they'd roll the bomb down and out over the lake.

As plans go, it was meager, but it was still a plan. Ben had been at a loss for what to do after he found the explosive device, and only after they'd secured the bomb in the back of the truck had he realized why.

He hadn't really expected to find it in the first place.

It was a miracle they'd stumbled across the bomb's resting place, and even more of a miracle that it hadn't yet detonated. Though he wasn't holding out hope that this next phase of their hacked together plan was going to work.

Still, he pressed on. *What good is a plan if it isn't tried?* he thought to himself. He wasn't sure if that was a real quote or just something that seemed to make sense, but he held on to it.

He now knew what it felt like to truly hope. To long for something to happen; to wish with all he had to accomplish something.

He'd felt pangs of it when his father had been in the ER, and then later as they stabilized him, but he'd forgotten the feelings of hope, longing, and even true despair.

This, he knew, was desperate.

They were racing at a breakneck pace, carrying a who-knew-how-massive explosive device that was *guaranteed* to blow in a matter o minutes, trying to find a place to dump it in a lake.

In a lake.

The thought struck him as funny for some reason, and he couldn't help but laugh out loud.

We're dumping a nuclear warhead into a lake.

He didn't know if the bomb was *actually* nuclear or if it was something else entirely, but semantics didn't matter to him at this point.

I've gone off the deep end, and I've taken Julie with me.

But as soon as he thought of Julie, his mind seemed to relax just a bit. They were still on a mission that would change the course of their nation's history, but knowing that she was with him—even in a separate car—made him feel better for some reason.

He hoped they'd get through it.

Flashing lights in the rearview mirror snapped Ben back to the real world.

Shit.

She flashed the lights again, and Ben stretched up a little to try and peer out the mirror and window into the truck bed.

He slowed the truck, trying to get the fallen bomb to roll around. He couldn't see anything out of the ordinary, and he didn't feel anything bump against the sides of the bed.

What's going on?

He slowed further, rolling to a stop. Julie pulled the police car up beside him, and he pressed the button to roll down the passenger-side window.

"What's wrong? You okay?"

"I see a boat down there."

Ben hadn't been paying any attention to the water. "Where?"

"At the shoreline," she said. "Instead of rolling it in from higher ground, why don't we just dump it overboard?"

"I like the way you think," he said, chiding himself for ever trying to rid himself of her. "But this only works if we can get it running. We don't have time to start rowing."

She nodded, already trying to find a road that led down to the lake. "I'll bet there's a turnoff up ahead. Keep your eyes peeled."

Ben nodded and began to roll up the window.

"Hey," she said.

He stopped and looked over at her.

"What's the time?"

He'd almost forgotten he'd been tracking the bomb's countdown timer with his watch's built-in timer, and he suddenly felt a wave of anxiety wash over him.

15 minutes, 14 seconds.

"15 minutes," he called to the other vehicle. Saying it aloud made him even more nervous.

They'd decided that they would try to allow for a five-minute window before the countdown timer reached zero, as a "safe zone." It was an arbitrary number, but Ben didn't want to take any chances that Stephens—or whoever else was behind this—hadn't programmed the timer to detonate the bomb before it reached zero.

That meant they had about ten minutes to get the bomb out onto the water.

He pulled away from the police car, suddenly aware of the one-way trip they were both on.

They didn't have time to get to the boat *and* get to a hill or raised area over the lake.

If they chose the boat option, it was their only option. Either the boat had fuel in it or it didn't, and if it didn't...

He didn't waste energy computing the outcomes of that scenario. Ben focused on the road in front of him, watching for a left turn that would lead them to the lake.

Another variable I've got to get right.

They didn't have the time to search multiple roads.

Luckily, the road they wanted was the first one that appeared in front of them. Ben wasted no time turning the truck and bouncing over the dirt ruts, all the while accelerating as the truck sped up downhill. He barely even checked behind him for Julie's car—it wouldn't matter much now if she was there or not.

The road ended by the water's edge at the put-in.

Mud and rocks made up the bottom half of the ramp as the road disappeared into the gently lapping waves of the lake, and Ben made sure to stop the truck well enough in front of the ramp so as not to have any trouble leaving the location when they were finished. Time was working against them, more than he'd ever imagined.

He hobbled to the small, green fishing boat moored at the shoreline. It has even smaller two-stroke engine and stick rudder attached at the rear.

At least that was good news. *Let's hope there's gas in it.*

He untied the boat, and immediately began pulling the cord to start the engine. Julie had parked her police cruiser haphazardly in a patch of mud on a steep incline off to the side, and she ran up next to him.

"Need help?"

"The keys are still in the truck!" Ben yelled over the sound of the sputtering motor. "Back it up here as close as you can."

She ran to the truck, and immediately kicked up gravel and mud when she threw it in reverse. Ben yanked the cord once more, hearing the engine cough to life. He just about had a heart attack when he looked up again. The truck was mere feet away and still moving quickly.

He jumped, ready to dodge the moving vehicle, when it stopped on a dime.

Julie stepped out and ran to him.

"Wow. You *can* drive that thing," Ben said.

"Who said I couldn't?"

"Here, help me get it off the truck." He released the latch of the tailgate and let it fall down, hopping onto it as soon as it lowered completely. He slid the heavy cylinder back to the gate and got back down, careful not to smash his injured foot into anything.

Together, he and Julie lifted the metal barrel, each holding the bottom with one hand and placing their other hand along its side, and set it on the boat's floor.

"I didn't realize that boat was so flimsy. I hope it doesn't fall through the bottom."

"Too late to worry about that now."

"How much time do we have?"

Ben glanced at his watch, then at the bomb's display screen. "I've got eight minutes, and that thing says thirteen."

She didn't respond. Ben understood what she was thinking. He was feeling the same way.

Doesn't seem like enough time.

"Ben! Look!"

Ben saw Julie pointing at a flashing set of police lights in the distance. The officer must have turned on the lights to ensure anyone around would see them coming.

"Get back in the truck. I'll be there in a sec," he said.

She seemed puzzled for a moment, but did as he said. Ben, meanwhile, aimed the boat at the center of the lake. He slid the bomb to the back of the small vessel. It would help get the boat on plane when it reached the proper speed, but he was more interested in steadying the rudder.

He made a snap decision and placed the cylindrical container on the left side of the rudder stick, preventing the boat from turning too far to the right. The way the lake was shaped, if he remembered correctly, was such that there was more open water to the left, where there was nothing but shoreline to the right.

Satisfied with his work, he took a final glimpse at the countdown timer.

11 minutes, 4 seconds.

He really hoped Stephens wasn't playing them for fools one last time.

He'd forgotten something.

The boat was, literally, dead in the water. He needed a way to hold the throttle down to get the motor to engage and push the fishing boat out onto the lake.

Come on, Ben. Think!

He pulled off his shirt and began spinning it into a long, spiraled rope. When he finished, he looped the shirt around the throttle section of the stick, careful to not cinch it tight just yet.

10 minutes, 31 seconds.

He ran one final check over their handiwork. The bomb was situated in the back-left side of the boat, standing on end and silently awaiting its detonation orders, and the engine was roaring, ready to engage. He had formed a loose granny knot with his shirt, now looped over the stick, and he abruptly pulled the knot tight. The tightening engaged the throttle, and Ben jumped backwards on the dock as the boat pulled away from its station. It accelerated, the small but powerful engine doing what it was made to do.

Ben watched the boat for only a moment before he turned back to the truck and police charger. Julie was already at the cruiser, and he yelled over to her.

"Get in the truck!"

He hobbled quickly back to the driver's seat of the truck and slammed the door after he climbed in. Julie joined him on the passenger side, and he hammered the accelerator to the floor, hitting the top of the small ridge of the adjoining road and turning onto it without slowing.

The police cruiser's lights receded into the distance, but Julie wasn't watching them anymore. Instead, she was staring directly at Ben.

"I, uh, wanted to make sure we'd both be able to get out of here," Ben said.

Julie looked at him oddly.

"You know—that police car… the way it was parked in the mud, and… I didn't, uh, there's a lot of mud, and stuff…" his voice trailed off as he realized how weak the excuse must have sounded.

I wanted to be with you.

"Whatever, Casanova," Julie said, a hint of a smile forming on her lips.

9 minutes, 11 seconds.

Ben couldn't get a signal. Julie's phone was useless out here as well, but she had a radio that worked.

"This is Julie Richardson. Anyone copy?"

She asked again.

"Officer Wardley. I copy. We've still got quite a few out and about looking for these caches, but there have been at least ten we've dropped into the lake already. Where are you?"

Ben grabbed the radio from Julie and gave him the update. "Wardley, we're around the Butte Overlook, heading northeast. We need to get everyone out of the park."

"Copy that, Ben. What about that bomb?"

"Heading into the middle of the lake. It goes off in nine."

"Nine minutes? Are you sure?"

Ben didn't respond, instead switching the radio to another open-frequency channel he knew a few of the officers were on. He repeated the message, much to the same reaction. He handed the radio back to Julie, who immediately called for Randy.

"Randy. Randall Brown, you out there?" Julie asked.

"Copy, Julie, I'm here. We're heading toward a rest stop a few miles from the lake. It's got a nice brick shelter and all, for what that's worth."

She looked over at Ben. He simply gave her a quick update. "I know where that is. Probably get there in six or seven minutes."

"We'll be there in a few," she said through the walkie-talkie. Randy confirmed, and told her he'd continue to track down the others and corral them together at the rest stop. Julie thought about what he'd said. *That brick structure will be useless against a volcanic eruption.* She appreciated the man's optimism, however.

"If that bomb reaches the center of the lake, we should be fine," Ben said, somehow reading her thoughts. "It'll detonate at the surface, which will obliterate the shoreline, but it should otherwise go straight up." He stopped for a second before adding, "Assuming it's not, you know, a nuclear holocaust."

Julie spied Ben's watch showing his altered countdown at less than three minutes, and she hoped it was an unnecessary precaution to have subtracted the five minutes from what was on the bomb's display screen.

She also hoped that this was all some sick dream; that she'd wake up in bed with a headache and only fading memories of the nightmare that had unfolded. But she knew that was probably an even longer shot than getting out of this alive.

"How'd you know, anyway?" Ben asked from the driver's seat of the truck.

"Know what?"

"Which cave it was in. How did you just guess the right one?"

Julie paused a moment before answering. "That's what I worked out with Randy, right after you left the first cave. He got me a map of the seismic activity below the lake, and how the hotspot's moved every year."

"Moved?"

"Well, like less than a centimeter, but yeah, over the course of millions of years, the hotspot has moved slightly northeast. Or to be more specific, the plate we're on has slid southwest, while the hotspot's remained stationary."

"And this hotspot," Ben began, "is what's caused all of the eruptions in the past, right?"

"Right. But it's also the reason there's a Yellowstone park at all. It's the source, generally, of all of the park's geologic activity. The Earth's crust is very shallow directly above it, and the lake is over a portion of that section. All I did was find where the crust was thinnest, where there was a known cave through that area, and then mapped those variables on top of the hotspot."

Ben nodded along, trying to follow her logic.

"I just figured that Stephens, or whoever he was working for, wanted to take the smallest risk of failure as possible, and that they'd want the location of their bomb to be directly above the most vulnerable section of crust."

"Preferably underground, so no one would see it," Ben added.

"Well, that, but also because the deeper it is, the more likely it'll cause a fracturing quake that would rip up the crust and cause the volcano. It turned out to be the only reasonable option when I looked at all the data, so I sent you down there."

"That all sounds pretty nerdy," Ben said. He shot a quick smile toward her.

"Yeah, well, it saved your butt."

Ben turned the truck onto a larger camp road, probably a main road toward the gate, and Julie saw him check his watch.

1:30.

6:30, if the bomb's countdown timer is accurate.

She noticed the truck's speed, how close they still must be to the lake, and wondered exactly how large this bomb blast would be.

---

2 minutes, 0 seconds.

"Everyone behind the wall!" Julie heard Officer Wardley shout.

There were seven others at the rest stop when they pulled up, including Wardley, Randy, and the officer he'd ridden with.

A few stragglers rushed way over to the rest stop's building, a simple men's and women's restroom with an outdoor water fountain, covered by a slanted roof. A brick wall stood at the other end, forming a short breezeway that Wardley and a few other men and women were now huddling behind.

Ben followed Julie as she stepped up onto the concrete floor of the pavilion and restroom.

"Glad you made it, you two," Wardley said as they approached.

With two minutes left, Julie thought. *Maybe less.* She wondered if it would have been wiser to just continue driving, see how far away they could get. But she knew it was irrational. Nothing they did at this point was going to change the outcome—either the bomb detonated with or without causing a cataclysmic eruption as well.

A few other officers were wide-eyed, as if they were staring at an apparition, and Julie knew they had questions—question about the bomb, where it was hidden, how Ben knew it would safely erupt over the water, and more. But Ben didn't seem interested in entertaining questions. He waited for Julie to press in to the group and stood stoically right at the edge of the pavilion.

She moved back a few steps to join him, and her hand found his. He turned to meet her gaze.

"You think this will work?" he asked.

"Stephens—they—seemed to have it all pretty well figured out," Julie said. "But I can't imagine the bomb's blast being enough to open a major fissure in the Earth's crust. The water will absorb much of the downward blast. This place has been here for 600,000 years without a major catastrophe like that, so I have to believe it's stronger than that."

"Right," was all Ben said.

"I have a question for you, now," Julie said. She noticed a few officers, as well as Randy, slowly making their way over to the pair at the edge of the concrete step.

"What's that?" he asked.

"How'd you know about the single occupant campsites? Why did it just suddenly hit you that Stephens or his cronies would be stashing the payloads at those sites?"

Before Ben could answer, Wardley spoke up. "Yeah, and why not just dump the powder in the woods, where no one would ever find them?"

Ben looked at each of the others in turn before he answered. "I took a guess."

The reactions were incredulous. "That's it?"

"You wanted more?"

Wardley shrugged. "Wouldn't hurt."

"Stephens was a loner. Livingston was a loner. Furmann was a loner. My mother, Diana Torres, preferred to be alone ever since my dad... left," Ben said, his voice hitching in his throat. "Stephens used that fact to murder her."

One of the officers stepped forward, looking confused. "That's a pretty wild guess, Bennett. I don't mean to sound accusatory, but I wouldn't be able to stand trial with evidence like that."

He seemed to be waiting for a response, as did everyone else, and Julie seemed surprised when he gave them one. "I thought about it long and hard, and the reason it was so compelling to me is that it lines up perfectly with my theory about this virus. About how to beat it."

Everyone's eyes, if they weren't already, were now riveted on Ben. Julie stared at him, too. They all waited for him to reveal his theory, but he wasn't given the opportunity.

A flash of light washed over Julie's eyes, and she took a stumbling step backward. Through the white haze, she saw the treetops of the forest bend and crunch under some unseen force, followed closely by a massive shockwave of dust and debris.

She tried to blink the light away, but it was almost immediately replaced by the loudest noise she'd ever heard. The cracking sound was like standing on a lightning bolt as it ripped open the earth, but it lasted longer.

Eyes bled. Eardrums rang.

Yanked off her feet, she found herself careening backwards and smashed against the brick wall. The roof above her was gone in an instant, and she saw the blue sky above her head. Dust filled every bit of the empty air in front of her face, and she felt it mingle with the saliva at the back of her throat, causing her to hack and cough.

Still, the force beat down on them. The bricks at the very top of the wall were the first to go, then she watched in horror as a larger section flew away entirely, like birds fleeing from a predator.

And just as quickly as it had started, it was over. She felt a heavy arm covering her, and it relaxed a little as the owner also realized the blast was finished.

"You okay?" she heard Ben's muffled voice whisper—or was he yelling?—into her ear. She nodded and stood up.

The others recovered from the shock quickly, and soon each of them were examining the wreckage and destruction. Julie struggled to her feet, looking in the direction from which the blast had come.

A large, blossoming, mushroom-shaped cloud, probably ten times the size of the one she'd seen only days earlier, had formed and was reaching up to the sky. It was a whitish-gray color, and she could see that toward the bottom of it, a layer seemed to be peeling off.

"It's the water," Ben said. He still had his arm around her and was now holding her close. "It probably offset a million gallons of water, but it doesn't seem like —"

A massive tremble directly below their feet caused Ben's words to be clipped short.

Julie panicked, running back onto the concrete slab, unsure of what to do.

"Julie—get away from the building!" she heard Ben yell. For some reason, she obeyed, though her mind felt like mush. She ran off the step just as the brick wall they'd been standing under collapsed.

And still the ground shook. She saw jittery images of a police officer screaming as the wall came down directly on top of him and another image of a stand of trees not a hundred feet from them simply disappearing into the earth.

The earthquake stretched on, growing more and more violent, but there was nowhere to go.

Ben held her, and together they waited out.

She thought every bone in her body was going to be shaken loose, and only then did she remember Ben's leg injury. She glanced up to him and saw that he was clenching his jaw, trying to steady himself. He was leaning almost completely on his good foot, doing his best to ignore the pain.

And then it stopped.

Just like the bomb's initial blast, the earthquake just *stopped*. It was as if the Earth was resetting itself, shaking itself off from a fight.

The entire brick structure was rubble, reduced to bits of brick and metal rebar. Trees had toppled; more felled there were still standing. A large crater had formed just on the other side of the road.

"Is it over?" she heard someone ask.

"No idea. I think if it was going to blow, it would have done so by now!" another voice yelled in response.

They waited for almost an hour, riding out the aftershocks.

And yet Yellowstone held.

Whatever was brewing beneath its surface had chosen not to incinerate life today.

As Julie and Ben headed to the truck, ready to return to civilization, a group of officers came over.

"Bennett," Wardley said. "You mentioned something about figuring out the virus earlier. What was that about? Did you figure it out?"

"Once Julie's hears back from her people at the CDC, I'll let you know."

Wardley's expression softened. "Ben, you've gotten us through this far. You were right about the caches, and you were right about the bomb."

Another officer standing nearby smiled. "Yeah. You know, you're either working for the bad guys or you're just smarter than you look. Tell us what you're thinking, man."

Julie saw Ben sigh. "Okay, maybe you can help me piece it together. Basically, Stephens—that guy we thought was on our side —had been leading us on this whole time. He wasn't just doing his job, though. It was personal to him, for whatever reason. He had more investment in this thing than we know. I think he was trying to make a point."

"What kind of point? That hates the United States? Point made, my friend."

"That's just it, back at the lab, I heard him say something like 'America isn't united *enough*...'"

"...To save itself," Julie finished. "I heard him say that, too."

"I've been thinking about what it all *means*," Ben continued. "We already know he wanted us to figure it out—he admitted that much himself. So I had to ask myself why he'd do it that way, when it would have been far easier to just blow the park and caldera silently, without taking us along for the ride.

"And that led me to thinking about the virus. Julie and I both had it —we were covered in the rash; they even put her in quarantine."

"But it worked its way out of your system, right? After it killed itself off?" Officer Wardley asked.

"It did, but when Julie and I were *together*, like physically close to one another, it didn't get worse. Only when we were separated was when it grew in each of us."

Julie was now confused as well. "Are you saying this thing can be beaten just by getting people to stand closer together?"

Ben shrugged. "It's worth looking into."

For Julie, the answer was too simplistic to be possible. She looked around at the others, and many were nodding. But the science…

"So what do we do?" she asked. "Get everyone together in a room and hope that it spreads, like chickenpox?"

"Maybe. I'll leave that up to your people," Ben said. "But I'd bet it's a start."

Ben and Julie spent the remainder of the day quarantined inside a massive white CDC tent set up just outside Yellowstone National Park. Her email had reached the highest levels of government, and each of the departments involved with the investigation of the *Yellowstone Virus* weighed in, including the CDC.

In the end, Ben's ideas were deemed sound enough to be fully tested and researched, and new quarantine locations were launched and data was gathered. Across the United States, each zone was given an updated protocol that included instructions based upon Julie and Ben's findings, with the expectation that each area would send their research back to corporate headquarters in Atlanta.

The tent outside Yellowstone was no different, and Ben and Julie found themselves helping with anything and everything to get the station set up and prepared, only to become the first test subjects. They'd explained everything that had happened so far, including Stephens' involvement, how Ben and Julie discovered where the caches and the bomb were hidden, and what they thought might be the way to defeat the virus.

Each of them had been assigned a separate bed, but because of their discovery of the "close proximity" rule, each bed was arranged close to another bed, and all of the infected patients were placed into the same large room, allowing the disease to proliferate and spread among them. Within a matter of hours, the CDC confirmed Ben's prediction that the proximity effect had a massive impact on slowing the spread of the virus, and within another few hours, they'd all but confirmed the suspicion that extended exposure to the virus led to an eventual recovery and inoculation.

They were released shortly after verifying that they were virus-free, and the research continued, using patients gathered from cities and towns in the surrounding two hundred mile radius around the camp.

Within days, news of the virus's weakness spread to major media outlets over television, radio, and internet sources. The key was proximity, and "recovery stations" were set up inside or near every major metropolitan area, including parks, arenas, stadiums, and larger government buildings. Smaller, more rural areas had similar stations, utilizing VFW posts, public meetinghouses, and judicial centers.

Large or small, the goal was the same: get as many people under one roof as possible, each with enough supplies to last a week. FEMA, Red Cross, and a dozen other agencies and organizations were simultaneously instructed to provide infrastructure support and training for the massive relief effort. And thanks to the efforts of large telecommunications companies, many of the relief locations were provided Wi-Fi access and secure data points, allowing work to continue without major conflicts.

Wall Street found little interruption in their operations, using mobile and wireless access points to continue trading and prevent any slowdowns in the US economy, and was able to ensure that losses in the major indexes were kept to a minimum. The government itself, operating for so long on pre-internet technology, seemed to be completely capable of keeping itself afloat without outside help.

Overall, the disaster relief efforts, while long and far-reaching, were successful. The nation watched as day after day, more public services were restarted, businesses were reopened, and municipal governments were resumed. Due to the staggering effect of healing the virus in phases throughout the population, as well as the increased desire to see America united again, many people were faced with nothing more than a week or two of vacation time while they were immunized against the disease.

Within a month, the *Yellowstone Virus* was deemed to be 'a minor threat' by the Centers for Disease Control, citing the work done by Ben and Julie as well as the data gathered by each of the quarantine stations. The virus/bacteria was expected to reveal itself in less than five percent of the population over the coming year, and while an actual cure was still out of reach, plans had been made to control the infection by forced exposure and proximity, eventually leading to full immunization against the disease.

"Valère, what happened?" Emilio asked through the screen.

Valère paced around the office, the speakers broadcasting the other man's voice directly to his ears, as if Emilio were not behind a computer monitor but instead right there in the room with him.

"I have sent over a detailed analysis of the events that transpire—"

"Not now, SARA," Emilio yelled. "I know you 'sent over' your little AI understanding of 'these events,' but I'm not asking that. Hell, it's all over the news! I know *exactly* what happened. I'm asking Mr. Valère."

Valère looked up, his eyes narrowed as he focused on the monitor. "Mr. Vasquez, I apologize for causing you undue stress. I assure you, our investments remain sound, as does our plan."

"Our *plan?*" Emilio shouted. SARA automatically reduced the sound level before it was sent to Valère's ears, so as not to cause any undue auditory discomfort. "Our plan has failed *miserably.*

This was supposed to *cripple* the nation, not create a more patriotic and united one!"

Valère let the man continue, uninterrupted.

"Stephens failed, thanks to that escaped *specimen* Fischer, and those two CDC—"

"One CDC agent, Mr. Vasquez. The other was merely a park ranger at—"

"SARA, enough!" Emilio yelled.

Valère turned to the screen, noticing the rage building in his partner's face. He held up a hand just as Emilio was about to start again. "Please, my friend, give yourself room to understand the true depth of what we have accomplished here."

Emilio sneered but remained silent.

"Our plans have failed, perhaps, when seen through the narrow lens of the project's parameters. But the Company remains strong, stronger than ever, perhaps, and that is in no small part due to the events that have transpired in America."

Emilio nodded.

"In addition, the Company has confirmed that research continues in Brazil, and preparations are underway in Antarctica. We remain beneath the radar and will continue operations while the governments involved clean up the mess."

"But at what cost, Valère? We failed. There is *nothing* we have accomplished by—"

"By what?" Valère asked. He steeled himself, pushing down the creeping anxiety snaking upward through his body. "There is nothing we have accomplished by failing? That is true. But what, exactly, do you think we were *supposed* to accomplish?"

Emilio frowned.

"Your parameters and objectives were the same as mine, and according to them, we have failed. Stephens was a loose cannon, and we have shown a lack of control over many of our contingencies. But what do you think the purpose was?"

"Of the failure?"

"Of even the *success*, were we to achieve it?"

"I—I don't understand where you're going with this, Francis."

Valère paused. "Of course you don't, Emilio. You were tapped for this project, and this one alone. But the Company has other interests, as I'm sure you're aware. So what could they *possibly* expect to gain from a project such as this?"

Again, Emilio frowned.

"Nothing, my friend. Nothing directly. This project is *busy work*. It was something that seemed large enough to matter, though not crucial enough to place the entire weight and infrastructure of the Company behind it."

"You mean..."

"Yes, Emilio. The Company needed us to create a distraction. One that would raise few eyebrows, regardless of success or failure. One that required little in the way of resources and management yet caused all eyes to focus inward."

"So the project—"

"The project was just that, Emilio. A *project*. A test, really. And we failed, but only in the sense of the direct mission. In this overall game, I believe we have achieved success. *Massive* success.

"Every eye in the developed world has been watching America, watching to see how they react. America is in fits, recovering, trying to stabilize itself. Whether it shall will be an interesting drama to watch. In any event, the Company was working on a much larger project when we discovered the enigma strain. The Yellowstone Virus is a side effect, a wonderful addendum to our research. I wrote the project's overview and had it approved as a way to divert more attention away from their larger goal."

"And may I ask what that goal is, Mr. Valère?" Emilio asked.

Valère smiled, his eyes heavy, as he reached for the control to switch off the monitor.

"No, Emilio. You may not."

59

The cold had been creeping in for the past few hours, and Ben's jacket seemed to be doing no more good. He sighed, watching his breath hang in the air and crystallize, the tiny specks sparkling as they collected and fell to the snowy ground.

He raised the long-handled axe and swung it once more. A satisfying crack reverberated around the tall pines, eventually getting lost in the white landscape. The block of wood split down the middle, sending the two halves in opposite directions, where two piles already lay. Ben examined his work, before heaving the axe up onto his shoulder, and walked slowly toward one of the piles. He filled a wheelbarrow and rolled the heavy load up a narrow dirt path.

As he exited the thick stand of trees, the sight in front of him almost stopped him in his tracks. The deep mocha-colored wood of the cabin's exterior stood out in stark contrast to the surrounding forest. A thin chimney piped out a few wisps of smoke from a fire he'd left unattended hours ago, but he could still smell the faint odor of burning logs.

He started up the path again, stopping only when he reached the front door. He set the wheelbarrow down on its mounts and stacked the wood in careful lines on both sides of the door. As he worked, he tried to calculate the fruits of the day's labor. *Half a cord, maybe more.*

Not enough, but not bad either, considering how slow he'd been lately thanks to his healing foot.

Finished with the wheelbarrow, he leaned it up against the wall of the cabin and reached for the door handle.

It opened before he got a grip on it.

"Took you long enough—it's getting a little chilly in here."

He smiled as he tried to think of a witty response.

"You know what? Think about it over dinner. You'll freeze if you stand there and try to get that brain of yours working again."

He stepped inside, immediately wrapped in the warmth of the dry air, and shut the door behind him.

Julie just watched. "Slowing down a little in your old age? Yesterday you got more than that, and you were done by four."

This time he wasn't caught off guard. "At least I'm doing something useful. What was that you tried to feed me last night?"

Julie's mouth hung open. "Oh, really? Good thing you're cooking tonight, then. We'll see how *you* do."

He removed his gloves and scarf and was now working on his boots as Julie came over and sat down on the bench next to him. He took off one shoe. Felt her arm slide underneath his when he went to remove the other.

She leaned her head on his shoulder, and he sat back against the wall. Ben felt her squeeze his hand, somehow causing the room to grow even warmer.

He smiled and closed his eyes.

THE AMAZON CODE

Continue the fun! Turn the page for a preview of the next Harvey Bennett novel, *The Amazon Code!*

1

THE WORLD ISN'T READY FOR a breakthrough like this. I'm not ready for a breakthrough like this.

Dr. Amanda Meron raced through the hallways of the small center, dodging metal carts full of trays of test equipment, computers and displays flashing and blinking. She lived for these moments, had dedicated her life to these moments, and she would not let them slip through her fingers.

For Amanda, it wasn't even about the research. Sure, she was fascinated by it, but it was the sense of *living* that accompanied the moments of pure scientific breakthrough.

How they must have felt, she wondered, *Einstein, Newton, Bohr.* Her childhood heroes, whom she now considered her friendly competition.

"Dr. Meron, in here. Just in time," she heard a voice call out from a room she almost ran past.

She knew this place better than anyone and yet her excitement caused her to momentarily lose her place. She slowed, turning into the glass-walled room, and took a look around. The faces of her peers, all smiling back at her, were assembled around the large computer monitor in the center of the room.

"We're ready when you are, Dr. Meron," the voice said. Dr. Henry Wu, the transplant from Stanford, stepped lightly to the side to allow room for their boss.

Amanda caught her breath and took her place next to Wu. She nodded. The screen flickered, and colors began to swirl around a central area of bursting light.

"We've transcribed over 10,000 more locations since our last neural bridge," Dr. Wu explained. "The map is now nearing 40% relational accuracy."

40%.

She almost couldn't believe it. Almost.

For the last few years — not to mention the years of schooling before that — she had been working toward this moment. Many in her field thought it couldn't be done, but the theoretical projections she'd used as a model in her doctoral thesis were more than just *whims*.

She knew it could be done.

She knew *she* could do it. If anyone could, *she* could.

"Data is now being transferred." All eyes remained on the screen. "Subject is nearing REMS, electrical impulses from the stem are now appearing in irregular rapid succession."

Amanda watched with confident delight. *This is it.* She reached out for something to hold on to, her hand finding the cold steel of a thick desk protruding out from beneath the computer monitor.

The subject, a Mr. Ricardo Herrera, was asleep in the room next door. A 67-year-old man from the nearby village, he had volunteered for a week of testing in the state-of-the-art facility Amanda had built. He and his family would be paid handsomely for his time, and with no expected side effects besides feeling wonderfully refreshed and well-rested, it would likely be the easiest money he would ever make.

"Are we recording?" she asked.

A younger technician answered. "Yes, of course. Digital and analog." He pointed to a rectangular box sitting to the side of the computer.

A VCR.

She smiled. *Haven't seen one of those in years.*

After a scare from a computer virus a few months ago, she'd decided to "go old school," as the techs called it: use analog recording technology in addition to their digital setup. The analog devices were slower, a *lot* bulkier, and plenty annoying to use in everyday situations, but they were almost completely hacker-proof. Someone wanting to tamper with their data would need to be physically present to do so.

"Subject is entering REM sleep." A dialog box on a separate, smaller monitor flashed a small message: *REM-S POSITIVE.*

The larger monitor flashed in the center of the screen again, and the colors began swirling the opposite direction. Tiny sparks of light, like miniature shooting stars, danced around the edges of the swirling vortex.

"It looks like something from a science-fiction movie," one of the techs whispered.

"It *is* something from a sci-fi movie," another responded.

The stars began to grow, then shrink, then grow again, before they died out, replaced by blackness, then a burst of color.

"Is this a dream?" someone asked.

"No," Dr. Wu replied, "our subject has only just entered REM sleep, but is currently dreamless. He is sleeping soundly, though, and we should see something soon enough."

"How will we know?"

Dr. Wu just smiled.

They all watched for another minute, then the swirling vortex of color shifted and faded. The blank screen stared back at them for a full thirty seconds. Amanda gripped the side of the desk until her knuckles were white, then released it.

Did they lose the connection?

She thought through the possibilities, trying to remember their hypothetical timeframes for these initial tests...

And the screen exploded to life again.

Blurry forms shifted around in front of her, some recognizable as people. They moved and interacted, melting into one another and changing shape.

Oh my God.

She swallowed, trying not to blink. Trying not to miss a moment.

"We've entered a dreamstate. Subject appears to be relatively lucid, attempting to focus on one of the bodies."

Her excitement almost got the best of her. Amanda's mind didn't even need to flash back to her papers and research to know what that meant; the answer was already at the tip of her tongue. If every single person in the room around her hadn't already been trained by her, she might have even begun a mini-lecture. *Dreamstate* was their term for mid-REM sleep during a subject's dream, and *bodies* referred to any "physical" noun — a typical person, place, or thing — conjured up by the subject's subconscious during a dreamstate.

It had taken two years to get here from their first attempt at viewing a subject's dream.

And now it was working.

The subject, Mr. Herrera, was trying to focus on one of the *bodies* in the dream. It was smaller than the rest, but more sharply silhouetted against the backdrop of swirling colors.

A person.

"Subject appears to be focusing on the memory of a child-body."

The narration confirmed what Amanda was watching onscreen. The image become a bit more focused still, and she could now see more of the "setting" body of this particular memory.

Herrera was in a "room" body, or at least it appeared so, as streaming rays of light glanced down diagonally from the top-right of the video. He was also moving, working around objects that were too blurry to make out.

Amanda forced her eyes out of focus, trying to break any of the involuntary paradigmatic functions they were attempting to use to make sense of the image. Forcing her eyes to make what she was seeing "blurry," the image might make more sense.

And it did.

She could now better understand what it was Herrera was remembering. He was walking through a house; a living room, then a dining room, passed by. The colors and shadows on the walls in the background established where in the image they were, and she could tell Herrera was moving quickly.

Chasing the small shadow.

Herrera was chasing a laughing child through the house.

The child stopped and turned to Herrera, and Amanda's eyes focused again on the image. Having now established a visual "baseline," she could now interpret the smears and blurry lines of the images, and in the picture recreated in her mind, she could almost see the child's face.

It was Herrera's oldest son, now in his twenties, somewhere between the ages of three and eight in the video.

She held a hand up to her mouth. *It's really happening.*

The blurriness could be fixed, as could the awkward lighting, through the use of more specific mapping techniques and — eventually — far more electrodes on the brain. After that, image manipulation and video effects rendering could sharpen it a bit more. She immediately considered the repercussions of this discovery, and tried to project how long her team might take to deliver a finished, test-worthy product.

"I — I can't believe this," Dr. Wu said from beside her. "The image is so... vivid. I never thought..." His voice trailed off as the first-person point-of-view Herrera again began following the child into another room.

"We're... *there*. Inside his head," one of the technicians said. "And we can improve the image quality by increasing the output of each of the electrodes, as well quadrupling the number of —"

"Go back!"

Amanda looked over to Dr. Wu, frowning.

"Sir?"

"Go back," he repeated. "This is being recorded, yes?"

"Y — yes, but —"

"I don't care about the current feed. Rewind the video back about three seconds."

"Dr. Wu," Amanda said, "we don't want to lose the —"

"I understand, Amanda, but I saw something..."

Amanda nodded, and the technician closest to the monitor reached out and fiddled with the controls on the computer below it. The screen changed to a computer desktop for a moment, then he double-clicked a folder and then a video file inside of it.

"Just changing from the live feed to the recording..." he said as he worked.

The video started over again, from the swirling vortex of colors to the blank screen. He dragged the cursor over the scrubbing track, "fast-forwarding" the file to a few seconds before the end.

"What did you see, Henry?" Amanda's voice was calm, but it hid concern. Dr. Wu was not the type of person to mess around or engage in hyperbole, especially not during a live testing period.

"I — I don't know. I'm not quite sure yet," he stammered, his eyes transfixed on the monitor display. "There! Stop it there, and go back a few frames at a time."

The memory they were watching was the same one as before: Herrera chasing his oldest son through a house. But Wu seemed transfixed not on the object of Herrera's active memory — his son — but on the background.

The video's point-of-view swiveled to the left, trying to keep up with the child, and it seemed as though Herrera was running past a window. They watched the screen until Wu spoke again.

"Hold it. Right there, on the right, outside the window. That is a window, correct?"

Heads nodded. Amanda couldn't see what it was that had Wu's attention.

"Outside, just beyond the window.

She blurred her vision again, then released it. The image came into focus more, and she felt her throat constrict.

"What the..."

"Is that a person?"

It was indeed. Amanda was sure of it.

The image was small — difficult to see even when she leaned in to the monitor — but it was sharply focused.

Eerily focused.

It was a man, covered in what looked like gold paint.

"It looks like a statue to me."

"But the detail..."

Amanda shook her head. "This is a joke, right, Dr. Wu?"

Dr. Wu just frowned at the screen.

"The man — or statue — is *completely* in focus." The gold-covered man in the image, standing outside the fuzzy outline of the window, was defined perfectly in the frame. It was small, and therefore easy to miss, but Amanda knew without a doubt what she was staring at.

A man, perfectly focused, stared back at them.

"Dr. Wu," she started again, "did you somehow layer this into the feed? Maybe there's an artifact from a previous —"

"No, Dr. Meron," he responded, his voice soft. "I did not interfere with this recording. What we are seeing here is part of the dreamstate created by Mr. Herrera's subconscious. The man we are seeing is, in fact, part of Herrera's memory."

"But how can it be so *clear*? So perfectly in focus?"

Wu shook his head. "I don't know yet. But let's see what happens if we jump a few frames at a time, forward and backward."

The technician nearest the monitor and computer assembly nodded and moved some controls. The frame jumped, skipping forward. Herrera's memory moved to the left, turning away from the window as he searched for the child.

All eyes were on the gold-covered man in the bottom-right corner of the screen.

The technician pushed forward another frame, then another.

"There!" someone shouted.

Amanda jumped, startled by the sound of the person's voice.

Or startled by what she saw.

The gold-covered man had *moved*. As Herrera's memory of the scene changed and shifted, the man in the corner, standing outside the window in the distance, turned and followed Herrera.

Amanda stared back at the man. She could see his eyes, deep black and sunken into his head, and his gold face, outlined by a shimmering light surrounding his body.

The eyes were looking directly at her.

2

"BUT HOW CAN HE BE *staring* at me?"

Dr. Amanda Meron was following her coworker, Dr. Henry Wu, through the halls of the facility to the staff conference room.

"He wasn't, Dr. Meron," Wu answered. "He was staring at the camera."

"The camera?"

"Well, you know what I mean. Our subject's projected memory. In this case, the memory of chasing his young son through his house, is remembered in first person, just like any dream you or I have."

"So the man was looking at Herrera? Our subject?"

"That's what we're going to find out," Wu said. "But yes, I suppose that is the most logical conclusion — the memory of the gold man would likely not have appeared unless it was a significant, yet repressed, memory. We need to ask Mr. Herrera who the man is and why he was dreaming about him."

"But why was he in focus? Once you pointed him out, it was as clear as looking at a photograph. I thought —"

"That the projections would all be distorted, blurry, out of focus? Yes, as did I. But for some reason, this memory of the man was so strong, so *reinforced*, that the electrodes were able to recreate it almost perfectly in the transmission."

"*Almost* perfectly?" another voice asked. Amanda noticed they had been joined by the same younger technician who had helped them navigate the computer's controls a few minutes ago. "He seemed pretty perfectly composed to me."

"Right," Dr. Wu said, not slowing his upbeat clip through the hallways. "But he was completely gold. The memory wasn't firm enough in its recall to recreate the man's proper attire, coloration, etcetera. Still, I do find it quite strange at the seeming insignificance of it."

"What do you mean?"

"Well, why was that man, in particular, the only thing in focus during that memory? Sure, we do not have the capabilities as of yet to recreate perfect images, but we've hypothesized on this before. The strongest memories, or the strongest *elements* within those memories, will be the things that show up the clearest."

"So that man is the most important part of that memory?"

"That's what our research suggests, yes," Dr. Wu said.

Amanda knew that, but it was encouraging — comforting, even — to hear it from one of her closest friends, and most trusted coworker. *I'm not crazy, then,* she thought.

"But why *that* man, and not Herrera's son? Or his house?" she asked.

"That is exactly the question we need to answer, Dr. Meron."

They turned and entered the conference room. Amanda had often thought the small room would be better served as a closet, but she held her tongue and pushed between the wall and the backs of chairs to get to a seat in the corner. This was her company, after all, and she was the last among them who would want to spend money on frivolous things like space and fancy conference rooms.

One technician and two other research scientists — Johnson, Guavez, and Ortega — were already there, seated across the table from Amanda. Dr. Wu and Nichols, the last technician, sat next to her.

She started immediately. "Team — as you know, our first neurological experiment using a fully-functioning, live human brain was a success. We will begin the project assessment and start assembling a response and hypothetical model as soon as this meeting is adjourned."

She continued through the required debriefing, not stopping to take questions until the end.

Thankfully, that was only a few minutes later.

"Okay," she said, wrapping up the session. "Any questions?"

Hands shot up around the room.

She smiled. "Let me guess — 'who do we think the gold-covered man is?' 'How was he so perfectly in focus?'"

Heads nodded in unison.

"I'm wondering those same things myself." Just then, the door opened and a small, petite woman shuffled into the few square feet of remaining space.

"Dr. Meron, the lab results," the woman said. She slid a folder across the table toward Meron.

"Thank you, Diane." She turned to the techs and scientists that had joined her around the table. "As you all know, I want this to be a fully open, honest forum. We're all part of this, so this is the first time *any* of us are seeing these results." Amanda opened the folder and began reading aloud.

"Upon waking the patient at 0900 hours, the following questions were asked. The transcript and responses to follow."

Amanda flipped a page. "1 — Were you able to engage in restful sleep? Response: 'Yes.' 2 — Do you remember dreaming during your most restful periods of sleep? Response: 'Yes.'"

She stopped for a moment and looked around the room. "I'm going to skip ahead a bit."

There were a few chuckles and nervous laughs, but she continued.

"7 — There was an object — what appeared to be a human male — in the dream. This man seemed to be covered in a gold paint. Brief pause. Who is the man? Response: 'I am sorry? I do not remember seeing a man.' 8 — This man seemed to be situated outside a window in the house. Do you remember the window? Response: 'I do. This was my house, my family's house. The window, uh, must have been the front window, looking out onto the street.' 9 — And yet you do not remember the man outside the window? Response: 'There was no man outside the window. I am sure of it.'"

Amanda swallowed, then closed the folder. Without speaking, she set the folder down on the table and placed her hands on it.

What the hell is happening?

Her first reaction was anger. *My research — my entire* company — *all of it is being sabotaged.*

She kept that feeling to herself. Unfortunately, the *second* emotion she felt — that of complete shock, of wondering what was going on, was plastered all over her face.

"Dr. Meron?" Dr. Wu's voice. "Are you okay?"

Amanda felt her head spin. *Am I shaking?* She tried to steady herself on the table. She looked over at Dr. Wu, nodding.

"Dr. Meron, I am sure there is a logical explanation for this. Perhaps Mr. Herrera had temporarily forgotten —"

"No," Dr. Wu said. "We need to run another test. Please have Diane prepare the subject for another round of REMS. He will need to expedite his regular daily schedule so we can have a test prepared for this evening."

Around the table, heads nodded. Amanda could hear the voice of Dr. Wu, but his words weren't registering. *We've been sabotaged,* she thought. *It's a joke. It's all a joke.*

Dr. Wu continued. "In the meantime, is there another subject prepared for a REMS analysis?"

Diane nodded. "Yes, Dr. Wu. Actually, we have a cousin of Mr. Herrera here as well. They signed up for the same examination week."

"That will be perfect." He turned to the technicians seated around the table. "Prepare the computer and fMRI system once more."

3

DR. WU DIDN'T BLAME AMANDA. For years she'd been building this project, working toward the ultimate goal and dream they both shared: recording human dreams.

The fact that she was currently overwhelmed with the reality of the situation did not surprise him. He would take the lead until she was ready to return. Knowing her, she just needed some rest and time to clear her mind.

He had been with her since the beginning of this final phase. Their careers were similar, though Amanda was certainly the savvy and creative mind that a research project of this caliber needed, while he was the lead scientist that provided the logical and analytical functions to keep it moving forward.

They were a perfectly matched team, as well. From day one they'd hit it off, her wit and charm matched by his seriousness and love for science. In most of his professional career he'd witnessed only cutthroat types vying for publication credentials, university positions, and curriculum vitae-building projects that would only further their careers.

But not here at NARATech. Neurological Advanced Research Applications was a firm like no other — focused solely on achieving the goals set by all of them, together, around the table inside that terribly cramped conference room. Political and bureaucratic considerations were, simply, not considered.

For the first years they'd worked together, he'd assumed that she had personally bankrolled NARATech — he simply couldn't fathom any other possibility for a company such as this. But after getting to know her, he overheard a few references to 'investors' and 'capital' and things of that nature, and he started wondering where Amanda had found the hands-off investors she'd collected to get this place off the ground. He couldn't imagine anyone willing to invest such hefty sums in an unproven market, especially without the massive oversight and earmarking along the way that always came with the investment money.

But NARATech seemed to be just such an organization. Headquartered in Maraba rather than Brasilia, the federal district of Brazil, NARATech was a billion-US-dollar research station with all the perks of a Silicon Valley startup, but tucked away from the bustle of city life. Dr. Amanda Meron ran the company, and Wu operated as the executive staff member.

That was it. No more, no less. It was a simple and elegant setup that allowed them to move quickly into the research areas they needed.

For Amanda's sake, Dr. Wu hoped this next test would go more smoothly. Specifically, he hoped that whatever strange phenomenon they had experienced the first time around would not plague them this time.

He motioned for the technician to begin. Again, they all stood around the computer and monitor, minus Amanda. The technician alerted Diane in the next room to switch on the fMRI scanner that would begin activating the electrodes arrayed inside the helmet their subject was wearing.

Wu watched as again the swirling colors danced and played on the screen, followed by the starbursts and sprinkling of light. It took longer this time for their patient to enter into a dreamstate, but after about ten minutes of watching, the screen went blank.

"Confirm recording," he said.

A technician confirmed just as the screen lit up in shining light. Wu was again stunned by the beauty of it. It was difficult to comprehend what he was seeing, but eventually things began to fall into place.

This particular dreamstate had much less structure than Mr. Herrera's. Abstract lines and shapes still danced in the background, fuzzy interpretations of something Mr. Herrera's cousin remembered from long ago. In the foreground, or what Wu assumed was the foreground, larger shapes — unknown bodies — moved back and forth on the screen.

The screen itself seemed to jump up and down as the shapes moved left and right. *It's a good thing I'm not prone to seizures*, he thought.

"Where are we?" One of the technicians, Johnson, asked.

Gauvez answered. "No idea, but it does look like a fun memory."

"Looks like a dance. Or a party."

There were a few chuckles, then silence.

Wu suddenly understood the context and setting. *It is a dance*, he realized. Mr. Herrera's cousin was also remembering a happy time, a moment of joy.

People, or at least their fuzzy outlines, danced around the screen. Two of the shapes — people bodies, as they would be called — embraced one another and swirled into one blob. The blob moved, turning to the side of the screen. Their subject moved its head and followed as the blob continued to move to another location in the memory.

They watched in silence for another two minutes until the two shapes reemerged from one and separated on screen.

And there, in the center of the screen, right where the two shapes split, the gold-covered man stood.

Watching.

Waiting.

Looking directly at Dr. Henry Wu.

Want to continue the story? Grab a copy of *The Amazon Code* now!

AFTERWORD

If you liked this book (or even if you hated it...) write a review or rate it. You might not think it makes a difference, but it does.

Besides *actual* currency (money), the currency of today's writing world is *reviews*. Reviews, good or bad, tell other people that an author is worth reading.

As an "indie" author, I need all the help I can get. I'm hoping that since you made it this far into my book, you have some sort of opinion on it.

Would you mind sharing that opinion? It only takes a second.

Nick Thacker

Instinct

The Gray Picture of Dorian

Uncanny Divide (written with Kevin Tumlinson and Will Flora)

ABOUT THE AUTHOR

Nick Thacker is a thriller author from Texas who lives in Colorado and Hawaii, because Colorado has mountains, microbreweries, and fantastic weather, and Hawaii also has mountains, microbreweries, and fantastic weather. In his free time, he enjoys reading in a hammock on the beach, skiing, drinking whiskey, and hanging out with his beautiful wife, tortoise, two dogs, and two daughters.

In addition to his fiction work, Nick is the founder and lead of Sonata & Scribe, the only music studio focused on producing "soundtracks" for books and series. Find out more at SonataAndScribe.com.

For more information, visit Nick online:
www.NICKthacker.com
nick@nickthacker.com